10

Tsutomu Sato

Illustration **Kana Ishida**
Illustration assistants **Jimmy Stone,**
Yasuko Suenaga
Design **BEE-PEE**

Honoka Mitsui

Class 1-A. Miyuki's classmate. Specializes in light-wave vibration magic. The type to jump to conclusions.

"Umm, Tatchu—!"

Miyuki Shiba

The younger sister of the Shiba siblings. Part of Class 1-A. An elite who entered Magic High School as the top student. A Course 1 student, called a "Bloom," whose specialty is cooling magic. Her lovable only flaw is a severe case of a brother complex.

"Umm, do they not suit me...?"

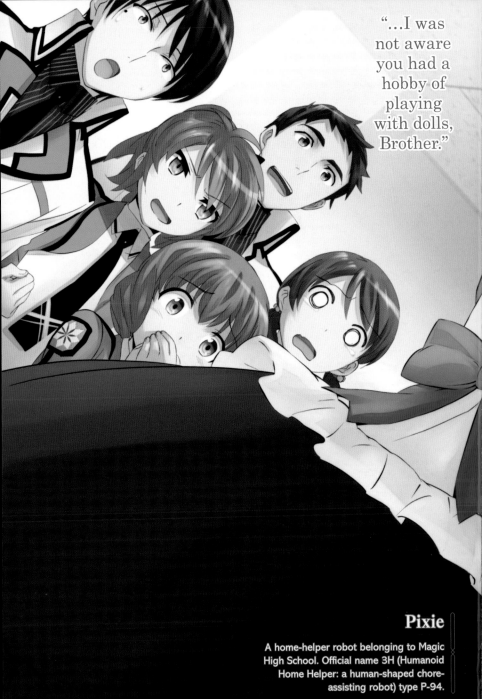

"...I was not aware you had a hobby of playing with dolls, Brother."

Pixie

A home-helper robot belonging to Magic High School. Official name 3H (Humanoid Home Helper: a human-shaped chore-assisting robot) type P-94.

"First of all, just calm down, Miyuki."

"I am subordinate to you. I want to do everything for you. I want to be useful to you. I want to serve you."

Tatsuya Shiba

The older brother of the Shiba siblings. A student of the National Magic University Affiliated First High School. Part of Class 1-E. One of the Course 2 students, mockingly called "Weeds." Specializes in designing Casting Assistant Devices (CADs), among other things.

Katsuto Juumonji

Senior at First High.
Former chairman of the club
committee, which oversees all
club activities. A powerhouse,
known as one of the three giants,
along with Mayumi and Mari.

"It seems
to have a
reason to
keep us here."

"Yes. If it
wanted to run,
it could do so
at any time."

Erika Chiba

Tatsuya's classmate. Has a bright
personality; a troublemaker who
gets everyone involved. Her
family is large and famous for
kenjutsu—a magical technique
that combines swords and magic.

"In other
words, it's
looking for
the next
person to
possess?"

"...The vampire's main body is a nonphysical entity called a parasite."

"The London conference definition, right? I know that."

Angelina Kudou Shields

A USNA (United States of North America) student who came to Magic High as part of a foreign-exchange program, switching places with Shizuku Kitayama. A blond-haired, blue-eyed girl with unequaled magical abilities.

State of the World in 2095

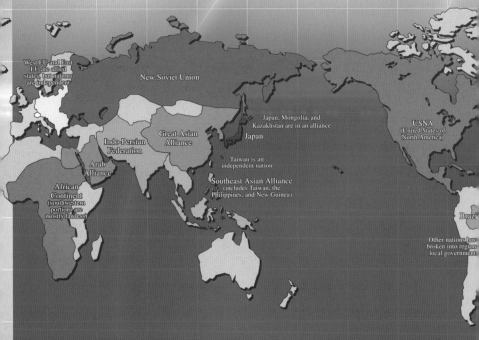

World War III, also called the Twenty Years' Global War Outbreak, was directly triggered by global cooling, and it fundamentally redrew the world map.

The USA annexed Canada and the countries from Mexico to Panama to form the United States of North America, or the USNA.

Russia reabsorbed Ukraine and Belarus to form the New Soviet Union.

China conquered northern Burma, northern Vietnam, northern Laos, and the Korean Peninsula to form the Great Asian Alliance, or GAA.

India and Iran absorbed several central Asian countries (Turkmenistan, Uzbekistan, Tajikistan, and Afghanistan) and South Asian countries (Pakistan, Nepal, Bhutan, Bangladesh, and Sri Lanka) to form the Indo-Persian Federation.

The other Asian and Arab countries formed regional military alliances to resist the three superpowers: the New Soviet Union, GAA, and the Indo-Persian Federation.

Australia chose national isolation.

The EU failed to unify and split into an eastern and a western section bordered by Germany and France. These east-west groupings also failed to form unions and now are actually weaker than they were before unification.

Africa saw half its nations destroyed altogether, with the surviving ones barely managing to retain urban control.

South America, excluding Brazil, fell into small, isolated states administered on a local government level.

The Irregular at Magic High School

VISITOR ARC ②

10

Tsutomu Sato

Illustration Kana Ishida

YEN ON

NEW YORK

THE IRREGULAR AT MAGIC HIGH SCHOOL
TSUTOMU SATO

Translation by Andrew Prowse
Cover art by Kana Ishida

MAHOUKA KOUKOU NO RETTOUSEI Vol. 10
© TSUTOMU SATO 2013
First published in Japan in 2013 by KADOKAWA CORPORATION, Tokyo.
English translation rights arranged with KADOKAWA CORPORATION, Tokyo, through Tuttle-Mori Agency, Inc., Tokyo.

English translation © 2018 by Yen Press, LLC

Yen On
1290 Avenue of the Americas
New York, NY 10104

Visit us at yenpress.com
facebook.com/yenpress
twitter.com/yenpress
yenpress.tumblr.com
instagram.com/yenpress

First Yen On Edition: December 2018

Yen On is an imprint of Yen Press, LLC.
The Yen On name and logo are trademarks of Yen Press, LLC.

Library of Congress Cataloging-in-Publication Data
Names: Satou, Tsutomu. | Ishida, Kana, illustrator.
Title: The irregular at Magic High School / Tsutomu Satou ; Illustrations by Kana Ishida.
Other titles: Mahōka kōkō no rettosei. English
Description: First Yen On edition. | New York, NY : Yen On, 2016–
Identifiers: LCCN 2015042401 | ISBN 9780316348805 (v. 1 : pbk.) | ISBN 9780316390293 (v. 2 : pbk.) |
    ISBN 9780316390309 (v. 3 : pbk.) | ISBN 9780316390316 (v. 4 : pbk.) |
    ISBN 9780316390323 (v. 5 : pbk.) | ISBN 9780316390330 (v. 6 : pbk.) |
    ISBN 9781975300074 (v. 7 : pbk.) | ISBN 9781975327125 (v. 8 : pbk.) |
    ISBN 9781975327149 (v. 9 : pbk.) | ISBN 9781975327163 (v. 10 : pbk.)
Subjects: CYAC: Brothers and sisters—Fiction. | Magic—Fiction. | High schools—Fiction. |
    Schools—Fiction. | Japan—Fiction. | Science fiction.
Classification: LCC PZ7.1.S265 Ir 2016 | DDC [Fic]—dc23
LC record available at http://lccn.loc.gov/2015042401

ISBNs: 978-1-9753-2716-3 (paperback)
        978-1-9753-2717-0 (ebook)

10 9 8 7 6 5 4 3 2 1

LSC-C

Printed in the United States of America

The Irregular at Magic High School

VISITOR ARC ②

An irregular older brother with a certain flaw.
An honor roll younger sister who is perfectly flawless.

When the two siblings enrolled in Magic High School,
a dramatic life unfolded—

Character

Tatsuya Shiba

Class 1-E. One of the Course 2 (irregular) students, who are mockingly called Weeds. Sees right to the core of everything.

Mikihiko Yoshida

Class 1-E. Tatsuya's classmate. From a famous family that uses ancient magic. Has known Erika since they were children.

Miyuki Shiba

Class 1-A. Tatsuya's younger sister; enrolled as the top student. Specializes in freezing magic. Dotes on her older brother.

Honoka Mitsui

Class 1-A. Miyuki's classmate. Specializes in light-wave vibration magic. Impulsive when emotional.

Leonhard Saijou

Class 1-E. Tatsuya's classmate. Specializes in hardening magic. Has a bright personality.

Erika Chiba

Class 1-E. Tatsuya's classmate. Specializes in *kenjutsu*. A charming troublemaker.

Shizuku Kitayama

Class 1-A. Miyuki's classmate. Specializes in vibration and acceleration magic. Doesn't show emotional ups and downs very much.

Mizuki Shibata

Class 1-E. Tatsuya's classmate. Has pushion radiation sensitivity. Serious and a bit of an airhead.

Subaru Satomi

Class 1-D. Frequently mistaken for a pretty boy. Cheerful and easy to get along with.

Shun Morisaki

Class 1-A. Miyuki's classmate. Specializes in CAD quick-draw. Takes great pride in being a Course 1 student.

Akaha Sakurakouji

Class 1-B. Friends with Subaru and Amy. Wears gothic Lolita clothes and loves theme parks.

Eimi Akechi

Class 1-B. A quarter-blood. Full name is Amelia Eimi Akechi Goldie.

Azusa Nakajou

A junior and is student council president after Mayumi stepped down. Shy and has trouble expressing herself.

Mayumi Saegusa

A senior and the former student council president. One of the strongest magicians ever to grace a magical high school.

Hanzou Gyoubu-Shoujou Hattori

A junior and the former student council vice president. Is the head of the club committee after Katsuto stepped down.

Suzune Ichihara

A senior and the former student council treasurer. Calm, collected, and book smart. Mayumi's right hand.

Katsuto Juumonji

A senior and the former head of the club committee.

Mari Watanabe

A senior and the former chairwoman of the disciplinary committee. Mayumi's good friend. Good all-around and likes a sporting fight.

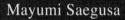

Koutarou Tatsumi

A senior and a former member of the disciplinary committee. Has a heroic personality.

Isao Sekimoto

A senior. Member of the disciplinary committee. Wasn't chosen for the Thesis Competition.

Midori Sawaki

A junior and a member of the disciplinary committee. Has a complex about his girlish name.

Kei Isori

A junior and the student council treasurer. Top grades in his class in magical theory. Engaged to Kanon Chiyoda.

Kanon Chiyoda

A junior and the chairwoman of the disciplinary committee after Mari stepped down. Engaged to Kei Isori.

Masaki Ichijou

A freshman at Third High. Participates in the Nine School Competition. Direct heir to the Ichijou family, one of the Ten Master Clans.

Shinkurou Kichijouji

A freshman at Third High. Participates in the Nine School Competition. Also known as Cardinal George.

Takeaki Kirihara

A junior. Member of the *kenjutsu* club. Kanto Junior High Kenjutsu Tournament champion.

Sayaka Mibu

A junior. Member of the kendo club. Placed second in the nation at the girls' junior high kendo tournament.

Koharu Hirakawa

Senior. Engineer during the Nine School Competition. Withdrew from the Thesis Competition.

Chiaki Hirakawa

Class 1-G. Holds enmity toward Tatsuya.

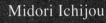

Midori Ichijou

Masaki's mother. Warm and good at cooking.

Akane Ichijou

Eldest daughter of the Ichijou. Masaki's younger sister. Mature despite being in elementary school.

Ruri Ichijou

Second daughter of the Ichijou. Masaki's younger sister. Stable and does things her own way.

Satomi Asuka

Nurse. Gentle, calm, and warm.
Smile popular among male students.

Kazuo Tsuzura

Teacher. Main field is magic geometry.
Manager of the Thesis Competition team.

Haruka Ono

A general counselor of Class 1-E.
Tends to get bullied but has another
side to her.

Yakumo Kokonoe

A user of an ancient magic called
ninjutsu. Tatsuya's martial arts master.

Toshikazu Chiba

Erika Chiba's oldest brother. Has a
career in the Ministry of Police.
A playboy at first glance.

Naotsugu Chiba

Erika Chiba's second-oldest brother.
Possesses full mastery of the Chiba
(thousand blades) style of *kenjutsu.*
Nicknamed "Kirin Child of the Chiba."

Anna Rosen Katori

Erika's mother. Half-Japanese and
half-German, was the mistress of Erika's
father, the current leader of the Chiba.

Harunobu Kazama

Commanding officer of the 101st
Brigade of the Independent
Magic Battalion. Ranked major.

Shigeru Sanada

Executive officer of the 101st
Brigade of the Independent
Magic Battalion. Ranked captain.

Muraji Yanagi

Executive officer of the 101st Brigade of the
Independent Magic Battalion. Ranked captain.

Kousuke Yamanaka

Executive officer of the 101st Brigade of the
Independent Magic Battalion. Physician ranked
major. First-rate healing magician.

Kyouko Fujibayashi

Female officer serving as Kazama's aide.
Ranked second lieutenant.

Ushiyama

Manager of Four Leaves Technology's
CAD R & D Section 3. A person in
whom Tatsuya places his trust.

Retsu Kudou

Renowned as the strongest magician in the
world. Given the honorary title of Sage.

Rin

A girl Morisaki saved.
Her full name is Meiling Sun.
The new leader of the
Hong Kong–based international
crime syndicate No-Head Dragon.

Zhou

A handsome young man who
brought Lu and Chen to Japan.

Xiangshan Chen

Leader of the Great
Asian Alliance Army's
Special Covert Forces.
Has a heartless
personality.

Ganghu Lu

The ace magician of the
Great Asian Alliance Army's
Special Covert Forces.
Also known as the
Man-Eating Tiger.

Miya Shiba

Tatsuya and Miyuki's
actual mother. Deceased.
The only magician skilled
in mental construction
interference magic.

Honami Sakurai

Miya's Guardian. Deceased.
Part of the first generation of
the Sakura series, engineered
magicians with magical capacity
strengthened through genetic
modification.

Mitsugu Kuroba

Miya Shiba and Maya Yotsuba's cousin.
Father of Ayako and Fumiya.

Ayako Kuroba

Tatsuya and Miyuki's second
cousin. Has a younger twin
brother named Fumiya.

Fumiya Kuroba

A candidate for next head of
the Yotsuba. Tatsuya and Miyuki's
second cousin. Has an older
twin sister named Ayako.

Maya Yotsuba

Tatsuya and Miyuki's aunt. Miya's younger twin
sister. The current head of the Yotsuba.

Hayama

An elderly butler employed by Maya.

Sayuri Shiba

Tatsuya and Miyuki's stepmother.
Hates them both.

Pixie

A home-helper robot
belonging to the magic
high school. Official name 3H
(Humanoid Home Helper: a
human-shaped chore-assisting
robot) type P-94.

Angelina Kudou Shields

Commander of the USNA's magician unit, the Stars. Rank is major. Nickname is Lina. Also one of the Thirteen Apostles, strategic magicians.

Virginia Balance

First deputy commissioner of the USNA Joint Chiefs of Staff Internal Investigation Office within the Information Bureau. Ranked colonel. Came to Japan in order to support Lina.

Benjamin Canopus

Number two in the USNA's magician unit, the Stars. Rank is major. Takes command when Major Sirius is absent.

Silvia Mercury First

A planet-class magician in the USNA's magician unit, the Stars. Rank is warrant officer. Her nickname is Silvie, and Mercury First is her code name. During their mission in Japan, she serves as Major Sirius's aide.

Mikaela Hongou

An agent sent to Japan by the USNA (although her real job is magic scientist for the Department of Defense). Nicknamed Mia.

Alfred Fomalhaut

A first-degree starred magician in the USNA's magician unit, the Stars. Rank is first lieutenant. Nicknamed Freddy. Currently on the run.

Charles Sullivan

A satellite-class magician in the USNA's magician unit, the Stars. Called by the code name Deimos Second. Currently on the run.

Claire

Hunter Q—a female soldier in the magician unit Stardust (for those who couldn't be Stars). The code name Q refers to the seventeenth of the pursuit unit.

Rachel

Hunter R—a female soldier in the magician unit Stardust (for those who couldn't be Stars). The code name R refers to the eighteenth of the pursuit unit.

Glossary

Course 1 student emblem

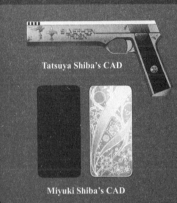

Tatsuya Shiba's CAD

Miyuki Shiba's CAD

Magic High School
Nickname for high schools affiliated with the National Magic University. There are nine schools throughout the nation. Of them, First High through Third High each adopt a system of Course 1 and Course 2 students to split up its two hundred incoming freshmen.

Blooms, Weeds
Slang terms used at First High to display the gap between Course 1 and Course 2 students. Course 1 student uniforms feature an eight-petaled emblem embroidered on the left breast, but Course 2 student uniforms do not.

CAD (Casting Assistant Device)
A device that simplifies magic casting. Magical programming is recorded within. There are many types and forms, some specialized and others multipurpose.

Four Leaves Technology (FLT)
A domestic CAD manufacturer. Originally more famous for magical-product engineering than for developing finished products, the development of the Silver model has made them much more widely known as a maker of CADs.

Taurus Silver
A genius engineer said to have advanced specialized CAD software by a decade in just a single year.

Eidos (individual information bodies)
Originally a term from Greek philosophy. In modern magic, *eidos* refers to the information bodies that accompany events. They form a so-called record of those events existing in the world, and can be considered the footprints of an object's state of being in the universe, be that active or passive. The definition of *magic* in its modern form is that of a technology that alters events by altering the information bodies composing them.

Idea (information body dimension)
Originally a term from Greek philosophy; pronounced "ee-dee-ah." In modern magic, *Idea* refers to the *platform* upon which information bodies are recorded—a spell, object, or energy's *dimension*. Magic is primarily a technology that outputs a magic program (a spell sequence) to affect the Idea (the dimension), which then rewrites the eidos (the individual bodies) recorded there.

Activation Sequence
The blueprints of magic, and the programming that constructs it. Activation sequences are stored in a compressed format in CADs. The magician sends a psionic wave into the CAD, which then expands the data and uses it to convert the activation sequence into a signal. This signal returns to the magician with the unpacked magic program.

Psions (thought particles)
Massless particles belonging to the dimension of spirit phenomena. These information particles record awareness and thought results. Eidos are considered the theoretical basis for modern magic, while activation sequences and magic programs are the technology forming its practical basis. All of these are bodies of information made up of psions.

Pushions (spirit particles)
Massless particles belonging to the dimension of spirit phenomena. Their existence has been confirmed, but their true form and function have yet to be elucidated. In general, magicians are only able to sense energized pushions. The technical term for them is *psycheons*.

Magician
An abbreviation of *magic technician*. *Magic technician* is the term for those with the skills to use magic at a practical level.

Magic program
An information body used to temporarily alter information attached to events. Constructed from psions possessed by the magician. Sometimes shortened to *magigram*.

Magic-calculation region

A mental region that constructs magic programs. The essential core of the talent of magic. Exists within the magician's unconscious regions, and though he or she can normally consciously use the magic-calculation region, they cannot perceive the processing happening within. The magic-calculation region may be called a black box, even for the magician performing the task.

Magic program output process

❶ Transmit an activation sequence to a CAD. This is called "reading in an activation sequence."

❷ Add variables to the activation sequence and send them to the magic-calculation region.

❸ Construct a magic program from the activation sequence and its variables.

❹ Send the constructed magic program along the "route"—between the lowest part of the conscious mind and highest part of the unconscious mind—then send it out the "gate" between conscious and unconscious, to output it onto the Idea.

❺ The magic program outputted onto the Idea interferes with the eidos at designated coordinates and overwrites them.

With a single-type, single-process spell, this five-stage process can be completed in under half a second. This is the bar for practical-level use with magicians.

Magic evaluation standards

The speed with which one constructs psionic information bodies is one's magical throughput, or processing speed. The scale and scope of the information bodies one can construct is one's magical capacity. The strength with which one can overwrite eidos with magic programs is one's influence. These three together are referred to as a person's magical power.

Cardinal Code hypothesis

A school of thought claiming that within the four families and eight types of magic, there exist foundational "plus" and "minus" magic programs that number sixteen in total, and that by combin-ing these sixteen, one can construct every possible typed spell.

Typed magic

Any magic belonging to the four families and eight types.

Exotyped magic

A term for spells that control mental phenomena rather than physical ones. Encompasses many fields, from divine magic and spirit magic—which employs spiritual presences—to mind reading, astral form separation, and consciousness control.

Ten Master Clans

The most powerful magician organization in Japan. The ten families are chosen every four years from among twenty-eight: Ichijou, Ichinokura, Isshiki, Futatsugi, Nikaidou, Nihei, Mitsuya, Mikazuki, Yotsuba, Itsuwa, Gotou, Itsumi, Mutsuzuka, Rokkaku, Rokugou, Roppongi, Saegusa, Shippou, Tanabata, Nanase, Yatsushiro, Hassaku, Hachiman, Kudou, Kuki, Kuzumi, Juumonji, and Tooyama.

Numbers

Just like the Ten Master Clans contain a number from one to ten in their surname, well-known families in the Hundred Families use numbers eleven or greater, such as Chiyoda (thousand), Isori (fifty), and Chiba (thousand). The value isn't an indicator of strength, but the fact that it is present in the surname is one measure to broadly judge the capacity of a magic family by their bloodline.

Non-numbers

Also called Extra Numbers, or simply Extras. Magician families who have been stripped of their number. Once, when magicians were weapons and experimental samples, this was a stigma between the success cases, who were given numbers, and the failure cases, who didn't display good enough results.

Various Spells

• Cocytus
Outer magic that freezes the mind. A frozen mind cannot order the flesh to die, so anyone subject to this magic enters a state of mental stasis, causing their body to stop. Partial crystallization of the flesh is sometimes observed because of the interaction between mind and body.

• Rumbling
An old spell that vibrates the ground as a medium for a spirit, an independent information body.

• Program Dispersion
A spell that dismantles a magic program, the main component of a spell, into a group of psionic particles with no meaningful structure. Since magic programs affect the information bodies associated with events, it is necessary for the information structure to be exposed, leaving no way to prevent interference against the magic program itself.

• Program Demolition
A typeless spell that rams a mass of compressed psionic particles directly into an object without going through the Idea, causing it to explode and blow away the psion information bodies recorded in magic, such as activation sequences and magic programs. It may be called magic, but because it is a psionic bullet without any structure as a magic program for altering events, it isn't affected by Information Boost or Area Interference. The pressure of the bullet itself will also repel any Cast Jamming effects. Because it has zero physical effect, no obstacle can block it.

• Mine Origin
A magic that imparts strong vibrations to anything with a connotation of "ground"—such as dirt, crag, sand, or concrete—regardless of material.

• Fissure
A spell that uses spirits, independent information bodies, as a medium to push a line into the ground, creating the appearance of a fissure opening in the earth.

• Dry Blizzard
A spell that gathers carbon dioxide from the air, creates dry-ice particles, then converts the extra heat energy from the freezing process to kinetic energy to launch the dry-ice particles at a high speed.

• Slithering Thunders
In addition to condensing the water vapor from Dry Blizzard's dry-ice evaporation and creating a highly conductive mist with the evaporated carbon dioxide in it, this spell creates static electricity with vibration-type magic and emission-type magic. A combination spell, it also fires an electric attack at an enemy using the carbon gas–filled mist and water droplets as a conductor.

• Niflheim
A vibration- and deceleration-type area-of-effect spell. It chills a large volume of air then moves it to freeze a wide range. In blunt terms, it creates a super-large refrigerator. The white mist that appears upon activation is the particles of frozen ice and dry ice, but at higher levels, a mist of frozen liquid nitrogen occurs.

• Burst
A dispersion-type spell that vaporizes the liquid inside a target object. When used on a creature, the spell will vaporize bodily fluids and cause the body to rupture. When used on a machine powered by internal combustion, the spell vaporizes the fuel and makes it explode. Fuel cells see the same result, and even if no burnable fuel is on board, there is no machine that does not contain some liquid, such as battery fluid, hydraulic fluid, coolant, or lubricant; once Burst activates, virtually any machine will be destroyed.

• Disheveled Hair
An old spell that, instead of specifying a direction and changing the wind's direction to that, uses air current control to bring about the vague result of "tangling" it, causing currents along the ground that entangle an opponent's feet in the grass. Only usable on plains with grass of a certain height.

Magic Swords

Aside from fighting techniques that use magic itself as a weapon, another method of magical combat involves techniques for using magic to strengthen and control weapons. The majority of these spells combine magic with projectile weapons such as guns and bows, but the art of the sword, known as *kenjutsu*, has developed in Japan as well as a way to link magic with sword techniques. This has led to magic technicians formulating personal-use magic techniques known as magic swords, which can be said to be both modern magic and old magic.

1. High-Frequency Blade

A spell that locally liquefies a solid body and cleaves it by causing a blade to vibrate at a high speed, then propagate the vibration that exceeds the molecular cohesive force of matter it comes in contact with. Used as a set with a spell to prevent the blade from breaking.

2. Pressure Cut

A spell that generates left-right perpendicular repulsive force relative to the angle of a slashing blade edge, causing the blade to force apart any object it touches and thereby cleave it. The size of the repulsive field is less than a millimeter, but it has the strength to interfere with light, so when seen from the front, the blade edge becomes a black line.

3. Douji-Giri (Simultaneous Cut)

An old-magic spell passed down as a secret sword art of the Genji. It is a magic sword technique wherein the user remotely manipulates two blades through a third in their hands in order to have the swords surround an opponent and slash simultaneously. *Douji* is the Japanese pronunciation for both "simultaneous" and "child," so this ambiguity was used to keep the inherited nature of the technique a secret.

4. Zantetsu (Iron Cleaver)

A secret sword art of the Chiba clan. Rather than defining a katana as a hulk of steel and iron, this movement spell defines it as a single concept, then the spell moves the katana along a slashing path set by the magic program. The result is that the katana is defined as a mono-molecular blade, never breaking, bending, or chipping as it slices through any objects in its path.

5. Jinrai Zantetsu (Lightning Iron Cleaver)

An expanded version of Zantetsu that makes use of the Ikazuchi-Maru, a personal-armament device. By defining the katana and its wielder as one collective concept, the spell executes the entire series of actions, from enemy contact to slash, incredibly quickly and with faultless precision.

6. Mountain Tsunami

A secret sword art of the Chiba clan that makes use of the Orochi-Maru, a giant personal weapon six feet long. The user minimizes the inertia on themself and their katana while approaching an enemy at a high speed and, at the moment of impact, adds the neutralized inertia to the blade's inertia and slams the target with it. The longer the approach run, the greater the false inertial mass, reaching a maximum of ten tons.

7. *Usuba Kagerou* (Antlion)

A spell that uses hardening magic to anchor a five-nanometer-thick sheet of woven carbon nanotube to a perfect surface. The making of a blade. The blade that *Usuba Kagerou* creates is sharper than any sword or razor, but the spell contains no functions to support moving the blade, demanding technical sword skill and ability from the user.

Strategic Magicians: The Thirteen Apostles

Because modern magic was born into a highly technological world, only a few nations were able to develop strong magic for military purposes. As a result, only a handful were able to develop "strategic magic," which rivaled weapons of mass destruction. However, these nations shared the magic they developed with their allies, and certain magicians of allied nations with high aptitudes for strategic magic came to be known as strategic magicians. As of April 2095, there are thirteen magicians publicly recognized as strategic magicians by their nations. They are called the Thirteen Apostles and are seen as important factors in the world's military balance. The Thirteen Apostles' nations, names, and their strategic-spell names are listed below.

USNA

Angie Sirius: Heavy Metal Burst
Elliott Miller: Leviathan
Laurent Barthes: Leviathan
* The only one belonging to the Stars is Angie Sirius. Elliott Miller is stationed at Alaska Base, and Laurent Barthes outside the country at Gibraltar Base, and for the most part, they don't move.

New Soviet Union

Igor Andreivich Bezobrazov: Tuman Bomba
Leonid Kondratenko: Zemlja Armija
* As Kondratenko is of advanced age, he generally stays at the Black Sea Base.

Great Asian Alliance

Yunde Liu: Pilita (Thunderclap Tower)
* Yunde Liu died in the October 31, 2095, battle against Japan.

Indo-Persian Federation

Barat Chandra Khan: Agni Downburst

Japan

Mio Itsuwa: Abyss

Brazil

Miguel Diez: Synchroliner Fusion
* This magic program was named by the USNA.

England

William MacLeod: Ozone Circle

Germany

Karla Schmidt: Ozone Circle
* Ozone Circle is based on a spell co-developed by nations in the EU before its split as a means to fix the hole in the ozone layer. The magic program was perfected by England and then publicized to the old EU through a convention.

Turkey

Ali Sahin: Bahamut
* This magic program was developed in cooperation with the USNA and Japan, then provided to Turkey by Japan.

Thailand

Somchai Bunnag: Agni Downburst
* This magic program was provided by Indo-Persia.

[8]

The morning after a night of madly dancing plasma and diamond dust.

Despite it being a Sunday, Tatsuya had come to school. Miyuki was standing next to him as though it was her proper place.

Like the days of old, schools didn't close just because it was Sunday. In fact, this school kept its gates open for those diligent in their club activities but, moreover, for students who had received permission to use the library, lab rooms, or practice rooms on their day off.

Of course, the Shiba siblings' destination wasn't a club room, or practice grounds, or the library, or a lab room.

Tatsuya and Miyuki had come to the student council room.

"It looks like nobody else is here yet."

As Miyuki had said, the student council room was empty. Upon hearing her remark, Tatsuya cracked a grin. "The cliché is that the person who calls the meeting always arrives last, but reality doesn't appear to work that way," he joked.

Miyuki smiled a little. "I see."

The remark was doubtlessly a courtesy.

And well... Tatsuya himself was aware that it had been a lame joke. He'd been amused simply because his council-mates had always been the ones to send for him, but today was a rare time that he was summoning them. That was what he found entertaining, at least more than whether tropes applied to real life or not.

On the other hand, just because Tatsuya was the one who called the meeting didn't necessarily mean he needed a lot of time to prepare. In the end, he didn't have to wait long.

"Good morning, Tatsuya, Miyuki."

Some of the people he was waiting for appeared quickly enough to be called punctual.

"Oh, Erika. You came here with Yoshida?" Miyuki noted.

"It was a coincidence!" she snapped. "...Is it just me, or do I feel a vague sense of malice in the air?"

"It's just you." Miyuki smiled back.

As the female high school students had a personable (?) conversation—

"Were you waiting long?"

"No, we just got here. Sorry for calling you on a Sunday."

—their male counterparts exchanged standard courtesies.

"Why does it feel like you're treating me and Miki differently...? Well, whatever. Anyway, what's going on? You never call us out on weekends, Tatsuya."

It was certainly an unusual thing. They hung out sometimes like high schoolers do, so meeting one another on weekends wasn't rare, but Tatsuya was always the one being invited in those cases.

Speaking of unusual, Erika's gaze was wandering restlessly, probably because the furnishings in the student council room—one whole wall covered in information appliances—were a strange sight. When he saw her doing that, Tatsuya reflected that this might be the first time she'd been in the place.

"Hold up on that for a bit. I want everyone together before explaining."

"There's more coming?" Mikihiko asked.

"Yeah. They should be here soon..." Tatsuya muttered in affirmation.

As though he'd been lying in wait for it, a knock came from the door. Part of him knew the person on the other side was probably the most familiar with this room out of all the currently enrolled students; he wouldn't find it strange for her to enter without the pretense of knocking. But here she was, being a surprisingly (?) conscientious and practical person. The fact that she'd knocked on the door without using the intercom did raise a question regarding her practicality, but Tatsuya himself opened the door manually rather than using the remote control, so he was just as bad.

"I apologize for calling you out here."

If Mikihiko questioned why Tatsuya would go out of his way to greet the newcomers, his doubts would have been dispelled as soon as the door opened. It was Mayumi and Katsuto.

"Yoshida and Chiba? Did Shiba call you two as well?"

Katsuto offered a plain question in the place of Mayumi, who looked more than just surprised.

"Ah, yes."

And Mikihiko gave a short reply in Erika's stead, who was also suddenly speechless.

"Let's get started, then," Tatsuya began before anyone could interject, prompting everyone to take a seat.

"Could you explain something first? Why did you call us here with the upperclassmen?"

"Agreed. I'd like you to start there as well."

Social emotions have a mirrorlike quality. Kindness brings about kindness, malice is responded to with malice, and hostility invites hostility. Controlling one's reactions in response to such emotions by factoring in one's personal interests is a form of adult discretion, but if people can't find a way to harmonize all their respective personal interests, they won't feel the need for discretion at all.

Mayumi's attitude was the classic example of an emotional reaction. She herself had nothing against Erika—in fact, she probably didn't even think about her much. Still, she had been dragged in by the hostility Erika displayed. Watching from the sidelines, Tatsuya thought to himself, *You're two years older than me, Mayumi, so I'd appreciate it if you acted a little more rationally.*

"I had something I wanted to inform you all of, regarding the capture of the vampire we're chasing."

Of course, Tatsuya didn't particularly mind if they stayed at odds. He decided to get this business over with without futilely trying to mediate.

"Let's hear it."

Katsuto was the first one to react, though it might be more accurate to say nobody apart from Katsuto reacted at all.

"Last night, I fired a synthetic molecule device into the vampire that transmits a specific pattern of radio wave every three hours."

He'd actually added paralyzing bullets to the mix as insurance in case the anesthesia didn't work, but as a result of a grievous miscalculation, it had turned out that his "insurance" was no longer reliable. Nevertheless, he couldn't effectively make use of the insurance on his own, either.

"The transmitter will survive for three days at most. Its radio wave output strength is weak, but the roadside cameras' surveillance antennae that detect and control illegal radio waves are able to receive it."

This time, everyone reacted. Or maybe it was more accurate to say they were completely incapable of not reacting.

"Wait a minute, Tatsuya," said Mayumi, eyes wide. "Last night? Where?"

"How did you find them?" Erika demanded critically, as if secretly frustrated.

"Synthetic molecule device—where on earth did you get something like that?" added Mikihiko, bafflement in his voice.

Tatsuya knew they were all reasonable questions anyone would want to know the answers to, but he had no plans to explain the background situation or the events leading up to it. That would require him to talk about part of the Independent Magic Battalion's technological power—an internal secret—and even Lina's true identity, which he was keeping under wraps for the moment.

"This is the radio wave frequency and pattern," replied Tatsuya, sliding a card to each of the four. "Mayumi and Erika, both your teams should be able to use the surveillance antennae, right?"

"...You want us to use this to find where the vampire is?" Mayumi asked.

Tatsuya nodded.

"...Why give this to us?" Erika interjected.

By *us*, she was asking why he gave it to both the Saegusa-Juumonji team and the Chiba family, and Tatsuya wasn't naive enough to misunderstand that. Nevertheless, he also didn't intend to instruct them one way or another. His goal was to tell the four assembled here about what he'd discovered thus far. Ignoring the question, he advanced the next piece of information.

"About the identity of the vampire we're chasing—it appears to be a magician on the run from the USNA Army."

Expressions of *you can't be serious* and *that makes sense* appeared simultaneously across four faces.

The unknown faction interfering with their search. Both Mayumi and Erika had sensed that they were at a high level, both individually and organizationally, and that they weren't something a simple illegal organization could bring here. If their identity was a team of USNA magicians chasing a deserter, then things made a whole lot of sense.

"Also, he's not independent. There are at least two deserters, and there could be as many as ten or so."

"Ten people deserted the Stars?" Erika balked.

"No, Erika, just because they're with the USNA Army doesn't necessarily mean they're part of the Stars."

"Wait, really?" Mayumi asked.

"...The Stars are a unit of handpicked magicians from the rest of the USNA Army who are exceptionally especially high magic-combat strength. There are, of course, plenty of other magicians in the USNA Army outside the Stars."

Tatsuya corrected Erika's misunderstanding and Mayumi's, too. The two beautiful young women had shown oddly in-sync reactions

(?), but they'd probably get mad if he pointed that out. He decided it would be in his best interests not to say anything he didn't need to.

"—And even if they're not Stars members, they've received combat training and also have these abnormal vampire powers. They won't be easy opponents by any means."

"You're right. Even ignoring their monstrous strength, we can't get careless with them," said Katsuto heavily, clearly hardening his feelings.

"But even if they're not Stars magicians, they're still from the USNA Army... I'd thought military magicians were strictly controlled in every country. Has USNA's military discipline loosened?"

Mikihiko's comment had no direct relation to the topic at hand. But Tatsuya had his own ideas about this. Instead of returning their "discussion" to its main thread, he proactively addressed the present doubt.

"Actually, it's probably the opposite."

"The opposite?"

"It would mean the parasites' influence was stronger than the military regulations placed on magicians, wouldn't it? Parasites change a human's nature, right? If that change was mental as well as physical, it wouldn't be strange for a host's sense of values to change."

"That's...true. Then why did the parasites desert?"

"Maybe they felt it was pointless to remain in the military, or maybe they have a goal they can't accomplish while in it. We won't know until we catch the parasites and question them."

"A goal... Most demons, not just parasites, want to sate their appetites or increase their own numbers, but I guess it's not worth wondering about right now. We can think about everything, but it'll be no more than speculation. More importantly, if military discipline hasn't loosened, that's an even more serious situation."

"Yeah. For some reason, these desertions appear to have happened despite military discipline being maintained."

"...So what do you want us to do anyway?"

It was Erika who had interrupted in a sulking voice as Tatsuya and Mikihiko were getting excited over a digression. Tatsuya saw Mayumi giving them a fed-up look, too.

"I didn't intend to tell you what to do."

Condemned for the derailment, Tatsuya, without showing a hint of awkwardness or clearing his throat, gave an immediate response, as though it were obvious.

Erika wasn't the only one who looked confused at the answer.

"They hurt a friend of mine, so I don't plan to leave them be. But at the same time, I'm not obsessed with personally making them regret it. If Public Safety or the MPD will deal with it, I won't meddle, and if the Clans Council takes responsibility for dealing with it, I won't complain. Of course, I couldn't care less if the Chiba family does their hunt on their own," said Tatsuya, who had already stood up and was moving away from the table. "I apologize for bringing you all the way here. With things being as they are, I thought giving these to you directly would be best."

"No, it's fine. You've done well," said Katsuto in thanks, preempting Mayumi, who looked like she wanted to ask something. "We're here together anyway, so we'll return after having a little talk."

"I see. Can I ask you to lock up afterward?"

"Sure."

Tatsuya bowed to Katsuto, traded glances with Miyuki, then left the room.

Mikihiko looked after him with a clinging sort of gaze, but he chalked it up to his imagination.

As Tatsuya was leaving school...

"Lina, would you please wake up already?!"

Yelled at by her roommate, Lina had finally crawled out of bed.

Ten minutes ago, her futon had been forcefully removed from her, and she'd gotten up without a choice. As she sat down at the dining table, Lina was still in her pajamas.

"I swear... I know it's Sunday, but you're being real lazy."

Amazed, Silvia placed a cup of hot milk with honey in front of her superior. With uncertain movements, Lina drank the contents a little at a time. After downing the drink, she exhaled and then finally woke up fully.

"Thank you... Silvie, has HQ said anything?"

She spoke in the perfect tone of the Stars commander—though her baggy, thick pajamas and unbrushed hair had no dignity or anything resembling it. Still, she wasn't hard to look at even in her disheveled state. Being a peerless beauty was a powerful asset. Silvia simply offered her a pained grin. She didn't say anything, but she was clearly thinking, *This is good in its own way.*

"As of right now, not yet. Still, I don't think we'll get away without any blame..."

"You think so, too...?" Lina hung her head and buried it in her hands.

Seeing her do that made her seem about as unreliable as she should be at this age, and even though she knew it was like attacking a fleeing enemy, Silvia couldn't help but ask her questions.

"Lina, what in the world happened last night? They may have been satellite-class, but they still had Stars codes. And four of them were disabled... Two of them had knife wounds on internal organs, plus brain contusions and spinal sprains. They're so badly wounded we can't expect them to return to duty."

"Ugh..."

"And then even you went missing for over three hours without any communication."

"Uuugh..."

Silvia probably didn't intend it, but her questions were pointing out Lina's failure.

"Did...did you lose?"

That was the last straw. Lina, cradling her head in her hands and groaning, suddenly collapsed onto the table. Even Silvia gave a start and winced, her momentum unintentionally delivering a finishing blow.

"I'm done for. I don't think I can keep doing this anymore. I'm turning in the Sirius code name."

"Huh? Umm, Lina… Commander?!" As Lina began to complain with her head on the table, Silvia began to panic. "Y-you'll be fine, Commander. You're carrying out your duty as a member of Sirius wonderfully…"

She thought she'd been asking normal questions, but she finally realized they were driving Lina's back against the wall. Flustered, Silvia started trying to soothe her.

"But what kind of commander would ever lose to a high schooler?"

Silvia felt like looking at the sky and sighing. It seemed like Lina was completely trapped in a morass of negative thoughts. "High schooler," she'd said—as though Lina wasn't a high schooler herself. Setting that aside for the moment, whimpering and whining like this was something teenage girls tended to do. Silvia herself had gone through that once upon a time. *"Angie Sirius" is a normal girl, too*, she thought, feeling an odd rush of emotion.

"Umm. That's right—you were just unlucky this time."

But Lina wouldn't be able to do her job like this. "Sirius" was the strongest combat force they possessed. Silvia got started trying to cheer her up in order to somehow reboot her.

"Commander, you lost to one of the Shiba siblings, didn't you?"

"…Both of them. Miyuki got in the way when I tried to capture Tatsuya."

"Oh! I knew those two weren't average high school students."

"…If that's what the average high school student is like, I wouldn't be able to stand it."

"Then wouldn't the task of fighting those un-average magicians at the same time be too much to ask of satellite-class soldiers?"

By deftly replacing "high school student" with "not average high school student" and "un-average *high school student*" with "un-average *magician*," Silvia eliminated the root cause of Lina's shock, aiming to bring her depressed thoughts up for air.

"It wasn't them!" Lina whined suddenly, her head coming up

forcefully. Silvia's plan had had a bigger effect than she had thought. "Besides Tatsuya and Miyuki, three ninjas showed up, too!"

"Ninjas…?"

Silvia knew that ninjas—*ninjutsu* users—were a kind of old magician. The reason she (mentally) reeled in surprise wasn't because she took the term *ninja* to be a product of dubious fiction but because the force of Lina's reply had pushed her back.

"We knew Tatsuya was connected to ninjas! But nobody even considered that someone with that level of skill might interfere!"

"Y-yes, you're right…"

"The only thing the intelligence data said was that a ninja was working as Tatsuya Shiba's trainer! I had no idea that particular ninja was master-class!"

"…Where did you get that intelligence?"

"I was told by the man himself. If I'd known such a strong opponent could get involved, I would have made a different plan. This is clearly a failing of the intelligence department. I'm not supposed to be doing intelligence work to begin with, so they should be giving me more reliable information for backup. Don't you agree, Silvie?!"

As Silvia intended, Lina seemed to have broken out of her self-deprecating loop of negative thinking. Instead, Silvia would now have to listen to her venting and complaining for the foreseeable future.

"Silvie, I'm sorry…"

Apparently having finished venting all the pent-up complaints and dissatisfaction, Lina was like her usual self again. Once she had recovered, the first thing that hit her was self-loathing at her disgraceful conduct.

"It's all right. Everyone needs to complain sometimes or they'll explode."

As Lina dejectedly apologized, Silvia gave her some more honey milk, smiled, and shook her head. Lina started trying to make herself even smaller after hearing that, but Silvia didn't mean anything by it.

II

She'd learned at a young age that one of a subordinate's jobs was to deal to their superior's temper.

"We don't have any instructions from HQ, but there are several reports I'd like your approval on. Ah, no, you can stay like that."

Lina had probably thought she had to fix herself up first and then come back. As Silvia's pajama-clad superior rose from her seat, Silvia waved for her to sit down.

"First, regarding the four wounded last night... Neither Titan nor Enceladus suffered any injuries. If we can't spot any aftereffects by the time the day is up, they should be able to return to duty. Like I said before, Mimas and Iapetus probably won't be able to do the same."

"...Once those two are up and moving again, we'll make preparations for them to return home."

"I'll handle that. The next report is from Commander Canopus. He says the Stars can't afford to dispatch any more personnel to Japan."

"...I see."

"He also mentioned he thought the General Staff Office seemed like it wanted to send Stardust reinforcements."

"Are they sending us more chasers?"

Research into evolving perception-type abilities into usable magic was lagging compared to functional magic already organized into the typed-magic system. Magicians with searching and tracking skills, even ones at Stardust level, were rarities. Even if you put the entire USNA Army's magicians into a group, it would be hard to say that there'd be enough of them. Now that some of the already few search-and-tracking personnel had been diverted to Japan, the Joint Chiefs of Staff would have little leeway in sending even more chasers here.

"No, soldiers." And sure enough, Silvia's answer was a *no*.

"I feel like the strength of Stardust won't be enough to deal with this situation, but... We have no choice."

There wasn't much of a difference in skill between satellite-class soldiers and Stardust. The only thing about Stardust's soldiers was that they couldn't withstand the enhancements, so they could fall apart at any moment. But for those fields in which they were enhanced, they displayed capabilities that compared favorably to Stars personnel. However, the satellite-class personnel dispatched to Japan had also been chosen with a heavy emphasis on their combat effectiveness, so compared with them, the Stardust soldiers would still have lower combat potential. Lina's sigh wasn't without reason.

"In terms of our other investigation, the other team hasn't gotten any noteworthy results yet."

Silvia, too, felt that Lina's concerns were valid, but it wouldn't do them any good to think about this and that, so she got right to the next report.

"In this situation, we need to prioritize dealing with the deserters, so we'll just have to have the other team do their best. But it would seem we can't make very deep inroads there."

The other investigation was finding the one who used the magic that the USNA diplomats and military were calling the Great Bomb, the strategic-class spell that caused the massive explosion. Lina was initially dispatched to Japan to figure out who that strategic magician was. The other team had arrived in Japan a step before Lina and her comrades infiltrated Magic University and its affiliated high school. That team was infiltrating magical equipment companies, starting with Maximillian Devices, to gather information.

"Come to think of it, I haven't had the chance to see Mia recently, either."

The name Lina mentioned as though just remembering it was one of the people on the other team living next door to them, whose real name was Mikaela Hongou. They were both of Japanese descent, but unlike Lina, you couldn't really tell Mikaela apart from a Japanese person. She'd taken on the false name Mia Hongou, written all in kanji, to infiltrate Maximillian Devices as a sales engineer.

"She's been running around until late at night for the last few days. She seems to be *at work* again today."

"We've been having to go all over the place until late at night ourselves, but... What a hard worker, going in on a Sunday."

Lina and Silva exchanged glances and giggled. Mia's camouflage as a sales engineer for Maximillian Devices was supposed to be just that—a camouflage—but they both remembered at the same time that Mia had said, the last time they'd seen her, that a coordinator at the university had taken a liking to her.

"Apparently, she'll be going to First High tomorrow," Silvia continued. "She says she's going with a delivery of CAD adjustment instruments."

"Huh?"

But when Lina heard this, her smile froze solid on her face. She was the Stars commander, yet she'd be seen playing the role of a high school student. She was feeling a sense of reluctance similar to when children didn't want to be seen in class by a parent.

"Her afternoon schedule is open, so why not go meet her for lunch?"

Lina, who had no real experience with student life, didn't really understand what was bothering her, but Silvia, who correctly grasped Lina's state of mind, made a suggestion—while hiding a smile at how her commander was uncomfortably averting her eyes.

"Tia!"

Amid the din, Shizuku turned around at a voice calling to her from behind. On the US West Coast, it was currently early evening on Saturday, January 28. Shizuku was at a house party being held where she was boarding.

"Ray," she replied after seeing the man (or rather, boy) waving his hand in an exaggerated fashion, raising her own a little.

His name was Raymond S. Clark.

He was the first male student at her school abroad to talk to her, and ever since then, the Caucasian classmate (likely a pureblood Anglo-Saxon, rare on the West Coast these days) would always find a reason to approach her.

She felt that he was probably making passes at her, but surprisingly, he was unobtrusive and good at keeping his distance, so she didn't hold any particularly bad feelings for him.

Incidentally, the nickname Tia was something Raymond had suggested. When she introduced herself, he'd asked her what "Shizuku" meant, and after explaining that it was the *drop* in *teardrop* or *dewdrop*, he'd given her the nickname Tia. Shizuku didn't exactly feel like the nickname was odd, but when she'd asked another girl in her class if she really looked that much like a crybaby, the response was that she matched the teardrop-shaped pearl image to a tee, and Shizuku hadn't voiced any objections since then—out of embarrassment. *Tia* had a nice ring to it anyway, so she let it go, and before she knew it, the nickname had stuck.

But getting back to the topic:

"That's a lovely dress, Tia. You look even more charming than usual," said Ray with a big grin, completely unashamed of the words.

"Really?" responded Shizuku—not in an unfriendly way but tilting her head in honest confusion.

Her black hair, which she wore in a somewhat long layered style, swung.

Ignoring Ray, whose gaze was growing even hotter, she looked down at her outfit.

A skirt long enough to almost touch the floor.

Her exposed back, shoulders, and arms.

Long gloves that went up to her elbows.

She'd heard the USNA clothing had, in places, reverted to traditional styles, but she'd been surprised at just how *classic* everything had become. It wasn't even uncommon to see women at normal parties wearing dresses that required squeezing into corsets. Shizuku's dress thankfully wasn't one of those.

"Those clothes suit you, too, Ray."

She'd bought the dress on the store clerk's recommendation, so she still didn't quite understand what about her dress was so good, but it was proper etiquette to return compliments when given. Raymond's tuxedo outfit was antiquated to her sensibilities (for someone from the same country, it was exaggerated), but it did suit his youthful, noble looks, so she felt no reservations about flattering him.

"Thanks! I'm honored you said so, Tia."

Besides, if he was going to be this happy about it, Shizuku didn't feel bad. Raymond's unabashed expressiveness reminded her somehow of her younger brother. She'd thought the established theory was that during adolescence, Aryans looked more mature than Mongoloids, but despite Raymond being the same age as her, he looked quite young to her eyes.

...No, it's not that he's that young, it's that Tatsuya seems mature, she corrected herself, looking back up at Raymond. "Are you by yourself?"

"I'd never think of escorting a woman aside from you, Tia."

Today's party wasn't the sort where you needed an escort to attend.

"I wasn't talking about that," replied Shizuku, pointing out his misunderstanding along with the doubt she had.

Raymond became amusingly bewildered. "Huh? Uhh, yes, I suppose I am...by myself?"

Don't ask me, thought Shizuku, but she didn't say it—she'd realized his lie after seeing the men constantly at work behind Raymond. (She didn't know it, but they were goading Raymond on.) Nevertheless, she didn't feel like blaming him for it.

"Umm... Tia, about what you asked me for..." said Raymond, clearly trying to change the topic as though he realized his outlook was grim.

"Ray," stated Shizuku. This was what she was after, but in her opinion, this wasn't the place to do it. "Let's go somewhere else."

The emphasis she placed on his name caused Raymond to close his mouth and nod at her suggestion.

They called it a house party, but it was being hosted where the Kitayama family's daughter would be staying. It was quite a bit more extravagant than parties that used any old hotel. The yard was open to partygoers as well, but given the time of year, it was rare to see anyone going outside.

Shizuku put a woolen stole over her dress and walked out under the star-filled winter sky. Her height wasn't particularly notable for a Japanese girl, but by American standards, she clearly fell into the category of "short girl." Her American-sized shawl covered her down to her waist, but she still had misgivings as to whether it would block the midwinter chill.

Using the CAD that was still in her handbag, Shizuku created a field of warmth around her. While she was at it, she extended its effective range to cover Ray as well. The heated zone also served to block out sounds.

"Thanks, Tia… Magic can be pretty convenient, can't it?"

"This isn't much. It shouldn't be uncommon."

Shizuku felt like he was acting a little too surprised for a follow-up remark, but Raymond shook his head strongly as though it really was incredible.

"You might not have noticed, since you just came to this country, but to us, magic isn't something *useful* like this. Here, you don't see people applying magic to daily life very often. It's something we use to display power, to flaunt intelligence, to parade our status."

"So you're stingy with it?"

"Ha-ha-ha-ha-ha… Well, yes." Raymond bent over laughing. But there was something a little off about his smile. "Here in the States, magic research is all about the fundamentals, military usages aside. Applying it to public welfare, daily life, and things like that is considered bad form. Though maybe not so much if it'll make a lot of money. Which is why… Err, I'm sorry. This isn't what we're here to talk about."

Ray didn't seem like he had any worries at first glance, but he must have had things on his own mind, too. Shizuku waited in silence for him to continue.

"Getting to the point," said Raymond, bringing up his face, which was pulled into a sharp expression, making him look like another person. "First, the news of a vampire appearing is true."

The "well-informed student" she'd told Honoka about. The information source she'd promised Tatsuya. It was Raymond here.

"The cause is unknown, but I found some information that seems to be related."

"Tell me."

"Of course. This is under a high-level information freeze, but in November, in Dallas, they did an experiment based on extradimensional theory to generate and evaporate micro black holes."

"Extradimensional theory?"

"Sorry. Even I don't understand the details."

"That's okay. What about it?" urged Shizuku, wondering to herself if Tatsuya would know if she asked him about it.

"I don't know the details of the experiment, but the vampires' appearance was observed right after they wrapped that up."

Shizuku thought about this for a few seconds, then spoke. "You think the experiment and the appearance of the vampires are causally related, don't you, Ray?"

"I did already say the cause was unknown," said Raymond, pausing to get his own thoughts in order. "But I'm certain that the black hole experiment was what called the vampires."

Shizuku didn't know where Raymond got his information or what basis he had to make such a statement. But in their short time knowing each other, she'd found out that he had a unique knack for discovering the hidden truth. For her, it wasn't important whether that was his own ability or that of an organization.

"…I see. Thanks."

The important thing was that she could trust his information.

"You're very welcome. I'd never turn down a request from you, Tia. If there's anything else I can do, feel free to ask me."

From a stranger's point of view, Raymond's approach was a very obvious one. But Shizuku herself thought only that his curiosity would wear off soon—— Whether this obliviousness of hers was innate or something she'd picked up from her friends recently, nobody knew.

◇ ◇ ◇

Tatsuya found himself faced with an unusual Sunday off. But that didn't mean he could just go wandering about in his school uniform. Tatsuya and Miyuki decided to return home first without stopping anywhere.

They weren't using his motorcycle today, instead opting for the train. As always, they sat down side by side in a two-seater cabinet, and as her brother stared out at the receding townscape, Miyuki watched his profile with a distressed gaze.

This incident had Tatsuya worried about something. Or maybe not so much worried as blaming himself. That was unusual for Tatsuya—he didn't normally fret over what might have been.

I wish he'd tell me, thought Miyuki.

She didn't think she'd be much help; not for a moment did she believe she could solve his problems. But even so, she could at least listen to him. She might not be able to overcome his anxiety, but she could at least share it.

That was what she thought as she continued to watch her brother's profile.

"I was naive…"

Had her wishes gotten through? Tatsuya had just muttered to himself.

"Brother?"

Suppressing her impatience, pushing her wish away, and pretending not to have noticed anything, Miyuki casually addressed him without saying anything, unable to put into words the question *What's bothering you?*

"I've been assuming that I'm unrelated, and this is where it got me. I'm behind on every little thing. Despite all the clues, I still don't know the most important things."

He was being abstract, but Miyuki instinctively knew what "clues" was referring to. "You mean…about Lina?"

Tatsuya's eyes widened—she'd unreservedly and correctly guessed what was getting at him. "Wow… I really can't keep anything from you, can I?"

The words *That isn't true at all!* rose to the top of her throat, but she prudently swallowed them. Most of the things Tatsuya thought about were beyond her comprehension. But she shouldn't be irritated with him for it, she told herself; instead, she should do her best to understand.

"I've known from the very beginning that Lina has been plotting something," he said. "I even had a chance to question her. I could have made my own chance for it, too. But I didn't want to make any waves in my own life, so I let her go, meaning I was slow to react as a result."

Tatsuya gave a self-deprecating grin.

Miyuki endured a painful tightening around her heart and waited in silence for her brother to continue.

"Well… I get it. Even if I had done something about it right away, that wouldn't have necessarily meant I could have prevented the damage. It's entirely possible I could have made the situation worse. But still… Faced with the fact that my friend got hurt, I can't help but think about it even though I know it'll do me no good."

This time, after hearing Tatsuya's confession, Miyuki couldn't stop a smile from coming to the surface. It wasn't because her brother had told her what he was thinking but because of what he'd told her.

"Brother… You've become a kind person."

"Miyuki? What's that all of a sudden?"

"No… You were kind to begin with. It was just hard to see, so…"

"I'm sorry, could you explain it in a way I understand?"

With Tatsuya making an utterly confused face, Miyuki didn't bother to hide her smile anymore. "I see there are things even you don't know, Brother. You may be smart, but you don't understand yourself, do you?"

"You think too highly of me. Of course those things exist. There's plenty of things I don't understand. I can't see myself without a mirror. I can only imagine what I look like from a flipped image."

"I should have expected you not to put up a show of strength about that. What I mean is…"

Miyuki paused meaningfully. Even knowing he was playing into his sister's hands, Tatsuya couldn't help but bend his ear.

"You can't forgive them for hurting your friend Saijou. And you don't want to be rough with Lina, because you're friends now, even if it's only been for a little while. That makes me happy, Brother—the fact that you have compassion for people other than me. Your emotions are far more human than you think."

Tatsuya turned to face forward again and shut his eyes.

It was funny to Miyuki that her brother was so clearly trying to hide his embarrassment.

It made her very happy that he let her see him acting like that.

"Yoshida, I confirmed the signal at the Tokyo Tower park. They're moving toward the Iikura intersection now."

"Got it. We're currently close to the Toranomon intersection on Sakurada Street. We'll hurry to Iikura."

"Within ten minutes, please."

"Understood. Arriving in two."

She hung up. Realizing that it seemed like they'd make it this time, Mayumi breathed a sigh of relief.

As a result of their discussion that morning, the student council members settled into a system where Mayumi would coordinate information while Katsuto and Erika led teams on the ground.

Both sides knew that squabbling among themselves would do more harm than good. But neither of them wanted to make concessions, so now they were doing whatever they each thought best. As a result, they were holding their own allies back.

In that sense, she'd have to thank Tatsuya for pulling a fast one on them and making a situation where they'd be forced to talk it out—but Mayumi felt like she'd been treated like a child, which annoyed her to no end.

Just you watch. I'm giving you the bitterest chocolate I can find for Valentine's Day.

Finding satisfaction in imagining Tatsuya's utter bewilderment, Mayumi returned her focus to the monitor.

Until yesterday, even if they got information on suspects for their search, the unknown third faction would always get the drop on them, and by the time they got to the scene, the suspects would have already fled.

How are they ahead of us when we're using the police's public security system? They'd even suspected an informant in their ranks. But now that the vampire's identity was all but confirmed, they had a guess as to who the third faction was. If it was a team of agents from the USNA Army, it would have search methods ready that they didn't. With unknown technology at their disposal, it was only natural they'd get the better of some civilian high school students.

Today, not only had the Magic High crew found a suspect, they had managed to pursue it without the third faction getting in the way, meaning the situation had taken a turn for the better. The clues Tatsuya had given them were certainly beneficial.

But the transmitter Tatsuya had put into the suspect wasn't very easy to use. It was difficult, in fact. Sure, Mayumi been able to catch the transmitter's radio waves using surveillance antennae. But in a city with such a highly advanced public transportation system, a person could move quite far in three hours.

One radio wave transmission lasted ten minutes. They had to capture the target in that time.

She'd only learned this after using the surveillance systems attached to the roadside cameras, but the cameras couldn't trace the parasite vampire. It wasn't that vampires didn't show up on camera, like in urban legends or fiction. But the legends and fiction weren't completely off the mark, either. No matter how much they adjusted the focus, the vampire only appeared as a blurred image.

From above them, it was especially bad. You couldn't see any features at all. The tracing systems in roadside cameras were based on facial recognition systems, so they weren't useful if you couldn't see any features. There was no communications interference happening, so the Saegusa family staff had speculated that vampires were probably using magic that disrupted optical devices.

That was how they'd gotten away three and six hours ago, respectively, and the team's search had continued into the dead of night.

But this time, it looked like the estimates were right on.

Meaning to narrow their search net, she called Katsuto, who was currently searching the Shiodome area.

In the classroom after the weekend was over, Tatsuya ran into a scene that had become familiar to him over the last few days.

Erika was slumped over her desk. It was good that she came to school early today, but it looked like it had taken all her energy.

Or maybe she was up all night?

"...Umm, should I wake her up?" asked Mizuki quietly. Tatsuya and Miyuki had met up with her at the station. Given how soundly she was sleeping, normal conversation probably wouldn't wake her up. Mizuki would have realized that at a glance as well, but she still lowered her voice, which was a very Mizuki-like thing to do.

"Let's let her sleep."

Tatsuya's response, on the other hand, was a frank one indeed. Perhaps it would be better to call it pragmatic.

It was pretty evident that if they forced her to wake up now, her brain wouldn't start working for at least the entire morning, and Tatsuya's mental state wasn't actually giving him the ability to care much about other people's affairs.

What had caused Tatsuya to lose his composure was an event that had happened about half a day before:

Essentially a moment after Tatsuya and Miyuki had finished dinner, their home phone had rung.

It wasn't a strange time to make a phone call—that is, for the ones on the receiving end.

But on the US West Coast, it was well past midnight. There was nothing strange about Tatsuya steeling himself, wondering what had happened.

"Hello, Shizuku? Has something happened?"

On the screen, as expected, was Shizuku. But what she looked like had been outside their expectations.

She was in her pajamas. What's more, it was a fashionable negligee, without even a gown on.

They shouldn't have answered the phone in the living room, either. The big, high-resolution display showed a vivid image that was just like seeing her in real life.

Was it silk? The faint gloss on the fabric wasn't doing much to conceal Shizuku's slender frame.

Tatsuya had seen her in a swimsuit during their summer vacation. But Shizuku's attire on the screen was more suggestive than that.

It was probably the "almost seeing, almost not" effect at work. If he just couldn't see *anything*, that would be one thing. But being able to see the fact that she had no underwear lines raised the effect exponentially.

As far as they could tell from the image, she wasn't wearing any underwear on her upper body, either. The ample sewn-on lace and the thin draping covered the important bits, but she was in such a state where a little loosening would be all that was needed to expose those bits.

Normally, even Tatsuya would have doubtlessly been flustered. Thankfully, most of his mind was taken up by worry, so he didn't make an unsightly display of panic, but...

"Shizuku?! What are you wearing?!"

...the other one looking at the screen with him, the same-gender Miyuki, was the one to blush—that was how disheveled Shizuku looked.

"Oh, Miyuki, good evening."

"Enough with the greetings! At least put on a robe!"

"...Okay, I guess?"

Her face seemed mystified, but as she was told, she crawled into a robe.

"Sorry for calling so late."

And then she bowed a little to them, meaning to restart the conversation.

"It's not that late for us here, but... Have you been drinking?" asked Tatsuya. Her vocal articulation sounded slightly—and suspiciously—different from mere drowsiness.

"Drinking what?"

"I meant—" began Tatsuya before canceling that sentence. He'd learned long ago that saying things like this was pointless. "Anyway, what's wrong?"

His ability to think had lowered somewhat, but she wouldn't have called them up without anything to tell them about. He decided they needed to attempt the maneuver quickly.

"Mm. I thought I'd tell you as fast as I could since you should know."

He didn't ask *Know what?* an insightfulness that probably deserved praise. "You found out already? That's amazing."

"Praise me more."

Coaxed by a level voice, Tatsuya felt a sudden sense of exhaustion. *Who's the one who let her drink?* She was clearly drunk. That seemed to be why she was acting so uninhibited. "Well, you really are amazing, Shizuku. Anyway, what did you learn?"

He was reluctant to come off like he was hurrying someone who took the time to call him in the middle of the night (by their time), but it would be best for both parties if they finished quickly. After all, she may have been drunk, but it didn't seem like enough to lose her memories.

"It's about why the vampires appeared."

But it was more sensational news than he'd thought. Tatsuya and Miyuki both leaned forward.

"Extra…extra something, I think. An experiment to create little dark holes."

"Dark holes? Shizuku, what are you talking about?"

After her unexpected gibberish, a whole host of question marks danced around Miyuki's head. That's right—over Miyuki's head.

"I don't know, either. I thought I'd ask Tatsuya."

"An experiment based on extradimensional theory to generate and evaporate micro black holes, right?" said Tatsuya in a low, hard voice.

"Yeah, that."

Shizuku didn't appear to notice that Tatsuya's voice had momentarily changed (she wasn't in a state that would let her), but Miyuki looked cautiously at her brother's expression.

"So something like that happened…"

The voice he spoke in was calm, the same as usual. No, even calmer than usual. But it was Miyuki who knew most of all that he was experiencing major shock.

"What is it?"

Miyuki was about to hang up the phone at that moment. She'd planned to give a lame excuse like *It's late* and end the conversation. She didn't want to damage Tatsuya's mood any more.

But Shizuku had asked a short question before she could.

"It's too much to explain in detail, so simply speaking…"

And Tatsuya went ahead and answered it:

"The experiment was to try to artificially create a very small black hole and harness energy from it. It's predicted that in the process of a generated black hole evaporating, its mass will be converted to thermal energy. They must have wanted to confirm that."

Having failed to interrupt the conversation, Miyuki had no choice but to listen to her brother's explanation—but her heart skipped a beat when she heard "convert to thermal energy." The warning they'd gotten from their aunt floated back up into her heart.

"Is that extradimensional theory? Taking energy from other dimensions?"

Of course, Shizuku had no way of knowing her concerns, and on the screen, despite her drunkenness, she asked a very academic...ish question.

"No, extradimensional theory isn't related to the actual process of harnessing the energy. Physics predicts that the tiny black holes will evaporate regardless of how they're generated. Extradimensional theory postulates that our universe is like a thin film of three-dimensional space enclosed within a higher-dimensional world, where the only physical force that can overcome the dimensional walls is gravity—in other words, the theory is that because gravity leaks a large portion of its energy into other dimensions, we can only observe it in this dimension as a much weaker force than it actually is. At extremely small, particle-scale distances, gravity acts upon other objects in this dimension before leaking out to other dimensions, which means gravity has a far stronger pulling force than we can observe at a normal scale. That's why, leaving extradimensional theory out of the equation, it's possible to generate infinitesimally small black holes. That's the theoretical foundation for the micro black hole–generation experiment, based in extradimensional theory."

"...*Did you get that, Miyuki?*" asked Shizuku, bobbing her head left and right.

"Unfortunately, I didn't understand much of it," agreed Miyuki with a shake of her head and a dry smile. She looked up at Tatsuya's face from up close and hedged, "But what part of that is related to the parasites appearing?"

Tatsuya looked down at his sister's face, glanced at Shizuku on the screen, and began to speak of what seemed at first to be something unrelated:

"Magic-induced event alterations don't need an energy supply. You also see no traces of physical energy having been supplied in the afterward. We also know for certain that in this physical dimension, there exists no nonphysical energy that can be converted into physical energy. But with movement and acceleration magic, we can observe ex post facto that there was a clear variation in the amount of energy at around the time the magic was cast. In this way, magic isn't constrained by the law of conservation of energy. It appears that the law of conservation of energy is being rejected by magic."

"They call that proposition the First Paradox of Modern Magic, don't they?"

"That propasition, err, I thought the propersition itself was connn-cluded to be incompleeete."

Tatsuya glanced at Shizuku's face on the screen for a moment. Her articulation was getting pretty bad—in fact, she could barely speak. But he couldn't see any signs that she was about to fall asleep on the spot. Her eyes gleamed with intellectual curiosity. She'd doubtlessly be unhappy if he told her he'd explain at another time. *Drunk people can be stubborn about the strangest things*, reflected Tatsuya, deciding he'd just keep talking.

"Yeah. You're right, Shizuku—it only *appears* as though the law of conservation of energy is failing. In the first place, the law is a deductive one, and it's impossible that any phenomena would go against it. In extremely short time frames like those applied to quantum mechanics, phenomena that disobey the law of conservation of energy can occur, but even then, if you look at it after the fact, energy equilibrium is always maintained. Since magic is also something that can have physical effects, at least in that category, it should obey the law of conservation of energy. The law says that in a closed system, the total amount of energy remains the same. If you did observe a variation in the total amount of energy, it would mean you've either made a measurement error or that the system wasn't closed."

"This world, in which magic is observed, isn't a closed system... That seems related to the extradimensional theory you explained before."

"I get it! The enershy you need for magic comes from another dimenshon?"

"More and more magical researchers are getting behind that sort of theory recently. I happen to agree; and if extradimensional theory is correct, then I think there must be some reason gravity is the only physical force that can act across dimensional barriers. Everything from this point on is just a groundless delusion of mine, but..."

As Tatsuya hesitated, Miyuki and Shizuku watched in silence.

"...Gravity acts on another dimension—wouldn't that mean it supports the walls between dimensions by doing so? Perhaps magic is drawing energy from a different dimension without breaking that wall. Magic is a phenomenon that doesn't need an energy supply, but that doesn't make it unrelated to energy balance. Even if we're just talking about what we can observe, magic that has a total energy balance of close to zero tends to be harder to fail."

Miyuki and Shizuku watched him closely, sorting out his thoughts as his gaze drew distant.

"Magic programs probably contain a process that calculates the lack of energy brought about as a result of the event alteration and draws that shortage from another dimension. You can't observe any physical energy supply, but if you consider that this extradimensional energy has nonphysical properties—magical energy, in other words—and that the magic program converts it to physical energy after the fact, things line up."

Even if they couldn't fully understand what Tatsuya was talking about, the two young women listened intently, because they instinctively realized he was speaking of things very important to their lives as magicians.

"Beyond the dimensional wall is a dimension in which magical energy is abundant, and gravity supports the dimensional wall so that it doesn't let that energy into our physical dimension. And magic crosses this wall, with the total energy balance drawing in the shortfall into the physical dimension so it all adds up to zero. I think that's the system that provides a solution to the First Paradox of Modern Magic. Nevertheless, if you generate a micro black hole using energy calculated based on extradimensional theory, the gravity acting across the dimensional wall would be erased by the black hole's generation. When that happens, for the instant the black hole is generated, perhaps the dimensional wall would end up wavering."

"What would happen if...the dimensional wall wavered?"

"*Magicwal energy you can't har-ha...control with magic programs would shpill in...?*"

Miyuki and Shizuku exchanged glances over the screen. The high-resolution cameras and displays showed the same emotion in their eyes.

"Energy structuralizes spontaneously, creating information bodies. Otherwise, the universe would have long ago homogenized and turned into a world of nothingness. There's no doubt the other dimension's magical energy structuralizes in the same way. And at the moment the dimensional wall wavers, information bodies of magical energy formed in that other dimension could potentially invade our world. That's what I think."

On the other side of the screen, Shizuku shivered.

On this side of the screen, Miyuki hugged her brother's arm.

Mikihiko finally showed up in class after second period had ended.

"Everything good now?"

He wasn't late. He'd been resting in the nurse's office again today.

"Tatsuya… I hate you."

Tatsuya had asked him out of worry, but what he got in response was a resentful complaint. "Hey, now. That's not very friendly."

He wanted to believe it was a joke, but there was a lot of emotion behind those words. Enough to make Mizuki, who was listening carefully, wince in fear.

"Let me at least complain about it. Do you have any idea how much my stomach has been hurting since then?" Mikihiko said, rubbing his stomach with a hand, no doubt remembering the pain. "All Saegusa ever does is smile and smile and never say anything, and Erika was clearly angry the whole time and stayed quiet… I had to talk on and on by myself. I felt helpless, like I was lying on a bed of nails…"

"Didn't Juumonji say anything?"

"Do you think he would make any comments about something like that?"

I see. That makes sense. All very "predictable" actions from those three.

"Umm… I don't really understand, but it sounds like you had a hard time."

When Mizuki displayed some heartfelt sympathy, Mikihiko seemed to recover a bit. On the other side of Mizuki, Erika was slumped over her desk, like usual.

It wasn't until lunch break that Erika finally revived. And no sooner had she opened her eyes than she grabbed Mizuki and started complaining.

"Are you listening? It was running away alone the whole time, but suddenly there were three of them. Don't you think that's unfair?"

Having the good judgment to know not to talk about this in the cafeteria where who knows who might have been listening, Erika had brought Mizuki into an empty classroom—a lab room Mikihiko frequently used—without even taking lunch.

"Umm, I suppose it is?" Mizuki nodded, overwhelmed, but she honestly didn't understand what Erika was talking about. At best Mizuki knew Erika was referring to the "vampire," but she had no idea what the situation was. She was thinking about how she never knew vampires came in threes.

"…Anyway, let's go to the cafeteria. Lunch break is almost over."

"Eh, I'm not really that hungry."

Mizuki *really* wanted to point out it was because she'd been sleeping this whole time, but she had a feeling if she did that, Erika would fall into an irreparable sulky mood, so she couldn't.

She sighed. *There's no helping it.* It wasn't as though she were dieting—the tradition (?) itself was abandoned these days anyway—but she decided to give up on lunch. Their schedule today didn't include any physical education or practice of the active sort, so she told herself skipping one meal would be fine. Besides, she was wondering about something else.

"Hey, Erika, how come you and Tatsuya are fighting?"

At that moment, Erika's shoulders twitched. "Wh-what are you talking about? We're not fighting. We're not, okay? Really." She shook her head and hands vehemently.

The long ponytail she'd been growing since the spring—Erika's favorite hairstyle lately—bounced to and fro in time with her head movements. It was plain as day that she was bothered by the question.

"You don't have to lose your head... I wasn't thinking you did something to him anyway. Tatsuya would just laugh it off if you got a little carried away, right? So if it was your fault, you wouldn't be fighting anyway."

"I...I can't tell if that's a compliment or an insult..." said Erika, crinkling her nose in *something approaching* an argument.

"It wasn't either. I was just stating the facts," replied Mizuki flatly, disregarding it.

"And I don't know if I can get behind you saying they're facts, either!"

"Okay, okay. Anyway, I don't think you're the cause of it."

Her indignant yet somehow unenergetic refutation was summarily washed away.

"Mizuki, you've grown strong..."

"If you don't want to talk about it, I won't ask anymore."

Even when she tried to pull things off track with a stagy line, a fastball was thrown back. Erika put her head on a table, her energy depleted. "We're not fighting... I'm just uneasy right now, and it's my own fault. I won't drag this on past today, so can't you let me go for now?" she asked, craning her head, timid eyes looking out from between her hair and arm.

Mizuki put a finger to her chin to think about it and tilted her head. Her hair, a shoulder-length bob cut with a tendency to curl at the ends, swayed along with her neck movement. She looked directly at Erika a moment later.

"If you can say for sure you'll be back to normal tomorrow, then that's okay."

Her feelings didn't seem to have slanted the way Erika was hoping. "Right... Ahh, this is no good."

Even Erika herself didn't believe that she'd be fine tomorrow without doing anything. She came back up, her face looking refreshed as though she'd accepted things.

"When all's said and done, all I'm doing is demanding attention from him. He never asked me to help him, but I figured he'd be on our side without saying anything. So when I saw him helping that *woman*, too, it made me mad, made me feel like calling him a two-timer... Great, and now I'm embarrassed about it again."

She covered her face with her hands, but bits of her reddened skin were visible. She wasn't just saying she was embarrassed. Seeing her oddly adorable appearance, Mizuki heaved a sigh.

"...Why do you sound like you're totally appalled?"

"Maybe not totally, but I am."

As Erika gave a sharp gaze through her fingers, Mizuki sent back an apathetic look of her own.

The sharpness vanished from Erika's eyes.

Mizuki moved in front of her (though all she really did was turn her chair and sit back down), reached out, and lowered Erika's hands from her face.

"Then you're just stuck being stubborn and hating yourself for it... I think they call that *tilting at windmills*."

"Urf! Your merciless words hit me right in the heart."

"I was being serious."

"...I'm sorry." Erika's body somehow seemed to shrink away.

"Erika, if I'm being blunt, Tatsuya is never going to be the one to meet you halfway."

"...You think so, too?"

"It isn't like he won't go after people who leave, but if you start thinking he's avoiding you, you'll be left behind forever. His mind is full of Miyuki already. You might not have to appeal to him, but you have to at least stay in his sight, or he might not even remember you."

"...That sounds like something he'd do."

"I can say for sure that Tatsuya doesn't care at all about what you think he does. I'm pretty sure just thinking about it would be a mistake."

"Yeah... You're right. He's obtuse— No, he's a lukewarm man with nerves of steel. I won't get anywhere by being embarrassed." Erika clenched a fist.

Seeing that, Mizuki gave her a somewhat detached smile.

That was exactly when Mikihiko came in the room.

"Oh. I figured you didn't have anything," he suddenly said as he entered. Before the two of them could ask, *What?* he held out the plastic-bagged sandwiches he was holding.

"Here, Erika. Carrot, tuna, potato. Shibata, you like egg sandwiches, right?"

"Huh? But why?"

"Th-thank you."

"You're welcome." That was his reply to Mizuki. "Don't *why* me. You have to eat something, or you'll get hungry while you're asleep." And that was his reply to Erika.

"Heh... Miki, that's very thoughtful."

"I'd like to say *you're welcome*, but Tatsuya sent me here with this. He said you seemed to be avoiding him and told me to bring it."

After hearing his answer, Erika and Mizuki exchanged glances.

"It doesn't look like you've been forgotten, but..."

"I've been left behind already..." Erika suddenly stood up, determination clear on her face.

"Wh-what?" said Mizuki, eyes wide.

Erika struck a powerful pose. "If that's the way it's going to be, I have ideas of my own, Tatsuya! I'm not going to let you treat me like air!"

"Says the one who runs away whenever he pays attention to you."

"Did you say something, Miki?"

"No. I just said to eat and make it fast," Mikihiko answered without meeting her gaze as he took out his own food. He was, after all, a childhood friend who had known her a long time. He might step on land mines once in a while, but he was well aware of how to handle this particular firecracker.

* * *

Once Erika sat down and the three were just about to bite into their sandwiches, it happened.

"Ow…!"

Suddenly, Mizuki scowled and shut her eyes tight. The sandwich fell from her hands, and Erika deftly grabbed it in midair. But that was a reflexive act; both her eyes and Mikihiko's were on their friend's suddenly distressed face.

Mizuki took her glasses off and pressed her hands to her eyes. Pained words escaped her lips.

"…What…is this…? I've never…seen an aura like this before…"

Mikihiko, who realized what was happening, immediately took out a paper talisman and formed a barrier that cut off any spiritual waves. It was taking advantage of a blind spot in the school rules that you weren't allowed to carry around CADs, but nobody present minded.

After directing his awareness outside, Mikihiko picked up on the waves as well.

"This is an evil presence…"

Waves not of psions but of psycheons. But Erika didn't understand and didn't realize it until she looked to where Mikihiko's awareness was focused.

Pure waves of "evil" were crossing the barrier and flowing inside. The waves were so strong it wasn't strange they could nullify the effect of Mizuki's aura-blocking lenses and affect her eyes.

"Shibata, put your glasses on."

But with the barrier softening them now, she should be able to block the waves with her aura-cut coating lenses. As Mikihiko predicted, after Mizuki put her glasses back on, she appeared to calm down.

Then, with enough time finally to think about what was happening—Erika and Mikihiko exchanged pale glances.

"Is the parasite coming to the school? In broad daylight? For what?!"

"It's got guts, I'll give it that! Where is it, Miki?!"

The chair she knocked over as she stood up made a clamoring noise, but Erika didn't take the slightest notice. She drew close to Mikihiko, almost pushing her face into his.

"Erika, calm down," answered Mikihiko in a calm but stern voice, standing up as well. "Let's get our weapons first. I can't rely on my talismans alone."

"...Yeah. Mizuki, you wait in the classroom."

"I'm coming, too."

Mizuki shook her head at Erika's seemingly sensible instruction.

"Mizuki?"

"I have a feeling I should go with you. I don't...know why, though."

Her voice was soft, but they could sense a determination within it that even a lever couldn't budge.

"...All right. But don't leave my side."

"Miki?" Erika's eyes widened.

But his answer wasn't simply one of getting carried away by the mood. "It'll be easier to deal with it if we're together than if it attacks her alone. Besides, Shibata's eyes should come in handy."

"Right... All right, Miki, but you have to take responsibility and protect her, got it?"

As if to say she'd be wasting time asking any more questions, Erika ran out toward the office where her CAD was being held. Mikihiko followed immediately after. Both he and Mizuki were well aware that this wasn't the time to be acting out a romantic comedy or coming-of-age drama. They just ran hand-in-hand lest Mizuki be left behind; he didn't have a choice—at least, that was the excuse he made to himself.

Warrant Officer Silvia Mercury First had been dispatched to Japan as Major Angelina Sirius's aide. Taking care of Lina, however, was not Silvia's only mission.

Stars members were classified into first-magnitude-class, second-magnitude-class, constellation-class, planet-class, and satellite-class. Of these, the first-magnitude-, second-magnitude-, and constellation-classes were treated as official combat personnel, while the planet- and satellite-classes were appointed jobs as rear support staff or illegal operatives. This was, of course, the standard role allotment. Lina, for example, was a first-magnitude-class but had been given a mission as an illegal agent.

Silvia's mission as the "first" member of the "Mercury" planet class was generally logistic support, and she specialized in the collection and analysis of information using her magical capabilities. For this mission as well, expectations for her information-processing skills in this area were high, and she'd been involved in psionic wave pattern analysis at a secret base prepared separately from the embassy.

The job she was grappling with now was the identification of the person in the white mask who had crossed swords with Lina and lived to tell the tale. She was working as part of an operational team matching their data against those involved in the USNA military and government personnel to see if any of them had the same psionic wave characteristics as the pattern they'd gathered from the mystery person.

The reaction stone, the centerpiece of a CAD, had the ability to convert both ways between psionic signals and electrical signals. In addition, whether magician or non-magician, a person always released psions a little bit at a time even when they weren't doing anything. Using the reaction stone to convert this psionic radiation into electrical signals and doing the appropriate processing, you could electronically record psionic wave patterns and display them on a monitor. Still, it was easier to quickly find slight disparities if you reverted them back to psionic waves to observe rather than displaying them on a flat screen. That was why a magician with training in psionic wave identification had been committed to a task that even non-magicians could perform.

She obviously didn't have data on the entire USNA military or all government authorities, but the data covered nearly everyone with a connection to magic. And anyone not related to magic was out of the Stars' purview. Silvia, while secretly hoping they wouldn't find any matches, continued her wave pattern search.

Confirming that nobody in the Stars matched the pattern was the first thing she'd done. Everyone found to have similarities within active service divisions outside the Stars all had alibis, too. Today, she had started her search through staff members assigned to the military's magical technology fields. And a little after noon, just when she was about to take lunch, Silvia—

What? No, that couldn't be...

—found an interesting data point.

As she had lunch with classmates from Class A—but not with Miyuki and the others—Lina wondered what she was going to do after this. Lunch break was an hour. About thirty minutes were still left. She'd probably finish her food in about five more minutes. Normally, she'd go somewhere else and have some postmeal tea or pay a visit to the student council room as a temporary member. Today, however—

...Should I go see Mia instead?

Mia, aka Mikaela Hongou, her next-door neighbor and in some ways her colleague, was on a visit to First High as an undercover employee of Maximillian Devices. Because Lina had been hung up on her deserter pursuit mission, she hadn't seen the woman for a few days. She didn't have anything to ask of her in particular, but it certainly was a good opportunity.

As she thought it over, not showing any opening in her motions or expression, responding without a pause whenever the conversation went to her, she had just emptied her last plate when, a moment later...

What's this?!

Lina nearly stood up out of reflex but held herself back only a couple inches from her seat. Thankfully, it appeared to the classmates sitting with her that she was simply adjusting her position, and they didn't appear to harbor any suspicions about it. Giving an inoffensive but insincere smile, she desperately suppressed the anxiety whirling through her mind.

An instant swelling of heterogeneous waves. The students around her didn't seem to realize it, probably because it wasn't a magical presence, just as psionic waves weren't. Lina herself could sense it only because she'd encountered it and fought against it several times recently.

But no doubt about it, it was the masked stranger, the vampire. She had a clue as to which direction it was in, if only roughly. It was toward the side gate where traders entered and exited.

That's right! Mia!

Once she thought about the location, it connected to her thoughts from just before, sending them back into her mind. Right now, Mikaela was scheduled to arrive at First High. And if she was visiting as a member of the supply team, she'd use the side gate.

"I'm sorry. I just remembered something I had to do, so if you'll excuse me."

With a polite farewell to the classmates sitting with her, Lina left her seat.

Anti-Stealth Field... I'd presumed them mere high school students. Was that a mistake?

A wordless voice emerged from inside the small Maximillian Devices trailer. A noise like a swarm of buzzing bees came back, waves of psycheons inaudible to the human ear. It was the "voice" the parasites exchanged via human thought. Seventy percent of the intent in that voice was affirmative, 30 percent negative. They weren't unified as one, but they also weren't separated as individuals.

Do you think I've been noticed?

The field was thick, spread out along the walls and gates. The parasites' psycheonic wave suppression and psionic wave stealth only wavered for an instant. Magicians who could distinguish psycheonic waves were rare, and regardless of their psycheonic signature, the psionic waves of the parasites weren't much different from humans'.

After the thought-produced question from the *individual* parasite in the trailer, the psycheonic noise came back *from inside her*. If a third party could have sensed the thought flow, it would have seemed to that observer that she was asking herself a question. And this time, the answer was 90 percent negative—judging that she had not been noticed.

I believe so as well, however... I knew I shouldn't have come here.

For her overt objective—gaining free entrance to First High property—today's job was her greatest chance. But considering her true objective, setting foot into a school guarded by sensors and anti-magic was an action that carried with it unnecessary risk. Given her ostensible position, she couldn't refuse doing this job, but perhaps she shouldn't have come here anyway, even if it meant abandoning her cover... Unease began to claw at her mind.

After finishing lunch, Tatsuya went to the school building roof.

Because Erika had put him in a bad mood today, their lunch group had consisted of him, Miyuki, and Honoka. A "flower in each hand," so to speak, from an observer's perspective. And, well, he really was doubly favored. Neither Miyuki nor Honoka bothered to hide their favor toward Tatsuya, after all. It wasn't that they didn't feel like it—it was more that they couldn't even imagine the idea of hiding it.

One might not be able to blame them, but people nearby were stealing looks. Even with Tatsuya's heart, it had been extremely uncomfortable. He'd come here to escape the cafeteria.

The rooftop of First High's main school building had been made into a hanging garden with elegant benches, making it a popular spot among the students. But it being the middle of winter, almost nobody was stalwart enough to spend time outdoors here exposed to the wind.

Today was humid, and while the wind chill wasn't incredibly cold, they were still the only three up there. One might think they should do something about the cold using magic, but aside from a few exceptions, students weren't permitted to carry CADs in the buildings. It wasn't that one couldn't use magic without a CAD, but nobody was fanciful enough to go out of their way to use CAD-less magic activation, something they weren't used to, just to secure spots for themselves during lunch break. The three present, though, were part of the group allowed to carry CADs around. Miyuki had already used a cold-blocking spell to give them a moment's relaxation.

To repeat that—Miyuki's spell was affecting all three of them. Her magic could lower the temperature enough to liquefy nitrogen. Even in the opposite direction, it was a piece of cake to shut out cold that wasn't even below the freezing point.

So there was no way it could be cold.

Nevertheless, Honoka clung tightly to Tatsuya's arm, not leaving any space between them.

The moment Honoka had performed that outrageous (?) act, Miyuki had given them a sober—or rather, a cold—stare, but now she was embracing his opposite arm as if to compete.

Thanks to them, Tatsuya couldn't move very well. He was shackled by both arms.

It would have been endearing if his face had started to steam even a little, but despite the voluminous chests pressing against him from either side, all Tatsuya did was grin painfully as if to say, *It can't be helped.* No doubt there were quite a few male students who'd tell him he had no right to complain even if someone stabbed him in the back.

Miyuki and Honoka had both been silent for some time now for reasons he didn't understand. When he looked at them more closely, he saw their ears and cheeks had reddened. It couldn't have been because it was cold, which meant it must have been *that* sort of thing, but he didn't grasp why they didn't just let go in that case—and though one might not call Tatsuya obtuse for thinking that, he wouldn't avoid criticism that he didn't understand a woman's heart.

Of course, he hadn't been thinking only about that this entire time. He was lost in thought, mentally away from the two quiet girls, meditating on the incident staring him in the face.

At first, he'd been thinking about what the vampire stood to gain by attacking people. At the moment, all he knew was that they were assaulting humans with high magical aptitude and stealing their blood and spirit energy.

Why were they targeting magicians?

Was there some meaning to stealing their blood?

And why did those deserters from the American army come to Japan in the first place? Was their objective only achievable in Japan, or were they wrapped up in another's schemes?

His thoughts wandered without an answer until, at some point, they came to the vampire's true identity.

The vampire's identity is for certain something classified as a parasite among old-style magicians.

It's valid to assume that Master's theory about parasites being independent information bodies originating in human mental activity is correct.

Shizuku's news, the micro black hole experiment in the USNA being the trigger, is also worth believing.

In that case, the incident was brought about by information bodies that invaded from another dimension... My own pet theory.

The issue is how the concept of information bodies invading from another dimension links to the concept of information bodies originating in human mental processes.

Where is the "mind" physically located in the first place? A different dimension? A higher-dimensional world? Or "nowhere"?

For that matter, where is the Idea? Where are the eidos?

Realizing that his thoughts were about to hit a dead end, he shook his head a little. The action served to reset his thinking.

There are two ways to think about this.

One, the parasites invaded from a different dimension.

Two, parasites that already existed in this world have been activated by uncontrollable energy flowing in from a different dimension.

In the end, if we don't know what a parasite—an independent information body originating in human mental activity—really is, I won't know any more.

In that case, what I should be thinking about is how to discover one and how to analyze it.

If they're mind-originating information bodies, there's a high chance they're made up of psycheons.

I should be able to locate them with my perception abilities, but I won't be able to analyze them…

His thoughts were interrupted by Miyuki suddenly stirring.

"Miyuki, what's wrong?"

Her movement had been an unconscious one born of unpleasant-ness, without any intent to play with him whatsoever.

The sound of Tatsuya's voice caused Honoka to realize his sister wasn't playing around, and she moved her tightly held body away. At the same time, she shivered. The cold-blocking spell had lost its effect.

"Ah, I'm so sorry."

Miyuki immediately manipulated her CAD, which she was still holding in her free hand.

The chill grew distant in short order.

But Miyuki's face was still dark.

"That's not important. What's wrong?"

Tatsuya didn't make any show of having felt the cold. Consid-ering all the training he'd gone through, literally face-to-face with death while using his self-restoration magic, this level of chill wasn't worth bothering with. More importantly, his sister's strange behavior concerned him.

"…I felt a terribly unpleasant wave, as though it grazed past my skin… But it must have been my imagination…"

Miyuki shook her head apologetically. She seemed to be feel-ing guilt over ruining her brother's relaxation time. Tatsuya, though, didn't accept the apology.

"Unpleasant waves? Were they psionic waves? Or psycheonic ones?"

Tatsuya couldn't put it down to her imagination; it oddly matched what he'd just been thinking about. But this question turned out to be pointless.

"I don't know... But if you didn't notice them, Brother, they must have been psycheons."

If it had been a psionic wave, there was no way Tatsuya wouldn't have noticed.

Tatsuya felt that she did well in one-upping him when he heard that, but he immediately corrected himself—now wasn't the time for such carefree thoughts. Magic high schools were equipped with terminals directly connected to the National Magic University, which held mountains of secrets within. From a security standpoint, this school would need the same level of protection as the university, and it was, in fact, furnished with an advanced system. Suspicious persons, sneak photography, and wiretapping were out of the question. But the countermeasures it had against magical interference were especially stringent.

The sudden wave of psycheons must have gotten caught in that anti-magic. If magical waves that made people feel unpleasant were always hanging around, authorities in Japan wouldn't possibly leave that alone. Considering she was unable to sense it anymore, he knew that whoever those waves belonged to possessed the ability to control them.

He couldn't judge the person right away to be harmful just because the waves felt uncomfortable, but there was even less reason to look at it optimistically. Especially not in a situation like the one they were in. It was more probable to assume that the person who had given Miyuki that unpleasant feeling was the parasite they were currently opposing.

Tatsuya made a mental list of methods with which to discern the source of the psycheonic wave, but as he began to investigate which would be most appropriate, his info terminal went off. It was the indicator that he was receiving a voice communication. Tatsuya put the phone unit to his ear.

"Tatsuya, it's terrible!"

Without any preface, those words leaped suddenly from the receiver. They were so forceful that a more timid person, even if the issue wasn't major—such as if *it's terrible* was followed by *my snowman fell over*—would have started to panic a little. Normally, one might think, *Could you please at least start with your name?* but now wasn't the time for that, and this was perfect timing for Tatsuya anyway.

"Saegusa, do you know the exact location?"

The operational lifetime of the transmitter he'd fired into the vampire in question hadn't run out yet. If the vampire who had infiltrated the school was that particular one, they could pinpoint its current location using the school's local positioning system. As the previous student council president, Mayumi would have known the LPS's administrator code. (Of course, the act would be in violation of the student council president's authority.)

"The vampire is in the— Oh, if you know, then this will be fast. The signal is moving from the side entrance toward the lab building's service entrance for materials. Maximillian employees were scheduled to come do a demo for a new measuring device today."

Which means it's mixed up with them, he thought quickly, before answering briefly for want of time. "Understood."

Why, for what reason, had the vampire come to First High now? He put that question, which related to his prior ideas, up on a shelf for the moment and quickly rose.

He pressed the button on the flight device attached to his belt and leaped over the fence.

After him, Miyuki triggered her flight spell as well.

Honoka, the only one who had been walking around without a flight device, was left alone on the rooftop.

At school, save for certain exceptions like student council and disciplinary committee members, students weren't allowed to carry CADs on their persons. Because of this, they left their CADs at the office when they arrived at school and picked them up when they left.

The office wouldn't easily return the CADs left there unless it was time to go home. During the incident in the spring, it was clear to everyone that it was an emergency, so they specially returned them. But today, only a handful of students and teachers noticed that something was going on. The office worker, unfortunately, was not included in that handful and wouldn't accept Erika and Mikihiko's requests for their CADs—not them alone anyway.

"What's wrong, Yoshida? …Ah. I'm surprised you noticed without a receiver."

As Erika was arguing with the worker, Katsuto arrived.

"Oh, hello, Juumonji," she said. Erika may have been a tomboy, but she had to admit Katsuto was superior and thus afforded him the courtesy. It didn't have to do with who was older—what she couldn't ignore was the difference in their talent and skill.

As Erika stepped aside, Katsuto placed a hand on the counter and leaned forward. With only that, the worker—a school faculty member—was overpowered by a student.

"I request CAD return due to an emergency."

As an unofficial rule, club committee officers were granted the right to carry CADs, but after giving the chairman's seat to Hattori, Katsuto had been conscientious about upholding the rules.

"B-but it's not yet time for—"

"It's an emergency."

It seemed like he didn't intend to let the rules confine him. Katsuto applied even more pressure to the female employee who was bravely trying to do her job. As a result, the grown adult quickly became pale.

"If we leave this be, it may cause disastrous results. The CADs, please."

"…Please wait a moment."

It wouldn't be accurate to vilify the employee as "weak." None could go against Katsuto's will unless they were considerably powerful.

"These two are my assistants."

"…All right."

But even so, the sight of her invited pity.

◇ ◇ ◇

Notwithstanding her energetic dash there, Lina found herself balking as she caught sight of the trailer Mikaela was in. She'd already felt a resistance to being seen by an acquaintance going about her high school life. It wasn't just the school uniform—she could handle being seen in those clothes. What embarrassed her, illogically, was being seen mingling with actual high school students, pretending to be one of them.

And now, the fear had cropped up in her mind that the sight of her going alone into a business trailer of a top manufacturer in the magic engineering industry might not be fitting for a high school student, either.

Disguising herself as a student and engaging in an intelligence mission was the task assigned to her. With another mission having interrupted, her spy activities were on hold. To add to that, the targets whose true identity she was supposed to find, Tatsuya and Miyuki, had instead found out *her* identity. Even Lina had to worry over whether she needed to pretend to be a student at this point.

But even if the siblings knew who she was, the other students and faculty didn't seem to. Tatsuya and Miyuki didn't seem to want to tell others about her USNA identity. What their intent was in keeping quiet, Lina couldn't possibly begin to guess. In a situation where she also couldn't silence the two who had discovered her secret, the most suitable choice would be to not do anything that could compromise her cover any more than it already was.

Now was a time she needed to avoid doing something suspicious, something that a high school student wouldn't do.

Thus, Lina was currently worrying about whether they would let her visit Mikaela in the Maximillian Devices trailer at all.

Unfortunately, she didn't have the option of not giving Mikaela a report. Naive though it may have been, she couldn't neglect her responsibility for a *fellow soldier.*

Caught between one sense of duty toward her mission and another toward her comrade, Lina ended up working by halves. For someone who had a propensity for sneaking around and avoiding people, she was starting to be careless in observing her surroundings.

Even when she saw Mikaela up close as she came out of the trailer, she simply sighed in relief.

Although they'd pinned down the location, neither Tatsuya nor Miyuki were of a mind to do something as reckless as fluttering down from mid-air on the spot. They knew for sure one of the vampires causing a mess in the capital had gotten onto school grounds…but that wasn't to say it was actually causing some sort of trouble right now. The visitors had probably been under surveillance since getting caught in the security spell, but the Maximillian employees had come to the school after going through proper procedures. They couldn't be rash without a clear reason.

And the fact that the visitors were under surveillance presented an inconvenience to Tatsuya as well. It was his first time against a monster rather than a magician. If he carelessly opened hostilities and was forced to use spells designated confidential, he'd have no end of covering up and silencing. Just thinking about it, as far as he could imagine, made him feel gloomy.

If they could just find out who the vampire infected with the parasite was, they'd have ways of going about this, but the Maximillian employees had come as a team of six. With so many moving around in one group, they wouldn't be able to discern which was emitting the waves. But that didn't mean he could erase—in this case, literally *annihilate*—everyone who witnessed it. Tatsuya and Miyuki hid in an empty classroom in the lab building and kept watch on the mobile laboratory (the trailer's cargo compartment), which had parked along-side the material delivery entrance.

"Lina?" muttered Miyuki suddenly.

Tatsuya had noticed her approaching the trailer before his sister said something, but he turned his attention back to the blonde transfer student.

Right on the heels of yesterday—their "duel" had ended very early in the morning, so it technically happened on Sunday—she had come to school as though nothing had happened. Her guts spoke to the fact that she was commander of a major power's elite forces, but this boldness now was oddly inattentive for her.

It didn't exactly feel like she was sneaking up on a target. Her attention was too scattered for that, and she didn't notice their eyes on her, either. She did seem like she was hesitant about something.

As Tatsuya watched her for no particular reason, she stopped next to the trailer, and a young woman who must have been a technician walked over to her.

Lina's lips formed the word *Mia*. Tatsuya conjectured the woman was a USNA Army agent sent to infiltrate Maximillian Devices.

During the questioning yesterday, Lina had said she was trying to capture the vampire. Her claim was that she wasn't merely pretending to be its enemy. But at the same time, she said that though she knew who the deserters who snuck into Japan were, she didn't know who was working with them. There was a high chance one of their own had turned into a vampire and was working as a collaborator with the deserters, but Lina and her allies hadn't discovered any information on who it might be.

The Sirius of the Stars couldn't possibly be unaware of the identity of an opponent she'd faced head-on and exchanged blows with several times, but...

As he thought about it, Tatsuya decided to take the risk and use his "vision" on the woman.

And then he noticed it. In his expanded awareness, he saw a different observer searching as well.

Several "spirits" were floating around the woman.

Not having expected Angelina Sirius to be the one to initiate contact on the First High campus, Mikaela Hongou felt perplexed and nervous. They shared the mission of discovering the mystery strategic-class magician, but their lines of command differed. Lina was higher ranked, but Mikaela didn't think she'd ever give her orders or directions. In this aspect, Lina was almost too fastidious—too naive to be kind and too obstinate to be mean. But Mikaela couldn't think of anything Lina would want to ask for her help on. She was the Stars commander, and Mikaela nothing more than a mere magical technologist.

Nonetheless, she couldn't ignore her just because she wasn't her direct superior. Doing that would be like asking others to suspect her. Mikaela got out of the trailer and endeavored to feign *normalcy* as she slowly walked toward Lina—

Shaking a hand at the spirits clinging about her as though batting away bugs.

When he saw the woman swat at the spirits *no normal magician should have been able to see*, Mikihiko knew she was the one.

"It's her. No doubt about it," he said in a hushed tone.

Without a word, Katsuto nodded.

"So that's what Lina was about. I see… She was an accomplice."

The low, anger-filled voice belonged to Erika, who had already expanded her armament device into its *kodachi* form. Tatsuya and Miyuki would have known that was a misunderstanding, but one couldn't blame her for thinking that way.

"I'll put up a barrier to block vision and hearing. It won't fool machines, but…"

"I'll do something about that."

Mikihiko and Katsuto nodded to each other. Behind Mikihiko, with a face unable to contain her fear, Mizuki was cringing.

"Not yet, Erika."

"I know," replied Erika, who, though certainly getting ahead of herself, gave a response that maintained a sense of calm.

Mikihiko threw the talismans in his hand. The six strips of paper slid low through the air as though possessed of invisible wings. They surrounded the trailer, then landed on the points of a regular hexagon.

"Here it goes."

Mikihiko's hands made a symbol.

His perception-blocking area magic, with a different spell logic than modern magic, activated.

"Mia... Is something wrong?"

Lina tilted her head dubiously when she saw Mikaela flitting her hands like she was swatting at bugs.

If it had been summer, the gesture wouldn't have seemed at all out of place. It wouldn't have been strange even in spring or autumn. But the season was winter. And not the warmer part—it was *cold*. Indoors was one thing, but there was no way any kind of insect would be flying around outside now.

"No, it's nothing to worry about."

Just hearing her voice, it seemed like it really wasn't anything important and that there was no hidden meaning. But the look on her face was definitely rattled. She'd made some sort of huge, possibly fatal mistake—that was the sort of expression she had.

What mistake had Mikaela made? She'd have to find out. That's what Lina's gut told her.

But first she had to tell Mikaela to get away from here. Lina's instincts screamed at her to figure out why she was bothered first, but her logic stressed that getting her away from the vampire threat took priority.

That hesitation stopped Lina for a moment. But thankfully (?), she didn't need to wonder about her decision any longer.

"...What's this? We're surrounded?!"

As the awareness-blocking area spell sprang forth to surround her, Lina's consciousness was stolen away.

◇ ◇ ◇

"Is this a barrier?!"

After the large trailer she'd been monitoring suddenly disappeared, even Miyuki couldn't help but be shocked.

As his sister turned to him with the question, Tatsuya nodded. "Yeah," he said. "Must be Mikihiko. He's quite skilled."

"This is Yoshida?" Miyuki couldn't hide even further surprise at the fact that a freshman boy, regardless of whether he was Course 1 or Course 2, could construct an information-blocking field with such a wide scope and thick density.

"Its effects are visual and auditory deprivation," mused Tatsuya. "It won't prevent the actual object from moving... I see."

He'd been uneasy because they hadn't made any advance arrangements to discuss what they'd do, but it would be far too much of a waste to let this thoughtful preparation be in vain. Tatsuya brought his voice call, which was still ongoing, out of suspend mode.

"Saegusa, it's Shiba."

"What is it?" the immediate reply came back. She must have been keeping her connection online, too.

"Please turn off the surveillance recorders near the lab building's materials delivery entrance."

If they'd been on the street, this would have been an unreasonable request even for the daughter of the Saegusa, but in school Mayumi had, in a way, been doing whatever she liked. She would be able to do this.

"I'd ask why...but you probably wouldn't answer."

"Thank you."

"Ha... There, it's off."

When Tatsuya thought about it, Mayumi was fairly easy on him. But he was somewhat indulgent with her at times, too, so it went both ways. A mutually advantageous relationship, so to speak.

"Let's go, Miyuki."

"Yes, Brother."

They exchanged glances, nodded, and then they jumped out from the classroom window they'd been hiding behind.

A white blade glinted before her eyes. The act of dodging it was wholly reliant on her instincts.

Lina pushed Mikaela aside, then used the recoil to roll backward herself. After she slid a switch on the side of her terminal, it split into a front and back piece. A tablet-shaped multipurpose CAD appeared from within them. It was a believable gimmick for an infiltrating spy to have, and her assailant—Erika—didn't hesitate over it, either.

Without even a glance at Lina, Erika turned to Mia, still on the ground, and pointed the tip of her *kodachi*, drawn back to lunge at her throat.

"Erika, what are you doing?!" shouted Lina, constructing a magic program.

She triggered the spell to blow Erika back.

However, it was blocked by the anti-magic shell surrounding Erika—a mass of event influence.

"Katsuto Juumonji?!"

Aghast, she turned around, and there was a giant boulder of a body. Looking at just its size, it wasn't an unusual physique in her eyes, but its sense of presence was more enormous than she'd ever seen before.

The preliminary report had labeled his strength as requiring caution. But now that she'd actually experienced it, she couldn't help but be shocked that there was still an enemy of this level of power hidden among them. The instant Lina's attention was on Katsuto, Erika closed the last step.

"Mia?!"

Her cry out of worry for her comrade changed into a cry of unbelieving shock.

Mikaela had caught the *kodachi* with her bare hand—and without using a CAD, surrounded it with a barrier spell.

She'd seen that magic before. It was the same as the strange person in the white mask.

"What is this...?" muttered Lina, stupefied, when a whisper came to her ears at that moment:

"Lina, can you hear me?!"

"Silvie?"

"Thank goodness, I finally got through!"

They weren't conversing through a communication device. This was the magic Silvia specialized in. Vibrating the air, then reading those vibrations as sound, without going through the flesh. If she could locate a person, their distance didn't matter, nor did the presence of obstacles, and she didn't need a communicator or a listening microphone.

She had to admit, the spell was useful for eavesdropping, but looking at it from a purely communication perspective, she could send messages just by vibrating the air in someone's ear canals, without fear of others overhearing. One couldn't expect secrecy from anyone who overheard the voice of whoever she was calling, but it was still a convenient spell for times like this when she had no room to carry a communicator.

"I've discovered who White Mask is!" In front of her, Mikaela put some distance between her and Erika while they continued glaring at each other, when suddenly Lina's attention was stolen by Silvia's voice.

"It was Mia! White Mask's identity is Mikaela Hongou!"

Lina's mind was filled with white. But that lasted only a moment.

"Mia, you were the one in the white mask?!"

For Lina, Mikaela was no more than a simple teammate. She lived in the apartment next door, and their relationship only consisted of having tea and chatting once in a while. Nevertheless, the fact that Mikaela had been the one in their battles to the death delivered no small shock.

As Lina was displaying an incredibly human reaction, Mikaela, who was staring down Erika, turned to look at her. But it wasn't to profess innocence, nor was it to declare remorse. It was a cold, inhuman glare, cautious of the enemy.

"What are you trying to pull, now of all times?!" Erika shouted.

Erika believed Lina and the vampire to be accomplices. Lina's shout sounded like nothing more than a bald-faced lie, so Erika pushed it aside and swung her *kodachi*, meaning to use the opening Mikaela had shown to slay her.

She took a step closer and horizontally slashed toward the woman's neck. But the weapon changed trajectory like some sort of parlor trick, weaving past Mikaela's outstretched hand to plunge directly into her chest.

Mikaela looked down in disbelief.

In a way, this result was inevitable.

Lina may have gone through close combat training, but she was still a magician.

Mikihiko may have studied martial arts, but he was still a caster.

And Erika may have learned magic, but she was still a swordswoman. When they fought sword versus fist, Erika's skill was far greater than any magician Mikaela had ever faced.

But a moment later, Erika was the one whose expression pulled back in tension. Completely unconcerned by the fact that she was wearing a skirt, she raised a foot and delivered a kick to Mikaela's gut. The impact shook the *kodachi* out, and with a pivoting jump, Erika pulled far back.

Mikaela's right hand sliced through Erika's afterimage. Her fingers had twisted into hooked nails, and a pyramid-shaped energy field surrounded them. Then, before Erika's and Lina's very eyes, the hole pierced in her chest closed up in an instant.

"Healing magic?! She healed that wound instantly?!"

"It looks like we're dealing with a real monster..."

Lina's voice was tight with shock, while Erika spat her words, still staring down her opponent.

"In that case, how about this?"

They heard that voice from behind the trailer.

As it spoke, the winter suddenly intensified. A pinpoint cold wave flew at Mikaela. The American, without any time to resist, either physically or magically, froze on the spot.

"Miyuki?"

Erika, her stance slipping, said the name in shock. The one who had appeared in her sight was, without any room for doubt, Miyuki. She could see Tatsuya behind her, too.

"What's going on?" Silvia shot into her commander's ear in a panic. *"Lina, are you all right?!"*

"I'm fine for now, but please send any free soldiers as reinforcements. This might turn into a rather messy escape."

"——Understood. I'll dispatch them immediately."

Lina gave her orders in a quiet whisper.

As this transpired, Tatsuya was walking up to Lina from her front.

"Cut."

Lina quickly said a single word. Silvia's spell ended. It might not have made a difference, but it was to hide their secrets. Tatsuya would have seen her lips move, but he didn't say anything to that effect.

"Lina, she seems to be an acquaintance of yours, but we'll be taking her," he said as he turned to her frozen sculpture of a neighbor and approached her.

"The Maximillian people… Did you kill them?"

At Lina's question, Tatsuya gave something that fell short of a pained grin. "What a scary thing to say. I just put them to sleep for a bit."

The Maximillian employees weren't collaborators and didn't know Mikaela's identity. They were just civilians who had been caught up in all this. If Tatsuya and the others caused a commotion now, it would give her the chance she needed to get out of the situation, but she also genuinely felt relieved that they wouldn't be causing the employees any more trouble.

"Wait a second. I can't let you just take her away."

Lina probably couldn't help it, but she'd been convinced and had withdrawn. Instead, it was Erika who was ready to appeal for a victor's rights.

"It may seem stupid to you, Tatsuya, but we have a sense of honor at stake here. If that woman is the one who hurt Leo, I won't give her to anyone else—not even you."

She hadn't taken up a fighting posture, but she readied the grip on her *kodachi*, without an ounce of needless strength or anything more than the power it needed so that she could shift into a fighting stance right away.

Actually, there was no need to gauge that slight action—one at the glare she was giving would explain everything.

Erika was 100 percent serious.

"It's not like I need her."

But she'd had an extreme misunderstanding.

"Huh?"

As expected, her expression turned to astonishment. Tatsuya's answer had been like clapping his hands right in her face.

"You're going to investigate the woman and deal with her, right?"

Lina's lips drew back when she heard "deal with her." Her face made it clear that she was desperately telling herself she had no right to comment.

"It's fine with me as long as you share what you come up with."

Tatsuya wasn't watching Lina when she made that expression. His eyes were focused on keeping both Erika and Katsuto within his field of vision.

"I'll contact you."

At Katsuto's words, Tatsuya responded with a bow.

Tatsuya watched Katsuto and Erika,

Miyuki watched Tatsuya and Erika,

Katsuto watched Tatsuya and Lina,

and Erika watched Tatsuya and Miyuki.

Only Mikihiko kept a close eye on the surround area, and he was the quickest to spot something wrong.

"Look out!"

The warning was so sudden that he only managed to get out two words. But it did its job. An airborne electrical discharge caused by an emission-type spell stopped on the barrier Katsuto had expanded and was erased by the anti-magic Tatsuya loosed.

Miyuki and Erika turned around to the caster who had fired the spell. Then they both stopped in place, dumbfounded.

The woman who had fired the electric magic attack was still frozen. A living human, or even something inhuman, couldn't be conscious in this state, nor could they ever use magic—that was what common sense dictated.

But that was now overturned. The ice sculpture was wrapped in electric light.

"Self-destruct?!"

Lina was the one to cry out.

"Get down!"

Katsuto and Tatsuya shouted in unison. Tatsuya scooped up his sister; Mikihiko protected Mizuki with his arms; and Katsuto, Erika, and Lina curled up, taking a defensive posture.

Mikaela's body burst out of Miyuki's ice and spat flames. It burned down to nothing in an instant like a dry piece of paper.

And then—from the empty spot where the dancing ashes had disappeared, magical lightning bolts attacked all five of the students on the ground: Tatsuya, Miyuki, Lina, Erika, and Katsuto.

Dull clouds hung in the winter sky, looking as though snow would start at any moment. But the rain of electric attacks hadn't come from the clouds; instead it had poured down from an empty spot in midair. It wasn't lightning. Their speed was far less than thousands of kilometers per second—the naked eye could perceive their movement. It was, at most, the speed at which a bolt would be fired from a crossbow.

But even a small, golf ball–sized orb of lightning was enough to take any human out of the equation. If ten of them hit at the same time, it would likely end in death.

And just because their eyes could follow them didn't mean they had any time to prepare defensive walls when shot at from a distance of less than ten meters. The only reason they stopped the initial barrage was because of the effects of the walls they still had up, which they'd expanded, mistakenly thinking the self-destruct earlier was an attack on them. If this attack had been unleashed out of nowhere, it doubtless wouldn't have left everyone unharmed. And this wasn't to say the crisis was gone now, either.

Tatsuya's magic erased the flash of light that appeared at Miyuki's back before she could turn around.

As for the ball lightning that appeared over Erika's head, it electrified the cloud of ice particles Miyuki had made and disappeared.

Katsuto's barrier halted an electric flash, and Lina's plasma scattered a lightning attack.

There was no sign of an activation sequence being used, but the ball lightning's creation and the addition of a movement vector to the lightning bolts had been event alterations caused by psion-constructed magic programs. Reading the signs of the event alterations—which involved watching which electrons separated from molecules and converged in midair—although the attack looked as though it was occurring at random points, they barely managed to make it in time.

There was no sign of a caster. At the very least, not one in range of Tatsuya's "vision." A magician wasn't what his "vision" had found.

That must be the parasite!

Magic fired from a clump of psycheons, floating in the sea of information.

Mikihiko and Mizuki had left the other five and hidden themselves behind the trailer slightly farther away.

The flashes of light that appeared in midair scattered before reaching their friends. That was what Mizuki was seeing now—she couldn't see any signs or aftereffects of magic. Instead, she saw a barrier that blocked most magical wave motion. Based on their experience a few minutes ago, Mikihiko had judged it necessary to establish that barrier for Mizuki, and thanks to that, they remained unexposed to the electric attacks. The information life-form, its flesh abandoned, wasn't equipped with a way to perceive light or sound. It seemed to be aware of this world by way of magical waves.

The situation their friends were in looked grim. The parasite's attacks were sporadic but sudden, and though they didn't seem to be overwhelming Tatsuya and the others, the group also couldn't counterattack. They simply didn't know where their opponent was in order to attack it. The monster's attacks couldn't hurt them, but they also couldn't take care of the monster.

"That's strange... Why doesn't it run...?" Mikihiko muttered.

Hearing that, Mizuki suddenly began to wonder about something she hadn't been concerned over before:

The thing that used to be a vampire, the parasite—why was it still repeating its ineffectual attacks?

She couldn't say for sure that the parasite had a mind or the ability to make decisions, but even if this was instinctual or mechanical behavior, there must be a reason it was so adamant about remaining here and continuing its assault.

But what could it be?

That was the question that ran through Mizuki's mind.

He dismantled the magic programs the parasite constructed before they could link to any event alterations.

At first, he couldn't get the hang of it, since there was no activation sequence expansion process, or anything to substitute for one, but now Tatsuya had a nearly 100 percent chance of shooting down the parasite's spells.

Now that they had some leeway in dealing with the attacks, he had time to start to doubt.

"Why do you think it is, Shiba?"

It seemed the same for Katsuto.

Right now, Tatsuya and Katsuto had taken up back-to-back positions, with Miyuki, Erika, and Lina between them. They couldn't see each other's faces, but Tatsuya had an easy time understanding the question.

"I don't know whether it's deliberate or instinctual, but it seems to have a reason to keep us here."

"Yes. If it wanted to run, it could do so at any time."

"I, at least, don't have a way to confine it."

"I don't, either. We don't know where it is to begin with."

Tatsuya and Katsuto were in a similar bind. They could see where it was located within the information dimension, but they didn't know where that location corresponded to in the real world. Its position in the physical dimension wasn't clearly defined. The relationship between it and physical beings was horribly weak, as though it was barely hanging on by a slender thread, just enough so that it could activate magic.

Moreover, the enemy was a psycheon information body. Even if they knew its position, if they didn't know its structure, Tatsuya had no way to attack it.

"Lina, you got anything?"

In the middle of his question, Tatsuya pointed his CAD behind him at Erika and pulled the trigger. The spell about to form next to her dispersed.

"…The vampire's main body is a nonphysical entity called a parasite."

At first, she'd decided not to respond to Tatsuya's question, but she seemed to rethink it—now wasn't the time. Lina answered in a reluctant tone.

"The London conference definition, right? I know that."

Lina was speechless for a good ten seconds after Tatsuya's response.

"…Who on earth are you people? Don't tell me all Japanese high school students are like this."

"Don't worry. We're exceptions in several ways."

It wasn't clear whether Lina understood the twisted state of mind hidden behind him saying *exceptions* and not calling them *special*.

"So?"

Tatsuya himself didn't have a clear awareness of it, either, so it wasn't strange she wouldn't understand.

"Parasites possess humans and alter them. There seems to be an affinity when it comes to who they possess, but searching for a host is apparently their behavioral principle, equivalent to a self-preservation instinct."

"In other words, it's looking for the next person to possess?"

"Probably."

"How?"

"That's what I'd like to know."

"…Useless."

"Well, excuse me!"

Even as they traded harsh words, Tatsuya and Katsuto combined their efforts to block every one of the parasite's attacks. But the parasite had to have an energy limit, too. At this time, what Tatsuya felt was not hope but concern.

An information life-form's energy metabolism system was an unknown for him. But he couldn't bring himself to think it could keep on firing magic endlessly. If it decided it wouldn't be able to possess anyone from their five—whether that was a deliberate judgment or an instinctive one—it could move to another place in search of a host.

But that didn't mean making it possess someone on purpose was a good idea. He wasn't overconfident in himself to that degree.

He couldn't see a way out.

"Not good… It's after Erika."

Mikihiko's remark as he protected Mizuki and watched his friends' backs was unintentional.

"Did it detect that Erika doesn't have any way to resist it…?"

Erika's magical faculties generally fell into close-combat skills against opponents with physical bodies. If distance was the only issue, she could blast someone with a somewhat-honed shock wave, but he was pretty sure she had no skills that would let her go up against an enemy without a body.

Mikihiko may not have wanted to acknowledge it, but he was impatient. If he'd been a little calmer, he might have realized that Mizuki was listening to him, and if he had, he wouldn't have been so careless with his next remark.

"If only we knew where it was, we could do something about it…"

After hearing Mikihiko's comment to himself, Mizuki hardened her resolve.

"Yoshida, please undo the barrier."

"Huh?"

It wasn't as though he'd forgotten she was there, but the unexpected request made his reply a confused one.

"Shibata, what was that?"

"I might be able to tell where it is."

At that point, Mikihiko finally realized he'd spoken aloud something he'd meant to keep to himself. He grimaced, regretting it.

That didn't seem to bother Mizuki. With a strong force of will in her eyes, she looked up sharply at Mikihiko.

"…I can't. It would be too stimulating. Remember how much it affected you even when its demon energy was suppressed? There's no telling what'll happen if you look directly at it now that the energy is released. In the worst case, you could go blind."

"When I chose to be a magician, I was prepared for the risks. Erika's in danger, isn't she? If I can't help now, the power I have doesn't mean anything, and there's no point in me being here."

He knew what she meant. He'd been raised with those exact values himself.

But he'd thought Mizuki had been born into a relatively affluent, ordinary—if you called not having magical aptitude ordinary—family, and that she was born with her demon-sight in a genetic throwback way. She was supposed to be a girl raised by parents with no attitude toward handling magic, of only a side-family bloodline, so thinly connected that if she hadn't been born, they wouldn't have even known there had been a caster in their lineage at all.

She had neither the reason nor the need to possess such resolve.

Mikihiko wanted to tell her not to say things like that. Considering yourself an accessory to magic gave certain kinds of magic fuel, and that was something only people like him, who had acquired a lot of security, needed to have. It wasn't meant for a *girl* who had simply been born with magical talent by chance.

After thinking about it and putting aside the fact that he was still no more than a *boy* himself, he said, "...All right."

In the end, he could do nothing but consent to his classmate's wishes. The very values constraining him as a magician from an elite family forced him to consent.

Mikihiko took a folded-up cloth out of his blazer pocket and handed it to Mizuki. When she took it, confused, he told her to try opening it. The cloth was thinner than she expected and about the size of a shawl. It was a Yoshida family magic tool, created based on a treasured Shinto item called a *hi-re*.

"Put it around your neck. If you think things have gotten dangerous, use it to cover your eyes. It should have a stronger effect than the glasses you wear."

Mizuki, probably spurred by the firm tone, didn't offer any questions and wrapped the thin cloth around her neck. A moment later, Mikihiko reached out to her, unwrapped the cloth, then made it hang down at her chest so that it was the same length on the left and right.

With her neck and shoulders being touched, Mizuki's body tensed nervously, but Mikihiko missed it altogether.

"Promise me. Promise me you won't do anything crazy. Erika wouldn't want someone else getting hurt for her sake."

"...I promise," nodded Mizuki, forgetting her embarrassment at the boy's fixed stare.

"Here goes," Mikihiko muttered, and Mizuki gripped the ends of the cloth he'd given her.

Just answering him with an unwavering *yes*, even though it was such a short reply, took all her mental energy.

She was so scared she couldn't even have lied.

But strangely, it didn't make her feel like running away.

She had an odd belief that this was her role.

Mikihiko murmured something she couldn't make out. A moment later, the chaotic wave came crashing over them.

She didn't even have time to think that her eyes hurt.

Intense pain shot through her body. But she couldn't even figure out exactly where the pain was.

As her knees threatened to give out, she used all her energy and opened her eyes wide.

And at that moment, she understood just how many things she didn't see—how many things she closed her eyes to—on a daily basis.

What she saw was now an alien world, with one alien thing that stood out.

Her gut told her it was the parasite.

It fired a spell, which collided with Katsuto's barrier and disappeared.

Hidden in that electric attack, she could see a slender, reaching thread.

Several of those threads were coming off the monster's "body."

They were long and thin, closing in on Lina and Erika, blocked by Katsuto's wall and shredded apart by Tatsuya's gunshots.

Those threads were mixed in with the electricity, and instinctively, she knew that they were trying to invade the girls' bodies through their bioelectric currents.

That was how it *looked* to her.

"It's over there."

Her mouth formed words, and her arm pointed, of their own accord. Mizuki was watching like a theatergoer on the other side of the silver screen.

"About seven feet above Erika, three feet to the right, and little bit behind—twenty inches. There's a point of contact there that the monster is using."

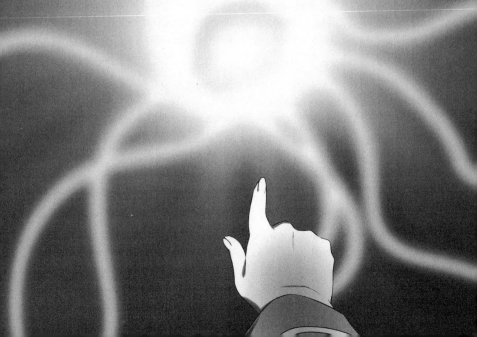

Mizuki had shown Mikihiko where the hole was, through which the threads were stretching into this world.

Considering even the time it would take to answer her to be a waste, Mikihiko's fingers danced over his CAD. His personal fan-shaped device unfolded into a strip of paper inscribed with the spell of the flames that surround Vidyaraja, the Wisdom King. He funneled psions into it, then collected the activation sequence that formed.

The anti-demon spell, Garudaflame—independent information bodies of "flame," whose objective it was to deal external damage to other information bodies—fired at the position Mizuki had indicated.

And then Tatsuya *saw* a magic program fire—one that possessed the concept of "burning" but did not materialize as an object-burning phenomenon, its information bodies cut off from real-world events.

The enemy was before him, but he couldn't help being surprised.

Tatsuya knew the basic tenets of SB magic, or spirit magic. It worked off a system that cut off from reality the independent information bodies floating in the information dimension, then actualized the phenomenon recorded within them.

The spell Mikihiko had just displayed worked under the same logic. The difference was that instead of actualizing it as a phenomenon in the physical dimension, it did so in the nonphysical dimension.

If you were using a spell designed to overwrite the information itself, its difficulty aside, it was neither rare nor original. The information body–dismantling magic he used was built, in a way, to overwrite the information itself.

But Mikihiko's spell had used the system underpinning magic theory—that information accompanied phenomena, and the information accompanying it was recorded in the information dimension—to generate only the phenomenon-accompanying information, thereby interfering only with the information dimension without interfering with the physical dimension. The "burning," which hadn't appeared in the real world, had caused an overwriting of information in the information dimension, telling it that something would burn at that location.

It was like the spell took the concept of what a magic system *should* be and turned it on its head. But what surprised Tatsuya more was how he'd suddenly started to clearly see exactly where the parasite was after being unable to get more than a vague impression of it. It was almost as though fuzzy parameters had abruptly been given concrete values.

The phrase *Schrödinger's cat* passed through the back of his mind.

The essence of that thought experiment, where you wouldn't know if the cat inside the box was alive or dead unless you opened the box, was, contrary to the intention of its proponents, that uncertain facts became definite upon being observed. Whether you applied the Copenhagen interpretation or the Everett one, the result would be the same: that for the observer, the uncertain fact would become certain.

In the case of a parasite—this information body called a "monster"—if someone were to observe it, would it become perceptible not only to the observer but to third parties as well?

By Mizuki perceiving it, had its existence in the physical dimension strengthened?

If that was the case...

...then now Mizuki is in danger!

There was no way the parasite wouldn't notice a gaze strong enough to apply changes to its attribute information.

Tatsuya hastily focused his "eyes."

There, he saw the scene he'd feared beginning to unfold.

Thoughts flew by in an instant.

Tatsuya stuck out his left hand, which was not holding a CAD, toward Mizuki.

Those who see can also be seen by those at whom they look.

One doesn't need to borrow Nietzsche's words; this is pure logic: You need a line of sight in order to see someone. And if there is a path for your sight, that means they can see you, too.

When Mizuki perceived the parasite, the parasite *moved its attention* to Mizuki.

"It's coming!"

Hearing Mizuki's shout—or maybe it was a scream—Mikihiko immediately reexpanded the barrier.

"Where?!" he demanded, reinforcing the hastily built defense as much as he could.

The defensive spell was activated mostly out of reflex.

It was mainly meant for concealment.

It provided little defense against things getting inside, and now that they'd been witnessed once, the concealment was only half as effective.

Mikihiko himself knew the necessity of being the one to attack. But Mizuki didn't have the mind to respond to that.

She simply covered her eyes and fell to the ground.

The boy couldn't blame her.

He knew she was a normal girl who had absolutely no experience confronting "evil." That was why Erika wanted him to protect her and why he planned to anyway. He'd already factored in Mizuki seeing the "evil" and losing agency—that was why they'd kept their distance.

Now, thanks to his own miscalculation, it was coming closer. As expected, Mizuki had fallen into panic, so how could he possibly blame her?

Besides—he hadn't the time to.

A "thread" reached out from the parasite. Mikihiko couldn't see it, but he knew "something" was hiding in the electric light, trying to capture her.

Well, Mikihiko wasn't just standing around doing nothing. Even if he couldn't spot the thing, he had ways of cutting off spiritual interference. Old-style casters like Mikihiko had always been experts in dealing with spiritual phenomena by intervening with physical ones.

But at the same time, there were a lot of traditional old-magic spells that needed time to prepare. It was inferior in its speed to instantly react, which the reason people had pushed modern magic as the main method and treated old magic as a mere branch.

Even so, Mikihiko took aim at the hole that opened in the barrier and used a spell called Cutting Exorcism to block evil interference. Though its power was inferior to ritual magic, it possessed speed that rivaled Swiftnine, used by magicians of esoteric Buddhism.

Psions shaped like a sword sliced the thread reaching from the parasite.

But it was, in the end, a simplified spell.

Even if it could sever the curse, it wouldn't be able to slay the main body.

Another thread immediately reached out and neared Mizuki.

Mikihiko, knowing this would be a stalemate, tried to use Cutting Exorcism again.

——But the blade never swung down.

Faster than Mikihiko could use it, a violent wind wrapped in an invisible light blasted the thread away, along with the main body.

The cloth Mizuki had borrowed from him did indeed shut out the discomforting waves that her glasses couldn't block.

But strangely, just because she couldn't feel the discomfort any longer, that didn't mean she couldn't see anymore. The figure floating in the air, lit by a subdued light and with several threads hanging off it, looked just like a floating jellyfish.

That, however, didn't do anything to relieve her terror.

Instead, it made things worse.

Even if she closed her eyes, the figure didn't go away. She saw the threads, and she didn't want to.

Ultrathin tentacles reaching out to grab her. That was what she could see. She couldn't think straight through the visceral fear.

If this had gone on for just a bit longer, it would have left a deep scar on her heart.

Her mind may have broken before her body was violated.

What saved her was a torrent of glittering psions.

The same light she'd seen half a year ago in the lab classroom was reproduced before her eyes with power more overwhelming than before.

It had been an instant thing, but it was impossible for there to be a lack of psion activity during magical combat. Tatsuya's right hand was the one that used dismantling-type magic, but unlike Program Dispersion, he could fire Program Demolition from either hand even without a CAD. Tatsuya collected psions to his right hand and mustered to the limits of his instantaneous output.

As he'd thought, being seen by Mizuki had made the thing into a concrete existence in this world. The closer the parasite got to her, the less its positional information distorted, and the more its distribution converged.

Before, he'd been able to see it as information but not know where it was or where to access it from. But now, Tatsuya understood the parasite clearly.

However, there was no time to tell the others. The tentacle—closer to a primitive amorphous organism's filopodia in his mind—that Mikihiko struck away had already re-formed and was reaching for Mizuki.

It frustrated him, but he had only one chance.

——He narrowed his eyes a little,

——set his sights, imagined a line pointing,

——and released the clump of compressed psions from his right hand.

The psionic current of Program Demolition, the emission point of which he'd set as his palm, shot toward the parasite and blew away both the tentacle and its main body.

"Shibata, are you all right?!"

As he heard Mikihiko's voice—the boy seemed about ready to flip out at how shaken up she was—Tatsuya lowered his left hand.

He wrestled with a feeling of bitterness at the result he'd expected to get from his own typeless magic.

Despite its name, Program Demolition was at heart a means to use a psionic current's pressure to sweep away information bodies, not one to demolish them. If the target was a magic program, then using it to rip the program away from the eidos made it function as an anti-magic spell.

In most cases, the shockwave that occurred when it did the separation would destroy the magic program's informational structure, hence the name "Demolition." However, Program Demolition's psionic current itself wouldn't destroy the information bodies. If the information bodies had a more robust structure than a magic program, they'd just be carried away without its informational structure being destroyed. It was a very possible result.

Even knowing that, he made the decision to use Program Demolition there.

To save Mizuki.

Because he couldn't think of anything else.

"It got away…"

Tatsuya didn't give a response to Katsuto's remark. By only blowing the parasite away with Program Demolition there, it was highly likely that it would flee without them being able to finish it off. Tatsuya had expected that, and that was how it turned out.

"That's fine. It may have gotten away, but it can't be unharmed. We should be thankful nobody got hurt this time."

Katsuto's comment wasn't only to make him feel better. The parasite had counterattacked in a way they hadn't expected, but their side did indeed have zero injuries. But they were the ones who had staged the encounter. It might not have even been planning to fight here.

They'd picked a battle that wasn't necessarily unavoidable, which meant the absolute minimum was everyone getting through unharmed. Their first objective was to capture the enemy, and the next best victory condition was to destroy it. In lieu of that: finding a new, powerful clue that would allow them to discern the full picture of the enemy's forces.

In other words, from the perspective of combat objective completion, this ending gave them close to zero points. They'd just barely managed to not go negative.

What a disgrace...

Only Tatsuya's pride made him keep that thought to himself.

If he'd said it aloud,

Miyuki would be concerned.

Mizuki would fret over it.

Erika would be hurt.

For Tatsuya, that would only be more disgraceful. That was the last sort of parting present he'd want.

[9]

It had become weakened.

It was not something that originally belonged in this world, nor did It wish to be present in this world.

It had the property of being drawn to strong psycheonic waves.

Rapture, anguish, abhorrence, and desire: Prayers, they could be called, these waves of crave-worthy psycheons. And by them, It had been dragged across a momentarily shaken "wall," from a world without form to a world written by form.

The shockwave when It crossed had caused It to split into twelve, and It resided in the humans It attracted.

To continue existing, It needed to absorb psycheons. Simply existing discharged psycheons, little by little. But in this *world with form*, It couldn't absorb psycheons without assistance. To replenish those psycheons, there was no choice but to become one with something with form that could gather psycheons.

As a result of using power so many times while still possessing only Its true body, It had lost a large amount of psycheons that had been accumulating ever since It arrived in this *world with form*. Moreover, It had been caught in a deluge of high-pressure psions, shaving away many of the parts that had intruded upon the physical dimension. That was when It lost the majority of psions as well. Psions were not essential to continued existence, but without enough psions, It would no longer be able to influence the physical dimension.

Its true body didn't possess advanced powers of thought. It was a mere monster, a result of reflecting and amplifying Its host's hidden thoughts and suppressed impulses. The true body only needed instinct-like thought processes to keep existing. Nevertheless, the minute intelligence It possessed understood how difficult it would be to bore a hole through the walls of willpower to gain a new host in Its current weakened state.

It needed a place to rest. A place with no minds and a large quantity of psycheons.

For example, within the blood of a body whose mind had vacated.

For example, in a mindless puppet that gathered psycheons through its human form.

After avoiding human presence and wandering, It found a container that could become a place to rest inside a warehouse on the edge of the First High campus.

The morning after the seven of them had driven off—not exterminated—the parasite:

"Good morning, Tatsuya."

"Good morning, Mizuki, Mikihiko… Erika's still like that, huh?"

In their classroom, Tatsuya encountered his female friend at her desk, face in hand, looking the other way and making every effort to appear displeased.

"Good morning, Tatsuya… Yeah, she's still sulking."

"I am not!"

After Mikihiko bowed with a pained grin, Erika snapped at him from the side, then once again returned to her *I've been offended* pose.

There was, of course, a reason she was so overtly grumpy.

After the vampire had achieved a transformation into a form they'd have to call an "information life-form" yesterday, even though they'd managed to drive it off with overwhelming six-to-one odds in their favor, Tatsuya had let Lina flee without capturing her.

Erika hadn't taken kindly to that. She still had it in her head that Lina had joined forces with the parasite. To make matters worse, Erika had been rendered completely helpless after the parasite had changed into its new shape.

This had been an issue of mismatched strengths, and there wasn't even a fragment of a reason Erika needed to be ashamed, but that didn't seem to fly for her on an emotional level. She'd made all sorts of objections to Tatsuya when he had tried to let Lina leave, and at the end had tried to cut her down.

The display itself had probably been venting. Erika hadn't really meant to kill her, and after being put in a full nelson, she had calmed down. (But when Mikihiko had put her in that hold from behind, she'd yelled "sexual harassment" and punched him as hard as she could.)

But that hadn't convinced her, either, and ever since lunch yesterday she'd been making sure everyone knew she was mad.

"Erika, give it a rest and cheer up already."

Tatsuya spoke directly to her, but his back was still turned.

"Didn't I explain this yesterday? Her *folks* were already starting to arrive."

He muddled the words in consideration of prying ears, but by *folks* he was referring to the reinforcements Lina had called in.

"It was already a huge mess by then. If more stuff happened, we wouldn't have been able to keep other students from wanting to know what was going on. If things went bad, there would have been a panic."

——Incidentally, it had been Mayumi who had ended up toiling to cover the whole thing up, not Tatsuya.

"I get that, but..."

Erika seemed to understand that much as well. She muttered in a sullen tone, her face still turned away.

"We also needed to patch up things with the Maximillian employees."

———In addition, it had been Tatsuya who created a situation where it was necessary to patch things up, but Lina (and her subordinates) who actually did it.

"I'm not about to say Lina's completely in the clear, but she wasn't guilty enough in that situation to recklessly go after her. If she really is guilty of something, she'll come attack again. And if that happens, she'll get no mercy."

Tatsuya's tone of voice was the same as always. But the dangerous intent in his words caused Erika to turn around without thinking.

"…Can we beat her?"

Erika still didn't know that the red-haired, golden-eyed magician was Lina. But even in just the battle against the parasite yesterday, she had felt firsthand that Lina was no ordinary magic user.

"Whether we win or lose is up to chance. Besides, it's not certain that Lina is going to try something on us anyway."

"But we'll have no mercy."

"Nope."

Tatsuya's manner of speaking was incredibly impassive, which only served to convey how serious he was. Mikihiko, who was listening from beside him, was cringing, and Mizuki was clearly frightened. But his attitude seemed to please Erika, and her mood made a full recovery.

On that same day, Lina (who hadn't gone to school) was getting what was probably the first taste of discomfort she'd had in her life.

She'd once been invited to a presidentially sponsored tea party, where she'd been forced to go through a thorough body check, which for a woman was nothing if not humiliating. But this hearing, under way at the USNA embassy, was uncomfortable enough to rival that.

"…Then, what you mean to say is the Sirius of the Stars was unable to do anything against a high school student, and the suspect was taken away?"

The plea that Mikaela Hongou had self-destructed and ultimately hadn't been stolen made it up to her throat, but even she knew that wasn't what the inquiry committee was getting at, so she quietly lowered her head.

"And the suspect was the operator living in the room right next door, wasn't she? You had a whole month, yet you didn't realize who she was?"

This time, Lina really wanted to shout back that their "suspect" was someone *they* had chosen as an operator... But she knew she couldn't possibly say something like that, which just stressed her out even more.

The nagging remarks continued. She may have been a magician with talent that spoke for itself, but she was a teenage major. More than a few people in the USNA military were jealous of her. The less actual combat experience a military official possessed, the stronger the tendency toward that, and right now, the men in front of her (for some reason, they hadn't chosen any women for the inquiry committee) were all the stereotypical high-ranking officers who knew nothing of real battle.

Their pointless disagreeableness went on. It started to seem silly to bother thinking seriously or getting mad about it, so Lina idly let their words flow by her.

"By the way, did your medical check come back with no issues, Major? You had several direct exchanges with the infected person, didn't you? Don't you think you should at least make sure there are no bite marks on you anywhere? If you haven't done that yet, you should check on that right now."

But when one came out with this abuse, this absurd remark that deserved the moniker of "sexual harassment," even she had to wake up. In the first place, they called their enemy "vampires" for convenience's sake, but they'd never bitten any of their victims. She was astonished they'd had the gall to sit here without having read any of the reports, but more than that—were these lecherous old assholes telling her to get naked right now, in front of them?!

"That would be incredibly rude to the major."

The only reason she could stop herself before making an outburst was because reinforcements appeared with good timing. Thanks to that, she could protect her reputation (and it was only a reputation) for being calm and thoughtful for one so young.

"Colonel Balance?"

More than one or two of the inquiry committee members moved to yell angrily at the woman who had suddenly burst into the kangaroo court calling itself an inquiry. But after realizing who she was, not one of them felt heroic enough to rebuke her for it.

Her name was Colonel Virginia Balance. Considering how the Stars organization worked, one would think her full name had to be a code name (Virginia for Virgo, and Balance for the scales of Libra), but it was her actual name. She'd just seen the last day of her thirties a few days ago, but the gallant *big sister–like* woman didn't really look it.

Of course, what made them scared of her wasn't the fact that she was a colonel, or the fact that she had a youthful appearance.

For one thing, rank wasn't an issue, since the majority of the military officials assembled here had done inquiries on generals before.

What was making them restrain themselves (in polite terms) was her job.

The USNA Joint Chiefs of Staff Information Bureau Internal Inspection Office's first deputy commissioner.

Reformed and rebuilt after the integration with Canada's military, the number two of the Internal Inspection Office, which kept a watchful eye on illegal acts not only by uniformed personnel but nonuniformed personnel as well. That was Colonel Balance's job.

Given the details of her duties, she wasn't out of place here. In fact, it was strange that they hadn't called her to begin with—because it was impossible, given her position and role, that the other committee members didn't know she'd come to Japan for this inquiry.

It was impossible to lay blame on her, despite her sudden entrance.

"Please, excuse me. May I have permission to make a statement?"

The colonel looked over the inquiry committee member sitting in the highest location with a stinging glance, then asked to speak, courteous in words alone.

"Y-yeah. Go ahead."

"Thank you. I will leave the question of why you didn't call me here for another opportunity."

Half the inquiry committee looked frightened, but Colonel Balance merely gave them a glance before turning back to Lina.

"The mission assigned to Major Sirius was not suitable given her duty and her skills, and it is my belief that her failing in her mission does not deserve laying the onus upon her person."

Whispering spread through the room. The reason they hadn't called Colonel Balance to the inquiry was because they knew they wouldn't be able to say anything careless with her in attendance—she was well informed in both military administration and military command affairs. Some thought that, as another woman, she would also side with Lina automatically. But for her to so frankly defend Lina caught them by surprise.

"Regardless, however, of where the responsibility for this lies, the fact that someone in the position of Stars commander was defeated in magical combat is something we need to be concerned about. After all, the Sirius is the strongest magician in our forces."

Lina clenched her fists tight. Colonel Balance's indication was something Lina herself felt more than anyone. It frustrated her so much that her back teeth nearly started to grate audibly.

"Of course, Major Sirius will no doubt also want a chance to vindicate herself. Isn't that right, Major?"

"Of course, ma'am!"

The colonel nodded at her response and moved her eyes to the group on the platform. "It is my opinion that we should have Major Sirius resume her current mission. I also suggest that we raise our on-site support to the highest level."

"The highest level of support, ma'am?" asked one of the committee members. "What do you mean by that exactly?"

Colonel Balance gave a fearless grin. "I believe I will remain here in Tokyo under the pretense of monitoring our military attaché."

The muttering that occurred this time didn't go away very quickly.

"In addition, the director general has already given permission to use the Brionac."

The muttering changed into a clamor.

Even Lina wore an expression of disbelief. "Colonel, ma'am, is that true?"

"It is."

The question wasn't very discreet from a rank order perspective, but the colonel answered it with a smile. And then, she added,

"I was the one who brought it here."

Silvia was waiting for Lina upon leaving the inquiry committee room.

"Silvie, where on earth did you go? That was awful!"

It had been nearly a day since Lina had seen Silvia in person. For some reason, when she safely *returned home* from First High yesterday, Silvia was nowhere to be seen, either in their apartment or in any secret locations.

Because of the stress she'd accumulated during the inquiry, Lina sounded like she was venting. Still, it was like an innocent joke from someone who was off her game, and Silvia would normally have smiled and ignored it. But Silvia accepted the *reproach* with a serious expression, straightened up, then offered, "I apologize, ma'am," in an unresisting voice.

"Huh? Silvie? I wasn't being serious or anything..."

"I know you weren't being serious, Lina. But I have to apologize to you."

Lina frowned, realizing this wouldn't be a conversation to have lightly.

"If I'd realized Mia's identity earlier, it wouldn't have driven you into such a disadvantageous situation, ma'am."

Saying *That's not true* would have been bravado. She'd been completely cut off amid the enemy yesterday. Lina was aware of that, so she couldn't deny Silvia's words.

"I was not good enough to fulfill my rear support role on this mission. I'm terribly sorry, *Commander.*"

"What's wrong, Silvie? You're acting like we won't see each other again—"

"Commander," said Silvia, her address cutting off Lina's response. "I've received orders from the General Staff Office to return home. Last night's investigation has diagnosed me as possibly *infected*, and I'll be undergoing a thorough examination on home soil."

"That's nonsense! That mutation isn't like a virus! There's no possible way a medical examination could tell you whether you have it before you change!"

"That's exactly why, Major."

"Colonel?!"

Addressing her from behind was Colonel Balance, who had just saved her from a tight situation.

"I apologize. I had no intention of eavesdropping."

"No, ma'am. We were the ones standing here making conversation."

"I see." Balance gave a slight smile to Lina as she did her best to stand on ceremony, then immediately went back to her stone-faced expression. "Regarding Warrant Officer Mercury's treatment, it's as you said, Major—we have no current way to detect the contagion before it changes you. In other words, we can't say for sure that the warrant officer hasn't been infected."

"Then why not me, ma'am?!"

"You're right. There's no proof that you're not infected, either. But if you were to oppose the military, Major, our forces would suffer grave losses. Therefore, we cannot allow you to return home until we know you're safe."

Lina's face paled. With no way to discern if the parasite had possessed someone, this was essentially a declaration of exile. At the same time, the pieces clicked together. This was the reason Balance had stressed that she continue her mission.

"On the other hand, were Warrant Officer Mercury to become a vampire and betray our military, considering her skill set, she could leak our military secrets to plenty of other nations. Therefore, she needs to return home at once."

That was logical as well. She felt emotionally opposed to it, but as a soldier who prioritized logical reasoning, Lina had to accept it.

"That's how it is. I'll assign you a different aide."

"No, ma'am. I don't need one."

Balance's proposal was based on her needs, but there was clearly also favorable consideration in it. Lina refused it outright.

"Anyone living with me will come under the same suspicion of infection. Thankfully, even living alone, Japanese apartments are set up so that I have no trouble."

"I see. If that's what you wish, Major, I'll arrange for nobody to be sent."

"Yes, ma'am."

After the two saw Balance off with a salute, Silvia gave Lina a teary-eyed smile.

"Commander..."

"Silvie, stop calling me that. It's too stiff. Please, call me Lina, like you have until now."

"...All right. Lina, it hurts me to go back home and leave you to your own oversleeping habits, but..."

"Now you're too informal! Besides, the day before yesterday was the only day I slept in, wasn't it?!"

As Lina's breathing became rapid, Silvia gave her a smile, this time without tears. "Lina, you haven't been infected. The demon has another thing coming if it thinks our Sirius is weak enough for it to possess her."

"——Of course. I would never lose to a mere parasite. The next time I find it, I'll burn it to cinders for sure."

"I know you will, so please finish your mission quickly and come back to HQ, Commander."

Silvia saluted, the smile remaining in her eyes, and Lina returned the salute, her attitude a deliberately confident one.

◇ ◇ ◇

Mitsugu Kuroba, who was on a business trip in Yokohama for his *legitimate* job, thought hard when the phone in his hotel room rang. He hadn't told the person he was in town to see that this was where he was staying. That person could contact him over wireless whenever they wanted, so he didn't need to tell them the hotel. And for the same reason, nobody related to him would call him over a landline, either. If it was for his *other* job, a call that went through the hotel front was even less likely...

"Hello?"

But he didn't feel the need to let the answering machine pick up. Just in case, he responded to the voice-only call without naming himself.

"Mitsugu, do you have a free moment?"

The moment he heard the voice drift from the receiver, his back unconsciously straightened. "Miss Maya... Yes, I'm quite fine right now."

His anxiety didn't come out of his voice, though, even when faced with the current leader of the Yotsuba. He was, after all, the leader of one of its branches—the one in charge of its information network. Maya and Mitsugu were cousins, though she was a bit his elder. The younger sister of the previous Yotsuba head was his mother, and his son was a candidate to be the next leader. Strictly speaking, he wasn't of direct Yotsuba descent, but using a more general standard, Mitsugu was extremely close to it. But it was exactly because the blood ran so thickly in him that he knew quite well how terrifying Maya could be.

It also immediately answered the question of why she was calling the hotel phone. This hotel was managed by a business the Yotsuba controlled in much the same way as Four Leaves Technology. The room he was using was also equipped with secret gimmicks for those with connections to the Yotsuba. In fact, he almost felt embarrassed for not immediately realizing the call would be from the main family.

Of course, he didn't mention that.

"It must be something urgent, yes? Please, go ahead and ask whatever you wish of me."

"*You know, Mitsugu… Can't you do something about that theatrical way you talk?*"

"Oh, my beautiful cousin, you wound me. Theatrical? I am always quite serious, I assure you."

He heard a tired sigh over the phone. He had a surprisingly good relationship with this terrifying cousin of his. She'd usually put in a courteous retort at his mannerisms, and so Mitsugu felt himself calm down completely through the exchange. That might have been his cousin's plan as well, but he knew he'd gain nothing reading too much into it.

"*I'll get to the point, then… Mitsugu, have you finished locating the parasite hosts?*"

The man was well aware that his face pulled back. This wasn't his legitimate job, or his other job—but his *real* job: the original role of the Kuroba. Mitsugu understood that, thus, he could not cut corners nor be unable to answer.

"Twelve in total. The US has dealt with four, and Miyuki and Tatsuya blew away another yesterday, so there are seven remaining. I've pinpointed where they are as well."

"*My, a fast worker as usual. I should have expected as much, Mitsugu.*"

"Not at all. You were the one working so hard to draw the attention of the Saegusa and Chiba. You saved me the effort of bringing it to light."

"*How modest of you.*"

Mitsugu didn't deny her this time—what he'd just said was, as Maya noted, nothing but modesty. He'd only finished finding all seven of them last night, of course, so he was just on time.

"*I actually received a request this morning from our client, telling us, and I quote, 'not to let these filthy monsters do as they please in Tokyo any longer.'*"

"Well, that's harsh. I don't recall Tokyo being under the Yotsuba's jurisdiction." Mitsugu frowned—a sincere gesture. It was for that very reason he had to be very delicate in moving his pieces around the city.

"I'm sure they have other pressing concerns. In any case, that's what things look like, so if you would please put an end to things for now."

"An end, you say?" he asked carefully. If he mishandled his reaction, he'd end up forced to overwork himself.

"Please remove all the hosts."

Maya's voice was incredibly plain. Her voice wasn't suppressing any emotion, nor did it sound cold or cruel. The Yotsuba head's voice was awfully—if the word could be used like this—routine.

"Not capture them?"

"Yes. Erase them."

"If the current hosts die, the parasites will apparently scatter in search of a different host. It will take a bit more time to locate their new hosts—"

"I don't mind. How does a parasite leave a host after death? How far is it able to move in an information body state? How much time does it need to fully merge with a new host, and how long does it take to resume its activities?"

"You'd like me to observe that and report to you?"

"It will probably give us valuable data. You can do it, can't you?"

With the receiver in his hand, despite this being a voice-only call, Mitsugu bowed deeply. "I am at your disposal."

"Please make another report after you've finished getting rid of them."

"I ask that you give me until the day after tomorrow."

"That will be fine. Thank you."

After Mitsugu assented to her command once more, the call ended.

Gathering psions in the palm of one's hand and grasping them.

That was the usual image for employing Program Demolition.

A normal Program Demolition would imply ramming those gripped psions into an expanding activation sequence or a functioning magic program. But the skill Tatsuya desired now wasn't to shoot down an information body using the actual body hosting it but to snipe an information body in the information dimension.

A means of directly attacking a parasite drifting through the sea of information.

He opened his clenched hand.

He left his arm at his side.

Any actions to complement his image of the physical direction would actually get in the way. Things like trails and trajectories didn't come about in the information dimension. If one defined what existed where, it was there.

Overlapping his targets, independent information bodies— apparently a type of *shikigami*—the clump of psions Tatsuya fired appeared in the information dimension, the Idea.

In a physical dimension, multiple objects cannot occupy the same position simultaneously.

But information had no such rule. An information body that existed in the information dimension didn't have a physical allocation restriction. Tatsuya's psions released from a compressed state at a "location" that overlapped with the independent information bodies, dissipated, and vanished without having any effect on the independent information bodies.

He grunted, clenching his teeth in frustration. As Miyuki looked on from the side with a worried expression, Yakumo, who had helped him with creating the targets, began to speak in his usual transcendental tone.

"It figures that even you'd have trouble with this," Yakumo went on drolly. "Well, this is one of those skills that those who can't do it will never be able to, no matter how hard they try."

Miyuki shot a murderous glare his way.

To Yakumo's credit, his expression didn't change. Although it did look as though a bead of something like cold sweat formed near his temple.

"Doesn't seem to me you have absolutely no compatibility with it, though, since you learned how to fire a farstrike in the true world in three days."

As Yakumo continued, somewhat flustered, Miyuki directed an even more criticizing gaze at him.

"Master, please set up the next ones."

But after Tatsuya requested to continue the training, Miyuki's attention turned to her brother.

——It had been one week since that day. The day when the parasite had invaded the school and the fight had come to a bitter conclusion. Tatsuya had asked for Yakumo's training the morning after, and today was now the seventh day.

Yakumo had tried to reassure him, but Tatsuya had gained a renewed sense of the walls to his own talent in these past two or three days. The fact that he'd learned to fire a psionic bullet at a target in the information dimension would have been rapid progress for a normal pupil. But Tatsuya had always been able to perceive information bodies adrift in the Idea. If you compared him with a normal pupil, he would have had a huge advantage before starting. So the fact that he couldn't make a psionic bullet *work* against a target was not the sort of thing that gave him an optimistic evaluation of himself.

"Well, sometimes you can't tell whether or not you have the affinity until you see the results. Part of spell casting means not being anywhere close one day and then suddenly being able to do it the next."

Perhaps picking up on Tatsuya's irritation, Yakumo gave him a few words of consolation.

"Although, it's also true that we don't have time to wait for eventualities."

Of course, he didn't end with just consolation.

"In your case, you know where you're supposed to aim, so I'd think putting together a different attack method instead of the far-strike would be an idea."

Upon hearing that, though he knew he was being rude, Tatsuya gave a bitter chuckle. "You can't develop new spells willy-nilly like that. I'll admit we're getting nowhere, but you think too highly of me."

"Do I, though? You're certainly incapable in certain fields, but you have extraordinary talent in spell improvement and development. Not a good idea to limit your own possibilities like that, in my opinion."

"That's right, Brother!"

As Tatsuya looked even less enthusiastic, his sister stepped up to encourage him.

"I know you can do it, Brother. You can make wonderful ideas reality, ideas that other people would never even think of."

…Actually, that was well past encouragement; it was sheer confidence. The way she said it didn't leave anything open to interpretation.

"I do not mean to intrude on Yakumo's strategy, but I believe you have no need to give up on either option. Couldn't you continue your first plan of using Program Demolition to directly attack, while you move forward with new spell development at the same time?"

If it had been anyone but Miyuki who said that, Tatsuya would have scorned it as ridiculous or settled it with a laugh, asking if the person wanted him to die of overwork.

But faced with his little sister's gaze, so radiantly confident that it far surpassed mere hope, he found that calling the idea impossible was instead what was impossible for him.

Tatsuya and Lina weren't the only ones who had gotten moving in the hopes of exacting revenge. Erika, Mikihiko, Mayumi, and Katsuto had all gone to work for the rematch against the overarching threat called the parasite.

But then, in the first week of February 2096, bad news drifted in from beyond the Pacific Ocean:

"Brother, this is…!"

The Shiba siblings learned of it on the news during their morning meal. It was as if the story had waited for morning to come; it was so shocking that Tatsuya was dumbfounded.

"…That's just what Shizuku told us, isn't it?" Tatsuya muttered darkly, after finally getting his voice back.

"…Yeah, though it seems like it's been dramatized quite a bit."

The news itself took the form of an anonymous whistleblowing report from a certain government-related official.

It went like this.

——Last year, on October 31, the United States government ordered its military magicians to develop a way to counter Japan's secret military weapon that they'd used on the southern shore of the Korean Peninsula. The magicians then went to the Dallas National Particle Accelerator Institute and forced the scientists there to perform an experiment to generate a micro black hole, ignoring the scientists' warnings. During the experiment, a hole opened in the dimensional wall, and it called forth a demon from another dimension.

The magicians tried to counter Japan's secret weapon by using the demon.

But they failed to control it, and it possessed their bodies instead. The true identities of the vampires who had been causing such a mess on the streets since the beginning of last year were the magicians possessed by the demon.

That placed threefold blame on the military for the victims. First: They failed to stop their magicians from forcing such a reckless experiment to go through. Second: Knowing the risks were high, the experiment went through anyway. Third: Magicians belonging to the military had brought harm to civilians, notwithstanding the high possibility they'd gone mad.

The underlying cause of this scandal was the military's failure to completely regulate magicians. Magic was powerful, but nobody knew when the supernatural ability would go out of control. Was using it truly within national interests? Shouldn't citizens be carefully rethinking their stance on the matter—?

"It's skillfully sugarcoated, but…"

"Then…"

"Yes, the expulsion of magicians is probably their true intention."

Tatsuya's voice was bitter as he answered Miyuki, who had grimaced, not so much in concern as from being appalled.

"The same roots as humanism... Non-magicians tremendously outnumber the magically inclined, so it doesn't bear thinking about which group the media would side with. The bigger issue is the news source."

Tatsuya reached out for the telephone console, but halfway there, he stopped.

Who had he been about to call...? Out of several candidates, for whatever reason, one face, who they couldn't call an ally, was the one that came to Miyuki's mind.

After hearing the sudden and unexpected bombshell news story—or maybe *scandal* was more appropriate—Lina's head was in nonmetaphorical pain. It wasn't just her imagination—she had a real headache.

Her honest feelings were that this was no time to be going to school. Still, a girl who was 100 percent combat oriented wouldn't be of any help in quelling a media panic; and besides, Colonel Balance had specifically instructed her to go about her business as usual.

After receiving a direct order from her superior officer, she couldn't claim ignorance and skip out on classes. As she nursed her throbbing headache, she went through the ticket gate at First High Station. From here, it was a straight shot to the school gates, but...

"Good morning, Lina."

Suddenly, a figure appeared in front of Lina. It made her forget all about her headache, turn on her heel, and dart away like a fleeing rabbit.

"What's the big idea, running away at the sight of us?"

"Ah, ah-ha-ha-ha-ha..."

Lina's escape ended in failure after just three steps.

Miyuki had gone around the turnstiles in advance.

With her classmate smiling sweetly and nowhere left to run, Lina seemed to settle on smiling and passing it off as nothing for now.

——Not that it meant much.

"That's fine. Well, it's not actually fine, but we don't need to be late because we wasted time here with pointless banter. There's something I want to ask you. Let's talk as we walk."

"…Talk about what?"

She obeyed and went with them, even with her caution clear as day. The reason was that Lina knew her current position; she couldn't cause a fuss in a place like this. Tatsuya knew from their short acquaintanceship that she wasn't a very patient person, so he got right to the point.

"Did you see the news this morning?" he asked.

"…Yeah. Not that I wanted to anyway," she answered, sounding genuinely displeased.

"How much of it is true?"

Lina didn't have any duty to faithfully answer his questions. But she felt like complaining to someone. As though she were thankful they knew everything about her, since she didn't need to hide anything at this point, she began venting her stress.

"All the important bits are downright lies!" She was still keeping her voice down, but her tone was severe. "They don't tell you anything except surface-level facts, which makes them even nastier! Typical information control!"

"So, as I thought, they're manipulating public opinion."

Lina tilted her head to the side—she couldn't understand why that seemed to make sense to Tatsuya. "What? As you thought? They're controlling opinions?"

"Well, it's just speculation. Anyway, the surface-level facts are correct, right?"

"…Yeah!" spat Lina in response, rankled that he'd so bluntly noted the one thing she didn't want him to.

"But those things should have all been naturally treated as confidential. I wouldn't think someone on the outside could find out about them so easily."

"…It's the Seven Sages, probably."

"Seven Sages? Not the Greek ones, I presume?"

"There's this group that calls themselves that. Nobody knows who they are, though."

Tatsuya couldn't help but be surprised at Lina's comment. "You don't know who they are? Aren't they a USNA-based organization? Is that possible?"

"It is possible! Frustrating though it may be!" Lina's expression betrayed genuine annoyance. "All we have is their name, which they gave us. No matter how much we investigate, we can't come up with anything. The only thing we know is that they call their officers Sages, and there are seven of them."

"Sages... That's rather on the nose, isn't it?"

"I'm telling you, we don't know who they are!"

"Hold on, Lina. Don't get mad at my brother for it."

"What? I—"

Miyuki's comment had been incredibly blind—she hadn't read the mood at all. Lina nearly exploded and shouted, *What was that?!* or *Are you saying it's my fault?!* but after a few deep breaths, she managed to stop herself from doing something that would draw attention.

"...Don't let it get to you, Angelina," she muttered under her breath. "Miyuki's the strange one here. If you start letting every one of that brother-obsessed girl's brother-complex remarks get to you, it'll never end. Don't think about the brother complex! No brother complex, no brother complex..."

Thankfully, nobody heard the calming, spell-like words well enough to find fault with them.

"Lina?" wondered Tatsuya.

"Huh? Sorry. What did you say?"

"These Seven Sages—is it possible they're linked to the humanist movement?"

As they walked, Lina returned to reality and considered the possibility for a moment—only to shake her head. "I can't deny it outright, but probably not. Judging from past examples, the Seven Sages aren't fanatical, and they don't abide by an ideology."

"Fanaticism aside, can any organization really not have an ideology?"

"…Sorry, that didn't come out right. They don't have an ideology in the normal sense of the word. According to our profilers, their mentality is transient and delights in committing crime. Stubbornly holding true to a single ideology wouldn't match their image. After all, they've even worked with us in the past. It was apparently pretty one-sided cooperation, though.

"That was when I learned the name," Lina finished.

Tatsuya nodded in understanding. They certainly didn't seem much like the humanists.

"One last thing, if it's all right."

There was still a short distance to the school gates, but Tatsuya told her he was almost finished.

"…What?" His voice was more serious than before, and Lina's own answer was replete with caution, too.

"Did they draw the parasite into this world on purpose?"

"No." Lina's denial was clear. "If you were serious about that, I'd be angry, Tatsuya," she added. She was already pretty mad—it was just that her anger wasn't directed toward Tatsuya alone at the moment. "We've already passed judgment on four of the infected. If you're suggesting someone did this as part of a scheme, I could never forgive them."

DD was a white male in his late forties with brown hair, brown eyes, and an average appearance. His real name was Donald Douglas, but almost nobody called him Mr. Douglas. Ever since he was a kid, people had just called him "Dee-Dee," a familiar nickname when put positively, and a lack of respect when put otherwise. His work colleagues and the other residents of his apartment thought of him as neither a poison nor a salve but as an ordinary person.

DD had been doing maintenance work in Dallas until three months ago. He was set up for a good career after graduating from a technical school with high marks, but because of a single misplaced button (he believed), he was unable to get a job that he could be fully proud of, and he changed jobs several times before getting married.

DD had been unhappy with his maintenance job, too. It was blue-collar work, though one offering a stable social position and a living-wage salary. In short, his standard of living was exactly average for those who lived in the old USA region. When you looked at the average for the whole USNA, including Central America, you could call it fairly high.

But he perpetually believed there was a job out there he was better suited for.

Nevertheless, after getting married, he'd put his family first and locked his ambitions deep inside. Fortune had seen to it that they weren't blessed with children, but one could call his relationship with his wife a happy one. He continued to be a good husband to her. Perhaps, though, his self-denial was too strong. If he'd stayed a little truer to his own ambitions, then maybe he wouldn't have been possessed by the demon that day.

On the day of the micro black hole experiment, he'd been doing a switchboard inspection on the outer wall of the building adjacent to the linear particle accelerator facility. That was when he gazed upon the giant experimental apparatus with longing eyes. His sealed-away unfulfilled ambitions transformed into pure longing, filling his heart. But that should have ended as a fleeting fantasy. Once his job was over, he would have exercised his usual self-denial and gone home a good husband.

——That is, if the parasite hadn't possessed him.

That day, he became a parasite. He'd had latent psychic abilities, and by merging with the parasite, that ability—Hypnosis Force—awakened. He used the power to trick his wife, then followed Their Own will and came to Japan.

DD's Hypnosis Force wasn't a very powerful ability. It couldn't make someone believe something remarkably against common sense, nor could it cause a person to behave contrary to deeply rooted moral or religious beliefs. Even the suggestion he'd used on his wife had been *A long business trip to Japan.*

But if something fell within a person's sphere of common sense or morals, he could order them to do it, even if it was a considerably odd command. For example, he easily got the real estate agent to believe all his necessary paperwork was in order and rented an apartment without going through a physical examination. Using this ability, he'd secured places to live for his comrades, who—including himself—had not been dispatched there by the USNA military. DD also used the sensible idea that *demons can't possibly exist* on eyewitnesses to warp their memories and cover up his comrades' activities.

But one week ago, they'd lost a succession of comrades central to their activities, and so they'd decided to move to a different location. He'd interfered with the minds of the USNA military staff to place him and his comrades at the back of the medical examination line so they'd be exempted from them. When his comrades who had fled the military in the meantime escaped their home country and entered Japan, he contacted the collaborator who had pulled the strings and arranged for their next hiding spot.

After cleaning up his things in the apartment, DD called upon his remaining comrades.

Are preparations for our move complete?

DD's question, which he directed within his mind, received an affirmative thought-response.

Even if there was someone with a strange ability that could intercept thought waves, they would have only heard a buzzing, like of bees' wings, regardless of the language. DD was the only one who communicated with human words—the parasites didn't need words to transmit their intent.

In the first place, they were essentially sharing a single consciousness. There was no need for everybody to think about what they should do; and now that the comrade who had previously been the main body of thought had completed their assimilation into a new host, DD became the new carrier of the main consciousness—the seat of humanlike thought.

Then we leave tomorrow morning. Be sure not to do anything conspicuous that might draw attention.

......

It's essentially already midnight. It would be more of a risk to move immediately.

The thoughts that came back contained three affirmatives and two negatives. And one death cry.

"What happened?!"

Without thinking, DD stood up and shouted in his physical voice. His "voice" went through the consciousness-sharing organ that had formed behind his brow. It had to have reached his comrades.

But the only thoughts that came back were death cries. At about the same time, his comrades' *minds* disappeared, one by one.

After counting four cries, DD felt something strange in his chest. Panicked, he looked down at it.

Right around where his heart was, there was something that looked like a black needle stuck in his chest. When he looked more closely, he saw that it was an accessory called a lapel pin. The end of the pin had only slightly pierced his clothing, and no blood was coming out.

Before DD could consider why something like this was stuck in him, he reflexively tried to pull it out.

But his hands didn't move like he thought they would. An instant after DD realized it was there, an intense pain shot through his entire body, so strong that it wouldn't allow him to retain sanity.

Pain tore through his heart, and his physical body ceased its functions permanently.

The cause of death was shock.

The postmortem certificate would probably read "commotio cordis–induced cardiac arrest."

DD never noticed the figure in black standing in front of him.

* * *

"Two seconds… I just can't get it to be as good as Uncle's."

While picking up the lapel pin that had fallen to the floor, Mitsugu Kuroba muttered to himself in a self-deprecatory manner.

The spell he'd sent the parasite to the grave with was an original he'd designed himself. "Poison Wasp" was the flavorless name he'd given the spell; it was a mental interference magic that infinitely amplified the pain felt by whomever he cast it upon, until they died. Because of how it worked, it wasn't impossible for a magician with high pain tolerance to use anti-magic to nullify the pain before dying of shock, and it exhibited no effects on those who could cut off their sense of pain. In terms of its lethality, it was a far cry from Grim Reaper, which was what his uncle, Genzou Yotsuba, previous head of the Yotsuba family, had used. Mitsugu's muttering originated in this difference being demonstrated once again.

But in terms of whether Poison Wasp was worse than Grim Reaper as a spell—that, he couldn't say for sure.

Poison Wasp's strongest point was that it could stop a target from breathing using, as its name implied, a wound as small as a needle. Grim Reaper was a spell that made targets inflict fatal wounds on themselves. It left a mark on the corpse, and blood would splatter everywhere. Poison Wasp, however, left such a small wound that one would never pinpoint it as the cause of death. Anyone who saw a victim of Poison Wasp was sure to first suspect death by poisoning, and then death by suffocation, but they wouldn't find traces of either on the corpse. In terms of which was more suited for assassination, Poison Wasp was the better spell.

The other aspect Poison Wasp excelled at was that others could use it besides Mitsugu. Unlike most mental interference magic, Mitsugu had written a nonindividualistic activation sequence for Poison Wasp and formularized its execution process. That meant magicians other than Mitsugu could use it, too. You had to have an affinity for it, of course, but Kuroba's entire team had already mastered Poison Wasp as a trump card.

"Boss."

Addressed by a voice from behind, Mitsugu slowly turned around. His pose, holding the soft cap on his head with one hand, made it look like he'd clearly read too many old novels (or so his subordinate thought). But the theatrical motion was quite fitting on him.

"We've finished cleaning everything up."

"Any casualties?"

"No, sir."

After hearing his subordinate's reply, Mitsugu nodded in satisfaction. These were the ones the USNA's pursuit team had been struggling so much against. A little lenience in his scoring when it came to his men was permissible.

"Orders from the head. Don't forget to track the mental body escaped from the hosts. We can't help ultimately losing them, but follow them for as long as you can."

At the order Mitsugu handed down, his subordinate made a subtle expression. The part of him that was lenient with them, the part that lacked strictness toward his men, didn't really mesh well with the part of him that calmly ordered multiple assassinations and sometimes impassively cut down his own subordinates.

Mitsugu Kuroba was an inscrutable man.

You could never see his real face through the several masks he wore.

He didn't even know if he had something to call a real face.

And the more closely one worked with Mitsugu, the more strongly one felt it.

[10]

Lina had outright denied any connection between the micro black hole experiment leak source and the humanist movement.

Tatsuya, too, had concluded that Lina's conjecture was an appropriate one.

However, as if to ridicule them both, the humanist-driven anti-magician movements had become the trend, and they were eroding the North American continent from east to west.

It was only a matter of time before the trend spread to the rest of the world, too.

Winter, three months after the season began, was about to arrive.

In the past, diplomacy either meant the gunboat kind or the behind-closed-doors kind.

Eventually, after the age of global power balances, diplomacy's fundamental direction had shifted toward major alliances, and diplomatic styles simultaneously saw conferences and ceremonies become the norm, but that didn't mean gunboat diplomacy and secretive diplomacy had disappeared.

Secretive diplomacy was an indispensable preparation for making such ceremonies succeed, and those involved in it changed from diplomatic superstars to diplomatic artisans, active even now in the world's shadows.

No matter when, and no matter where.

The seeds of the world's conspiracy would never run out.

Not tonight.

Not even in this country.

"...I must say, these fanatics are simply incorrigible."

"Ha-ha-ha, yes... It's easy to make them act but difficult to take the reins."

On one side of a table, a suit-wearing middle-aged man encouraged the man across from him, also a middle-aged man in a suit, though a Caucasian one, not a Mongoloid.

As though he'd been in Japan for some time, or perhaps because of his hobbies or education, the Caucasian man let the other pour the clear liquid out of the sake bottle he'd extended and into the small sipping saucer, then, following proper etiquette, brought it to his lips.

"Now that I think about it again, this alcohol you call *sake* is quite mysterious and—how should I put it—refined... It's undistilled, and yet it has no color."

And flawlessly, he remembered to interject flattery toward the other nation.

"Oh, not at all. I cannot deny that it lacks beauty when compared with the vivid reds of wines. Of course, when it comes to the flavor, I believe I've provided something that will satisfy you."

The one on the receiving end of the flattery also remembered to make a display of modesty.

The thing the two facing each other had in common was that neither would reveal what they were really thinking.

"And you have indeed... As much as I would like to get comfortably intoxicated, those fanatics I mentioned before never seem to get tired of lawbreaking, so I cannot take too much time."

"I cannot thank you enough regarding your special consideration for the safety of our countrymen who reside in your nation."

Their tones of voice remained the same. Their faces, too, still held slight smiles. But anyone who lived in their world would have sensed that the air had changed since just a moment ago.

"Not at all—it's our natural obligation. Still, these people are mad, and logic will be ineffective… For example, you could explain to them that the massive explosion that decimated the Great Asian Alliance fleet was the work of scientifically systematized magic and not the work of the devil, but they would never listen."

"Yes. After all, they may turn a deaf ear, but that doesn't excuse any harm befalling foreigners who need to be kept safe… I humbly ask for your empathy here."

The two men each tilted their bottles at the other, and as though that were a signal, they gulped down the contents of their sake cups at the same time.

"I want you to take what I'm about to say as a complaint. If you would even reveal a thin outline of that Great Bomb, I think we would be able to calm them down."

"…Likewise—please take this as a complaint of my own. The military has complete control over information regarding the weapon used on the Korean Peninsula's southern end. No matter how confidential it may be, civilian control is the basis of democracy…but why must military men be so obstinate?"

Sparks flew between the men's gazes for an instant, and after that instant, both their eyes had turned into empty smiles.

"You heard them."

Fujibayashi stopped the wiretapped conversation recording and brought her face up.

"Our diplomats seem to be trying pretty hard this time. Even they understand how important and singular the strategic-class is."

"And besides..."

Tatsuya stopped before he said it. Fujibayashi angled her head and said, "Hmm?" to get him to continue.

"...And besides, ma'am, I'm sure the Ministry of Foreign Affairs has its own honor to uphold. Three years ago, Japan faced an unprovoked invasion. Even facing criticism for information leaks from within, the government made every effort to find a nonmilitary solution. And now they've been mocked to their faces for that effort."

"You mean the Great Asian Alliance did, right...?"

To Fujibayashi this was preaching to the choir, but Miyuki didn't quite seem to grasp it.

Even Tatsuya had enough common sense to know, well, that was normal. "Japan and the USNA are allied nations, but we're also potential rival nations in the Pacific Sea," he said. "A moderate weakening of Japan is in the USNA's interests."

After seeing his sister nod slightly, Tatsuya continued his explanation.

"On the other hand, while the Great Asian Alliance may be big, they're not strong enough to face the Japan-America alliance directly. It would be a big gamble, and not one their nation is in a desperate enough state to take... Why, then, did the GAA commit to the reckless Yokohama invasion?"

Tatsuya paused for a moment to give Miyuki time to think about it. He didn't want her to be only a pretty doll at the end of the day.

"The GAA isn't strong enough to take on Japan and America at once... America is allied with Japan, but they'd be fine with Japan being a little weaker than it is now..." she said to herself. Then her face lit up, and she put a hand to her mouth. "Wait, then... The GAA and the USNA have secretly joined forces?"

Tatsuya gave her a satisfied smile for a job well done. Seeing them, Fujibayashi let out a dry grin.

"Saying they've joined forces might be going too far," Tatsuya said, "but I think it's very possible for them to be in some sort of conspiratorial relationship." He looked over at Fujibayashi before she lost her smirk and nodded slightly.

"Conspiring to, for example, make the USNA's Pacific fleet deployment late to respond to a GAA military invasion," she offered, affirming Tatsuya's speculation. "And when you think about it in hindsight...the USNA's fleet movements were unnaturally slow at the time."

"In all likelihood, the GAA's objective wasn't to occupy territory or destroy crucial facilities—it was to kidnap scientists and steal technology, wasn't it, ma'am?" asked Tatsuya.

"Probably, yes. Considering the location and their combat strength, they couldn't have hoped for anything more. Mobilizing their fleet was a backup plan in case the operation failed. Of course, that came back to bite them. They poked the grass, and the snake came out."

"I don't believe the pheasant would have been shot if it hadn't cried. After all, we're actually the ones concerned about the snake now."

Tatsuya maintained his poker face, but...

"That's really something, coming from the one who was most involved in it."

...Fujibayashi seemed to see through it.

"Anyway... I should get going," she said. "I might be here under the pretense of early recruitment, but a soldier staying too long in a civilian household is an unnatural thing."

"Thank you for coming all the way here today."

As Fujibayashi stood up, so did Tatsuya, who offered his thanks.

He didn't express any modesty by saying something along the lines of *though we didn't offer much hospitality.*

She wasn't aware of it, but Miyuki had been the one offering the hospitality, so there was no way anything would have been less than perfect. That was how Tatsuya processed it in his head.

When they followed her to the front door to see her off,

Fujibayashi said, "Oh, right," and reached into her purse. Though the suddenness was all an act, of course.

What she took out was a small, thin, neatly wrapped box.

"Here you are. I know it's two days early, but some friendly chocolate."

"The obligatory kind, ma'am?"

It was a refreshing honesty, without a shard of expectation involved.

For obligatory chocolate, it had a very stylish wrapper. But Tatsuya knew as well as she did that she never cut corners with anything, so he didn't misunderstand things for his own convenience.

"Are you unhappy with it?" Fujibayashi smiled mischievously.

That moment, Miyuki's eyes shone with a sharp light, but...

"Not in the slightest."

...at Tatsuya's immediate response, the light vanished entirely as though it were nothing but an illusion.

After saying their good-byes and closing the door, they heard the young woman burst into laughter from the other side, but the siblings pretended nothing at all had happened and quickly returned to the living room.

Ever since the war (World War III), there had been a strong impression that cultural trends had changed completely in this country.

But in reality, it wasn't that major a change, and many so-called frivolous customs had continued unabandoned to this day.

One of those was Valentine's Day, which was coming up the next day. One could argue all one wanted about St. Valentine's Day originally being far from frivolous, or the whole chocolate-giving thing being a sweets company conspiracy, but it wouldn't matter. Young people were fully aware of all that, and they jumped into it anyway.

With Valentine's Day coming up the next day, the First High

campus was also laden with a giddy air. In this respect, magicians (in the making) were normal boys and girls, too.

"...Mitsui, you can get going early today if you'd like."

They were in the student council room after school.

An error noise had been repeatedly going off for a while.

Azusa had asked the question of Honoka, its source, not because she thought Honoka was angry, but because she thought she wasn't feeling well.

"She's right, Honoka. You should go home for today."

Lina, who was acting as a temporary council member, stressed the point, her vivid blue eyes clouding. Despite her identity remaining unknown not only to normal students but to Azusa and Isori as well, it was quite a bold move—but of course, she also had no other option to choose at this point.

"No, I'll be fine," answered Honoka bravely, seeming clearly not fine.

...She knew why she wasn't fine. Part of it was that she would have been embarrassed to take them up on the considerate offer. But everyone who knew her as the opinionated girl who felt too much responsibility and tended to go overboard only worried even more.

"Mitsui, I think it's great you have such a sense of duty, but taking a break isn't a bad idea."

Honoka still couldn't say *Okay, I'll take a break, then* when Isori said it, so Miyuki had to be the one who drove the point home.

"Honoka, you really shouldn't push yourself. No matter how hard you try, you won't be able to do any work, right?"

Miyuki, too, was (on the surface) making a deeply concerned expression. Her beauty was mystical, and it made you forget she was a real person, but when she made that sort of face, it very much suited her, enough to make Azusa, Isori, and Lina all nod in unison.

But for Honoka, who realized that Miyuki had guessed why she wasn't fine, it was a very uncomfortable suggestion. Especially the part about her not being able to do any work.

"I...I guess. All right..."

After a moment's hesitation, Honoka energetically rose to her feet and gave a bow. "I'm terribly sorry! I'll be going home early today. I'll work hard again tomorrow!"

"Yes, do your best tomorrow," replied Miyuki in advance (in spite?) of the two upperclassmen. Azusa felt it odd for Honoka to say "again tomorrow," but the only one here who knew what she meant by it was Miyuki.

After bowing and excusing herself, Honoka spun around on her heel as her cheeks reddened.

"...And that is why Honoka went home early," Miyuki explained to Tatsuya as they went down the path from the school to the station.

"Right... To get ready for tomorrow, huh?"

"Yes, no doubt."

While Miyuki nodded confidently, Tatsuya grimaced against a creeping chill.

"She's definitely the type to put a lot of effort into things like that..."

"Are you happy, Brother?" Miyuki teased.

"It's not that. I just feel bad." Tatsuya gave a verbal shrug. "I can repay any gifts, but I can't return what really matters," he finished gravely.

Miyuki hesitantly took his sleeve. "...Please, you don't need to worry about things like that. Honoka and I want only for you to be happy from the bottom of our hearts."

"...Really?"

"Yes. All you need to do is accept that without comment."

"Uhh, I don't want to be a third wheel here, but..." interrupted Lina with some difficulty, her face less reserved than grudging. Tatsuya looked over at her, his sister still gripping his sleeve.

"Third wheel? That's a strange thing to say, Lina."

Your brains are what's strange here! Lina wanted to protest, but she'd already been made plenty aware that she couldn't beat Tatsuya with words, brute force of tone aside. Lina decided to follow the results of her acquired knowledge: that being forthright and immediate at times like this was the best solution.

"Essentially, Honoka wasn't looking well because she was worried about giving you chocolate tomorrow?"

"You did well to notice, Lina. I had thought chocolate-giving was a custom unique to Japan."

Lina had asked the question while looking at Tatsuya, but the answer came back from Miyuki, as though such an exchange were natural.

…However, in this particular case, Tatsuya had no way of answering her question, so Lina wasn't particularly offended.

"No, not at all," Lina replied, a little huffy. "Valentine's Day chocolate is a famous bit of Japanese culture, but a lot of kids do it in the States, too. Plus, our other classmates here in Japan have been talking my ears off about it."

"Hmm, I see… To whom will you give your chocolate, Lina?"

"Even you're asking me that, Miyuki…?"

Judging from the unpleasant frown on her face, others must have persistently been asking her the same thing. Regardless of what form it took, such interest (or curiosity) itself was the same as it was a century ago, and it would doubtlessly be unchanged after another century.

"I didn't plan on giving chocolate to anyone."

"Oh, but not even obligatory chocolate? Or did nobody tell you how that custom works?"

"Come on, I know what that is."

"In that case, a lot of people would be happy if you gave them some, wouldn't they? Like people who helped you out when you came to study abroad."

Lina frowned at Miyuki, but she couldn't glean any emotion other than mild interest from her expression. "If I gave individual gifts, it would cause all sorts of problems."

"Really? It must be difficult being so popular."

Miyuki's remark made Lina catch her breath.

She felt like the Shiba sister was putting her popularity ahead of

her actual ability, but Lina also understood that this was she herself trying to play the victim.

"You're amazingly popular yourself, Miyuki. Who will you give chocolate to? Will Tatsuya get the real thing?"

Lina had taken for granted that the object of Miyuki's chocolate-based affections would be Tatsuya, and that she'd tease them to no end for trading amorous words, but...

"What are you saying, Lina? Brother and I are siblings. It would be strange for me to give him homemade chocolates."

"......"

So this is what it's like to be struck dumb... thought Lina, feeling it from the bottom of her heart.

"...Hey, Izumi, what do you think she's doing?"

"I think... I think she's making chocolates, but..."

"Well, then... Why is she giggling like that...?"

Kasumi and Izumi Saegusa, twin sisters of the Saegusa family currently in their third year of middle school, exchanged hushed whispers by the kitchen entrance.

"It looks like...she's having fun. I think."

"I don't know if that's what this is."

Their eyes were turned to Mayumi as she heated a sheet of baking chocolate in hot water. But though she seemed to be having fun, a girl in love would never be smiling like that on the day before Valentine's.

"...Who might she be wishing to inflict it upon?"

Mayumi's giggles had already gone beyond "hee-hee-hee," turning into something closer to "fu-fu-fu-fu..." or "ku-ku-ku-ku-ku..." It was as though she were planning to poison someone. The twins exchanged glances.

"Kasumi, about the chocolate our sister is using..."

"Ahh, yeah... It's the ninety-five percent cocoa, zero percent sugar kind..."

Products boasting that they had 99 percent cocoa content had been sold in the past, but currently, the most bitter chocolate available for purchase was Mayumi's ingredient of choice.

"And that bag..."

"It's espresso powder, isn't it...?"

"I wonder if something bad happened to her..."

——A compacted psionic bullet appeared in the Idea, flew in a short arc, and collided with the independent information body.

"That one was all right. Let's call it for this morning."

"...Thank you very much."

As Tatsuya caught his breath, turned to Yakumo, and bowed, Miyuki ran over with a towel in her hand.

Large beads of sweat had formed on Tatsuya's forehead even though it was midwinter. Miyuki, after watching him wipe the sweat, spoke to Yakumo, her gaze concerned.

"Sensei, Brother's exhaustion seems rather extreme for Program Demolition..."

Yakumo shook his head and held a hand up in front of Tatsuya to stop him from answering her himself.

"Can't help a little bit of exhaustion. The concepts of 'movement' and 'exclusion' don't exist in the true world, and Tatsuya just brought them into it."

After last Monday, Miyuki had declined attending his training, saying she'd be in the way. Today was Tuesday, a week and a day since she'd last been here. So she didn't know what things Tatsuya, to whom it had been suggested to devise a new anti-parasite spell (Yakumo had suggested it, and Miyuki had pressed him), was trying until she asked Yakumo. A new spell was one thing, but all Miyuki thought was that he was simply practicing trying to use Program Demolition in the information dimension.

"Is it...an arrangement of some sort that would cause side effects?"

She had complete faith that her brother was the strongest of magicians, but she knew there were plenty of things he couldn't do. Even if they needed it to achieve victory, if it harmed his mind or body—by shortening his lifespan, for example—then she was willing to immediately do whatever she had to in order to get him to stop, even if it meant persuading him through tears.

"No, I don't think it is." Contrary to her feelings on the matter, Yakumo's answer was a bland one. "Tatsuya is only changing his way of seeing things. Instead of directly *striking* the target, he sets the coordinates every 1/32nd of a second to be right in *front* of the target, and by linking that setting through his unconscious region, he created a conceptual bullet of *exclusion* that *moved* to the true world—isn't that right, Tatsuya?"

"That's right, Miyuki. Since I'm using the full extent of my thinking and cognitive abilities, it's only mentally…no, *neurologically* exhausting. I promise there's no danger of any side effects, so don't worry."

"I see…" With Tatsuya putting it so clearly to her, Miyuki seemed relieved for the moment. "Then your prospects for finding a way to attack the parasite are looking better?"

As his younger sister looked up at his face with eyes glittering, as though enamored by his constant successes, Tatsuya accidentally showed her a pained grin.

"Well…"

"It could probably destroy newborn 'children.' But it might have trouble against a 'parent' whose existence has solidified over many years."

Tatsuya had been about to shake his head, still grinning painfully. Yakumo had cut him off and given a delicate evaluation.

Thanks to that, the siblings got through it without needing to feel awkward.

Miyuki hadn't come with Tatsuya this morning on a whim, nor did she want to check up on his training progress.

This was the third time, after last year and the year before, that she'd come to Yakumo's temple on the morning of February 14.

The reason went without saying.

After returning to the priest quarters, Miyuki took a neatly wrapped package out of her bag and offered it to Yakumo.

"You may think of it as a heretical custom, but please accept this gift. You're always taking good care of my brother."

Right then, Yakumo's face broke into a complacent grin. "Oh no. Even foreign pagan customs deserve to have their good parts accepted."

He says the same exact thing every year... thought Tatsuya, and he certainly wasn't the only one.

"Master, everyone is watching."

But Tatsuya was the only one able to chide him for his overly careless expression.

"Hmm? Oh, I don't think it matters. It'll be an incentive for their training."

Still, it didn't seem at all like Yakumo had responded to the candid advice.

"Are desires of the flesh not contrary to your precepts?"

"It doesn't matter so long as it doesn't lead to lust."

He was answering the questions in a transcendental tone of voice, but his face was still locked in that foppish grin.

There's just no dealing with him. Tatsuya sighed in resignation, and many of Yakumo's pupils offered wordless agreements.

If the mass-transit commuter trains that had been used until mid-century had any winning point over personal train cabinets, it would be the predictability of arrival times.

Given how they were used, cabinets didn't have any sort of time schedule. There were also never any traffic jams, so they never arrived significantly late. But there was no legal speed limit on the tracks, so one could arrive quite early. That could make it somewhat inconvenient for meet-ups.

Even Tatsuya and his friends, who had frequently met up at the station to go to school together in their first semester, had fallen into a pattern of meeting up in the classroom instead.

"Good morning, Tatsuya."

"Good morning, Honoka."

However, youthfulness still acted as though that inconvenience were nothing.

Or perhaps it was love.

Both were probably correct.

"Oh, good morning, Honoka."

"Good morning, Mizuki."

And for a maiden in love, for today, she didn't like the thought of anyone going with her. Honoka, too, thought there was no helping Miyuki being around, since it was the default.

But other than Miyuki, even though they were friends, they were honestly nuisances. No—it was because they were friends that she wished they'd guess from what day and what month today was.

——Her feelings probably showed on her face.

One could say that Mizuki read the mood from the slight change in Honoka's expression.

She suddenly began to fidget. This was quite uncomfortable, but saying *I'm going on ahead* or *I remembered something I have to do* out of nowhere would also be too obvious.

It was a deadlock, where their thought processes aligned but she couldn't make a move, but rather surprisingly (?), the one to break it was Miyuki.

"Mizuki, is there something on your uniform?"

"Huh?"

Not expecting the sudden comment, Mizuki did her best to crane her neck and look over her shoulder at her back.

There was no way she'd be able to see her back like that, and there was no dirt or anything on it in the first place, so it was no more than fruitless labor, but—

"Come here. I'll get it off for you. Brother, I apologize, but please, go on ahead. Honoka, you go on, too."

"Oh, I see," agreed Tatsuya blandly from next to Honoka. Honoka, for her part, grew flustered; he gave her a simple chin nod to urge her on.

She followed after him, her gait unsteady as she threw a look of appreciation over her shoulder.

Miyuki smiled a little and nodded.

The unexpected turn of events, with just the boy and girl going to school, sent Honoka's nervous excitement through the roof. Even when Tatsuya said something to her, it was all she could do to nod and respond with "uh-huh." And hoarsely, at that. Tatsuya was actually walking slowly, and yet, her joints felt so tense it seemed like her feet would get tangled and trip over nothing at any moment.

Her self-assessment told her that it was social anxiety, which was the undeniable truth.

But once they got into school, the entrances used by Course 1 and Course 2 students were different. Even Honoka understood that would mean wasting this perfect chance.

Not making the most of an opportunity a rival provided was the same as betraying them.

"Umm, Tatsuya!"

Once they'd gotten through the school gates, Honoka called out and stopped him.

"Could I maybe take up a bit of your time?!"

Her manner of speaking was stiff and formal, like a subordinate speaking to an officer many ranks higher than her or an executive several strata above.

"Sure."

Tatsuya accepted it with a reserved smile, not a hint of annoyance, and nodded.

"Please… Come over here."

Honoka hurried toward the rear yard, sneaking to try to avoid drawing attention (which just made her stand out more), and Tatsuya chased after her, careful not to fall behind or overtake her.

——With an expression that said he knew everything.

"Umm, Tatchu—!"

In the shade behind the robotics club garage, known by the school as a tête-à-tête (confession) spot. (Though there were no particular legends about it.) Honoka went out in front of Tatsuya, forcefully held out a small, meticulously wrapped box in both hands—and, with all her might, choked on her words.

After which, she froze.

Her long hair, pulled into two tails that hung to neck length, didn't hide how red her ears were.

Her downcast face was crimson from the middle all the way to her forehead, peeking out through the gap in her bangs, which hung to either side.

She couldn't budge. She couldn't speak. She couldn't advance or retreat like she wanted to. Her arms trembled, and her heart pounded out of control. Similar waves were rippling out from all over the rest of the school, but the ones her heart created were as strong and large as anyone else's. They were beautiful, unsullied waves, like the tones created by a tuning fork—— She'd lost her heart, and the waves made her very soul tremble, guiding her to come into herself.

"Thank you, Honoka."

From Honoka's hands—still stuck out, as she couldn't move, constricted by her own too-strong feelings—Tatsuya gently took the small chocolate box, careful not to damage the wrapper. And in exchange, he placed a small, palm-sized paper bag into her hand and closed her fingers around it.

For a moment, at least, her curiosity about the unexpected act overrode her embarrassment. Honoka brought the paper bag to her breast, then looked up with a blank expression.

"Umm, Tatsuya, what's...?"

"A little something in return. It's separate from next month, so you can expect something then, too."

Honoka hastily wiped the tears that suddenly formed in her widened eyes and gave a clumsy smile.

"I, um, is this, I can't... Umm, Tatsuya, may I open it?"

"Of course."

Honoka took the present out of the bag and gazed at it listlessly...

"...Honoka, we should get to class."

...Until Tatsuya said something to her, breaking her out of a standstill.

Tatsuya had been carefully attentive to whether anyone was peeping or listening in on them.

Still, he hadn't gone so far as to use Elemental Sight. He couldn't risk revealing a skill designated as top secret just for a Valentine's Day event.

However, he should have used it.

There had been nobody trying to eavesdrop. Because It hadn't had a mind until just a moment ago.

Inside a garage built in a corner of the First High campus, It had been dozing within a doll without a heart when It awakened to a wave much like the one that had dragged It into this world.

The term *awakened* might invite a slight misunderstanding.

Bathed in strong, pure thoughts, similar to prayers, a new ego sprouted for It.

It would probably be more accurate to say Its ego was reconstructed.

As It slept inside the soulless doll, a mind was born for It.

The puppet now had a mind of its own.

After arriving in the classroom, no sooner did Honoka put her things down than she ran into the bathroom—and dragged Miyuki with her.

They weren't headed for the stalls; instead they went before the mirrors.

With vexation, she pulled out the bands tying her hair, then pivoted and, with careful motions, smoothed it out.

The finishing touch was what she'd just received from Tatsuya—a pair of hair accessories. The elastic hair bands had a simple design, with two small spheres laid into a setting hanging from them. But though the design was simple, their construction and materials were not the cheap sort. For one thing, the bands didn't tie into a loop but went through the settings to form loops around the entire rear covers. Plus, the silver-colored settings were shaped like tiny nails holding the spheres, and those spheres were perfect crystals with high purity.

Rock crystals were valued more for their use as a magical assistance medium than as a decoration these days (it was said they gave sharper direction to the waves of your thoughts). The crystals were the type of precious stone most familiar to the girls at magic high schools, and Honoka understood their worth as well. Though doubtless she would have been overjoyed even if they'd been cheap glass balls, since they were a gift from Tatsuya. She was all the more touched for it.

"Hey, Miyuki, how do they look? They don't look weird, do they? Do they look good on me?"

Putting her hands to the hair ornaments, Honoka asked a little uneasily.

Miyuki, without smiling or appearing annoyed, gave her a completely serious answer. "Don't worry, Honoka. They look great."

"...Really?"

"Really. Brother would never choose a gift that looked bad on you, would he?"

Honoka nodded, blood rushing to her face.

Too occupied with her happiness, she didn't notice the strange emptiness in Miyuki's voice, as though she were reciting a script.

* * *

On the short path to his own classroom after parting with Honoka, Tatsuya was fighting against the self-loathing rising within him.

His sense of guilt for what he'd done to deceive her and his regret at making his sister an accomplice were a pain like a toothache, slowly spreading through his heart.

The hair ornaments he'd given Honoka were, in truth, things Miyuki had picked out.

If that was all, then it was just a little white lie. It didn't change the fact that it was a gift from Tatsuya, and there was no need to purposely disappoint the girl.

But the reason he'd given her that present wasn't anything so innocent.

Tatsuya had known that if he gave her a gift in return for the chocolate, her mind would be saturated by that alone. He'd predicted that it wouldn't give her the time to think about anything that went along with the giving of Valentine's Day chocolate, like words exchanged to express their "feelings," or "promises" to link them in a relationship—and that's what had happened.

That was why he'd prepared a return gift for the day of, and Honoka's response had been exactly as Tatsuya had calculated.

Tatsuya had toyed with her heart.

He'd given up on himself a long time ago.

There was no helping the fact that he was a monster who didn't understand human emotions, and he knew that if other people's goodwill ran out or he received retribution because of it, it was well deserved. (If one were to point out that this wasn't resignation but a so-what attitude, they'd be exactly correct.)

However, when it came to using his sister for an underhanded plan to buy time while knowing she'd never disobey him, he couldn't help but feel regret.

——The very fact that he had these thoughts was proof he wasn't as far gone as he might have assumed, but unfortunately, there were no adults in his life to tell him that.

"Yo. You look kind of exhausted, and the day just started."

He must not have switched gears in time. The moment he entered the classroom, that was the comment he got.

Leo, straddling his chair, raised a hand in greeting, and Tatsuya returned it.

"And you seem good as new, even though you just got discharged."

"You know, the proper greeting is 'good morning.'"

Then Mikihiko interrupted, making a resigned sort of grin.

"Right. Good morning, Mikihiko."

"Heya."

Contrary to Tatsuya, who listened and gave an actual morning greeting, Leo seemed to want to stick to his own way of doing things—though he probably didn't mean anything by it.

"Good morning. Leo, you're back to normal, huh?"

When Mikihiko said "back to normal," he meant "the same as ever," but...

"You got it. The doctor really didn't want to discharge me, so I've got a ton of pent-up energy."

...whether or not Leo understood that, he answered the question literally.

His initial diagnosis was that he'd be living in the hospital for at least another month, but Leo had a nonsensical ability to recover from things. The doctor would inevitably have been rather skeptical of it.

But since they could see nothing actually wrong with him, and the patient himself wanted to be discharged, they couldn't keep him in the hospital forever. With all that, he'd returned today.

"What about you, Tatsuya? You get in a fight with your sister this morning?"

"Of course not."

That wasn't Tatsuya's remark but Mikihiko's.

Tatsuya wasn't exactly happy at the immediate declaration, but it wasn't a misunderstanding, either, so he couldn't argue the point.

"He's probably tired out from the battlefield, right? Today is Valentine's, after all."

"Oh!" Leo gave a big nod.

That pushed his buttons, too, but if he got mad at that, he'd be stuck in the swamp.

"I don't have a significant other, so there's no battlefields for me... Mizuki. You're late today."

Tatsuya feigned ignorance, using the girl who had just entered the classroom as an obvious way to divert the topic.

"I just stopped by the club room. Good morning, Yoshida, Leo."

With Tatsuya being so unsubtle about the change of topic, Mikihiko et al. were making somewhat frustrated faces, but given her qualities, Mizuki didn't notice it at all.

"You're coming to school again, Leo? I'm glad you recovered faster than we thought."

In actuality, they'd heard he'd be discharged yesterday and coming to school today when they visited him last week, and Mizuki obviously would have known.

So normally, this comment would have sounded strange, but Tatsuya, Mikihiko—

"Yep! Thanks for coming to visit so many times."

—and Leo all grinned it away.

No sooner did Mizuki sit down than she handed small, palm-sized boxes to the three of them. Her attitude about it was very bland, without a hint of haughtiness, nervousness, or embarrassment.

It was the face of someone who saw this special day rationally, as a mere annual event.

There was approximately one boy who looked a little unhappy about it, but he appeared to be trying to keep a straight face, so the other two said nothing.

It was the mercy of the brave.

Incidentally, that one person was not Leo.

However, Leo was simply staring in curiosity at the small box he'd received.

Apparently, this was the first time he'd received chocolate on Valentine's Day from anyone outside his family.

It felt quite unexpected, but they didn't know what sort of student he was in middle school, so neither Tatsuya nor Mikihiko made their surprise known.

The one who did was Erika, who had just come into the classroom.

"I thought you were out of the hospital early. You were after the chocolate?"

Although her remark went little beyond an expression of surprise, from Leo's point of view, it was abuse that he couldn't let slide.

"Of course not! Don't be stupid, woman!"

Not only did he retort, he kicked his seat out and stood up.

"Oh, was I right?"

Certainly, if you wanted to read into it, his reaction was extreme enough to interpret that way.

——If you really forced the interpretation, that is.

Leo began using a compound skill that combined a growling and a grinding of teeth. Tatsuya, however, had just been teased earlier, and as retribution, he didn't offer any particular aid to his friend in need, leaving him alone as he addressed Erika:

"Good morning, Erika. You're late today."

Erika turned around and responded, "Morning, Tatsuya."

The natural consequence was that Leo got left behind.

"February 14 is awful every year," she continued. "It's because we got so many men around in our dojo."

Erika didn't originally intend to mess with Leo—those were her honest complaints—but it seemed like her mind was shifting in that direction.

"More than a few of them get all pouty like children if you don't give them anything, but they're also the ones who improve their skills the most, so I can't ignore them. It's awful."

Her repetition of *awful* probably showed just how strongly she felt it.

"Can't you just give it to the ones who want it?"

"Then a couple others start pushing their luck, complaining it's unfair... And then suddenly, they decide to organize. Normally, the word *unity* isn't even in their vocabulary." A truly disgusted expression rose to Erika's face. "At least my parents pay for it, pretending it's to foster friendship with the pupils, and the female students come shopping for it with me, but..."

Her face was so annoyed it made Tatsuya want to show her some pretend sympathy. "That really does seem like a lot of work."

"It is! It's so annoying... Valentine's Day can go jump off a cliff for all I care!"

Erika's stress must have erupted while she was talking. She was seriously indignant.

"Miki, you must have it nice." As often happened at times like these, she went straight for venting. "You've got a lot of girls among your pupils, don't you?"

This time, she'd chosen Mikihiko as her target.

"You get your pick of the litter every year, don't you?"

"Yoshida... Is that true?" Mizuki interjected.

She didn't really know why she'd asked it.

Or rather, she wasn't thinking about the reason.

And Mikihiko, too, took more damage from Mizuki's remark than Erika's words themselves, but he didn't bother trying to find out the reason.

"That's not true!"

Instead, he gave a reactionary answer.

This conversation would have been quicker if he'd thought about the context a little more, but maybe it was too much to ask of a sixteen-year-old boy.

"Anyway, if I were that frivolous, I could never do any real training."

But that was a careless remark.

"Oh no you don't, Miki. What about our dojo are you trying to say is frivolous?"

"Uh, wait, I didn't mean that—"

"Then what in the world did you mean?"

With Mikihiko starting to sweat, Erika locked her gaze onto him, and Mizuki made a somehow similar expression as she, Tatsuya, and Leo exchanged pained grins.

The magic high school curriculum was a *normal* high school–level program, plus a magical program. All modern educational systems, not just magic high schools, promoted specialization at an early stage. In concrete terms, educational practices placed importance on students concentrating on fields such as literary programs, science programs, arts programs, or physical education programs in order to improve their skills in a single category starting at the high school stage. This meant that, excluding certain high schools that boasted comprehensive educational programs, students had a jam-packed curriculum that included both general education and field-specific education. But even so, it was said that magical curricula sported especially little wiggle room.

Consequently, magic high school students were diligent. The kind of "play" that implied wasting time, like gossiping during class or thinking about off-task things, was essentially absent. Perhaps it should be called unfortunate that at First High, this impulse was stronger with the students in Course 1 than in Course 2. Perhaps the reason was that their sense of fear at being left behind was stronger than their fighting spirit to overcome the odds against them.

But here, too, there were exceptions. During the general program's physical education period, set up to be separate from magic practice, the tense atmosphere had a tendency to settle down. It was especially prominent on days like today, February 14, when students hadn't been able to fully focus on classes all morning, and a giddy mood drifted among them.

*　*　*

The girls' school uniforms took more time to change into and out of than their male counterparts'. This wasn't particular to First High—most schools had the same thing going on. And it wasn't particular to school uniforms in the first place. Most men and women hadn't wanted the unisex fashion culture advocated by certain gender discrimination abolitionists.

During the short times between classes, the pre–phys ed changing rooms were constantly filled with a hurried air. In a great rush, but careful not to damage anything, they removed their clothes, hung them on hangers, placed them in their lockers, and changed into their gym clothes. The lockers had biometric authentication, and more than enough of them were available to give one to each person. Each time a student used one, it would register their vein patterns, so the student had to take that time into consideration, too.

Nevertheless, the students were used to it by February, and now they could talk to nearby girls while their hands moved briskly, leaving them enough time to even be worried and reassured by turns (?) over what their classmates looked like in their underwear. Today, the changing room was experiencing a greater stir than usual.

By this time of year, the students had more or less staked their claims upon a locker. As always, Miyuki got changed in front of a locker in the middle of the right-hand wall. To her left was Honoka's. To her right was the one Shizuku normally used, but at the moment, when class 1-A was having phys ed class, it was an extra locker.

Today, though, Lina had come up on Miyuki's right side.

"Oh, hello, Lina. Is your usual spot taken?" asked Miyuki as she put her CAD and information terminal away in the compartment in her locker.

The locker Lina usually used was the one close to the entrance. At first, all the girls in class A figured she'd use the same locker Shizuku had been using, but Lina had purposely chosen an unpopular, unused locker near the door. When Miyuki told Tatsuya about it, he had said, "She probably chose it so she can get out in a hurry," which had been enough to convince her. There was no guarantee his speculation was right. What she could say for sure was that this was the first time Lina was getting changed next to her.

"Well, no."

Miyuki didn't ask *Well, why then?* Instead, with a simple, uninterested "oh," she put a hand on her outerwear.

But Lina, who maybe thought her answer was a little too unfriendly, supplemented her remark while taking off her own outerwear. "When you asked who I'd give chocolate to... I know you weren't trying to be mean, but now it's bothering me a little."

"Everyone wants to know. You're cute, after all," said the Shiba sister seriously as she slipped her necktie off.

Lina puffed out her cheeks, dissatisfied. "Then why aren't you... getting bombarded with questions?"

Lina's objection cut off in the middle the moment Miyuki opened her uniform's dress and was about to take out her right shoulder. It was a very simple action with no real meaning behind it, but it glued Lina's eyes to it and temporarily stopped her tongue from working.

"Who can say? I suppose I don't have the sex appeal."

When Miyuki said that, Lina got mad for no reason—or rather, without knowing the reason. She didn't consciously pull off her own uniform dress as if to compete with her.

As Lina's half-naked body appeared from under the uniform, this time it was Miyuki who breathed a sigh of admiration.

"Lina, you have a nice figure. I envy you." As she said that, she unabashedly stripped down to her own underwear.

"Was that sarcasm? What reason could you possibly have to be jealous of me?" Glaring at Miyuki's seminude form, Lina put a hand to her hip, drew herself up to full height, and snapped.

"Your waist and your butt have just the right amount of firmness. They're very sexy. You're not just skinny, you're really in shape, you know?"

Miyuki reached out with her right hand and rubbed the narrow part of Lina's waist. It was, in a sense, an innocent way of touching,

without any sort of lust involved at all. But even though Lina knew there was no sexual desire involved, she found it hard to maintain her presence of mind. They heard a few gulps from here and there in the changing room—the scene was enough to make people lose their cool from simply watching.

Of course, Lina didn't have time to worry about the peanut gallery. "Th-that goes for you, too," she said, reaching out with a hand. But just before reaching Miyuki's skin, she hesitated and pulled back. "You have a very feminine body, not muscular at all. It makes me jealous."

With Lina blushing and her eyes wandering, Miyuki gave her classmate a mischievous smile and released her hand from her waist.

Then they heard a loud *slam* come from behind Miyuki.

Miyuki turned around, and Lina looked over.

Honoka was clinging to her locker, paralyzed.

Miyuki cast a vague look around and saw her classmates, in the middle of changing, blushing and looking away in their immodest states. She had been naturally ignoring the stares like she always did, so it was only now that she realized everyone's attention was on the scene they were acting out.

"...We should finish getting changed."

To this proposal of Miyuki's,

"Yes."

Lina, who felt the same way, answered readily.

The giddy mood exploded after school ended. Between classes, the students had probably been exercising self-restraint. Like a dam had broken, bittersweet acts were playing out here and there on campus, some of them the sort you'd want to throw rocks at.

Their aspects were varied, too.

For example, gift scenes with a little too much energy in them, not only between nearby friends but even between parentally approved fiancés. Specifically, the disciplinary committee chairwoman, Kanon, barged into the student council room and used her smile to pressure the accountant, Isori, into eating, right on the spot, the homemade chocolates she'd packed into a thick paper gift box fancy enough to be someone's high-class bento box.

For example, cases where girls were being a little shy but stubborn. Specifically, the kendo-*kenjutsu* couple, with the female student, not caring about things like "obligatory chocolate" or "pride," storming into a Course 1 classroom, a high threshold for a Course 2 student to cross, blushing and averting her eyes as she offered a red ribboned box, and the male student's eyes widening in an expression of surprise and taking the box with an attitude suggesting he might start to dance right then and there.

For today alone, the First High students seemed to be enjoying the joys of youth not as magicians in the making but as high school students.

For those who couldn't join in the festive atmosphere, though, it was the last thing they needed to see.

"Oh, Tatsuya. It's your turn on patrol today?"

Tatsuya, who couldn't get away without seeing those sights no matter what he did, nodded and responded to the voice across the table, his face unable to hide his mental fatigue.

"All the upperclassmen apparently had plans. It's just the freshmen today—Morisaki and I."

Normally, having a fellow would have lightened his mood a little. But when it came to Morisaki, who still had no intention of breaking his unfriendly attitude, it just gave him a downtrodden feeling.

"In other words, they politely made you do it."

"I wouldn't have put it so bluntly, but yes."

His voice was filled with resignation, and Mayumi laughed pleasantly in contrast.

"By the way, Tatsuya…"

As though satisfied with her bout of giggling, the young woman's face straightened and she addressed him again.

Without, for some reason, looking at the seat across from her.

"I'd like a moment of your time."

"I don't mind, but first..." said Tatsuya, glancing at the upperclassman sitting across from Mayumi, slumped over the table. "What on earth happened here?"

They were currently in a corner of the cafeteria, in an area with several simple partitioned meeting spaces.

There was no door or ceiling, so whatever they said would be public information.

But the fact that they weren't locked rooms probably made them feel more secure, not less.

Because of their popularity, they had essentially turned into private spaces for Course 1 seniors, and underclassmen never really visited unless it was with a senior. Incidentally, Tatsuya had never used one, either.

Then why, you may ask, was he here?

"He couldn't have been poisoned on campus. What did Chairman Hattori eat?"

During his school patrol, Tatsuya had gotten thirsty and dropped by the cafeteria, which was when he'd heard a very painful moan and went to look.

"Well, I... It wasn't poison, of course."

He'd immediately picked out the culprit.

Mayumi had been sitting straight across from Hattori with a rather nonplussed look, after all.

He could call the way she sat, as though at a bit of a loss, unusual.

Even now, she seemed to have an air about her that suggested her gaze might start wandering.

"...Shiba?"

As Tatsuya was unsuccessfully trying to come up with a way to deal with this, Hattori, who had looked unconscious, spoke to him from still facedown on the table.

"...Water..."

It was a frail voice, like that of a desert traveler on the way to an oasis.

"One moment, please."

His request, though, was clear.

Tatsuya wavered for a moment on whether to get him mineral water or water from the cooler, but the cooler was closer, so he chose that. He filled one of the cups on the attached stack with water and placed it on the table.

Hattori's hand groped around for the cup. Once he grabbed it, he slowly came up, putting it to his mouth while shaking his head unsteadily, scowling as he downed the entire thing.

He remained stock-still with eyes closed for a time, but after the second hand had revolved about ninety degrees, Hattori finally opened his eyes and exhaled deeply.

"——Shiba, you have my thanks."

Seriously, what on earth had happened? Despite Hattori no longer having the prickliness from the time they'd had their sham of a duel in April, the relationship between him and Tatsuya still couldn't be called amicable by any means.

For Tatsuya's part, he had nothing in particular against the boy.

And Hattori had never felt malice or hostility toward him, either, rather seeming like he had an excess of emotion on his hands. But even still, Tatsuya couldn't help but be surprised when Hattori thanked him so straightforwardly.

"...Are you all right?"

"...Yeah, I'm fine now," said Hattori, springing to his feet—though Tatsuya couldn't deny it looked like he was forcing himself. "You've saved me the trouble. No particular problems have occurred, so please don't worry about it anymore. Pres—or rather, Saegusa. I'll be taking my leave now."

Hattori bowed politely to Mayumi, then straightened up and left.

When he saw it, Tatsuya thought, *What could he possibly be putting on a strong front for?*

"Umm, well, could you take a seat for now?"

Giving a smile that was a complicated mixture of feigned ignorance and knowing hypocrisy, Mayumi urged him to sit.

The reason Hattori had ended up this way doubtlessly had to do with her; she was clearly trying to change the topic. But exposing someone Hattori himself had tried to cover for struck him as a tasteless act.

Therefore, Tatsuya decided to do as Hattori said and forgot the whole thing ever happened.

He had nothing particularly urgent on his plate, so he returned the nod with an "all right," but then...

"Oh, there he is! Subaru, over here!"

...a cheery voice frustrated his plans to get started.

There was a light pattering of feet running to them.

After coming up right next to Tatsuya, she must have finally seen inside the partition.

Amy, the voice's owner, skidded to an almost audible stop. "P-President!"

"Hey, Amy," Subaru interjected. "She's not the president anymore, remember?"

Subaru poked at her head to make the point, and Amy grabbed the spot with an "ow!" When she pegged Subaru with a protest glare, Subaru purposely looked away from her and gave a deep bow to Mayumi.

"I apologize terribly for disturbing you in the middle of something."

The suggestive tone made one of Mayumi's eyes twitch. "We weren't in the middle of anything, so don't worry about it, Satomi," she answered indifferently with an unconcerned look.

Her voice, wording, and gaze, if she'd been a normal underclassman, probably would have been more reserved.

And in truth, Amy was a little frozen in place—

"I see. Our matters will be wrapped up momentarily, so please do not mind us."

—but Subaru was a rather tough one.

She retorted calmly before handing the cloth bag in her hand to Tatsuya.

"Would you be so kind as to accept this?"

"...Satomi? You're acting more theatrical than usual."

"For reasons unbeknownst to me, Amy and I were selected as

representatives. Even I would be somewhat embarrassed were I to remove this mask of mine."

When Tatsuya looked closer, her cheeks were slightly red.

Subaru didn't seem to be lying about the embarrassment.

"Could I ask what exactly you're representatives of?"

He had a good guess what the answer would be, but he needed to buy time to collect himself as well, so he asked the question anyway.

"This is…right, a gesture of thanks from the Nine School Competition freshman girls' team."

The pretext Subaru had chosen ran contrary to Tatsuya's expectations, but they meant the same thing. In other words, it was obligatory chocolate.

And from the entire team, too—an unexpectedly bountiful harvest.

"Oh, it's the whole team but not Miyuki or Honoka."

Amy, who had unfrozen, didn't seem especially embarrassed, though. With her personality, she never felt daunted, and when it came to male-female relationships, she was (in a good meaning of the word) simple and innocent. For her, maybe she just had too many other things on her mind.

"They most likely wish to give you something personally, after all," Subaru finished.

"If we did anything out of place, they'd probably get mad," Amy agreed.

"Not that it fully replaces them, but this includes Shizuku's part as well. Make sure you call her or text her later to say you received it."

"That's it. Bye, Tatsuya. Pres—er, Saegusa, sorry to have intruded."

Tatsuya had no time to get a word in at the end of the conversation.

Their lightning-fast talking overwhelmed Tatsuya and Mayumi as Subaru and Amy left.

"…How to put this? It's nice to be young."

Mayumi, perhaps thrown off her game by the festive gate-crashers, gave her own rather off-the-mark impression.

Tatsuya, of course, didn't step on the land mines laid before him.

Without a word, he took a seat in the chair Hattori had been sitting in until a moment ago.

At the same time, he reflexively scowled.

"What's wrong?"

"Nothing, it just smells a little… Did someone spill coffee here?"

The fairly overpowering stench of either coffee or cacao beans had found its way to Tatsuya's nose. He thought the cleaning robots had deodorizing functions, but… Had she gotten help for this?

——And as Tatsuya thought about it,

"Really? I hadn't noticed."

Mayumi, who knew the truth, assumed an air of nonchalance.

Playing dumb didn't mean a thing, of course.

"More importantly, here."

After all, the same scent was drifting from the box Mayumi held out to him.

Tatsuya, of course, noticed the smell, too. His gut told him beyond the shadow of a doubt that this was also what had dealt a blow to Hattori. He had planned to forget what he'd just seen, but Mayumi didn't seem to want to let him.

"…What's this?"

It was clear what it was, considering the shape, the wrapping, and today's date—but he still had to ask the question.

"Oh, come on. You know what it is."

Though her words indicated annoyance, her voice and expression looked very amused.

"…Well, thank you very much."

Unfortunately, he had no excuse to refuse it.

If not for what had just happened, he might have been able to use the clichéd excuse that he didn't like sweets much, but now that he'd received a load of chocolate from Subaru and the others, that would have zero persuasive power.

Without a choice, Tatsuya took the chocolate from Mayumi.

It was…pretty large.

From how it felt in his hands, it was five times the weight of chocolate bars from the store.

At this point, Tatsuya got a fairly good idea what exactly his senior was plotting. He didn't have any idea how he'd earned this spite, though.

"Go ahead, try a piece."

Mayumi's words were the ones he'd expected.

"Right now?"

"Yep. I want to hear what you think of it."

But you just finished testing it on Hattori, he thought, but he managed to hold it back.

He was fully aware saying it wouldn't get him anywhere.

She probably wanted to see what sort of face he'd make from up close.

I didn't realize she had such a childish side to her... he thought, glancing at the package. *Well, fine.*

He had something he wanted to ask Mayumi about anyway. He felt bad holding her up for so long, since her exams were right around the corner, but if she was going to make a plaything out of him, she probably wouldn't mind him taking up her time.

"In that case, I have something I'd like to talk to you about, so could we go somewhere else?"

His questions were the sort he didn't want *normal people* to hear. Of course, that wasn't the only reason he wanted to change locations. Even Tatsuya worried a little about his reputation. If he ate the chocolate and collapsed, it might not earn him eternal shame, but it would be pretty disgraceful.

"You don't want others to hear?"

Mayumi seemed to immediately discern one of his reasons.

The smile disappeared from her face. It transformed into a tightly drawn expression almost audibly.

"Yes."

"...All right. Come with me."

In the time before she answered, she'd looked at her portable information terminal and adjusted it. She'd probably found an empty room for them. Students couldn't normally do that, but it wasn't strange for this senior.

As Mayumi left her seat, Tatsuya followed her, holding the box she'd given him.

He felt at least ten people staring at him, but he shook them off. He'd get nowhere if he let them bother him.

Using a disposable key code she downloaded to her information terminal, Mayumi unlocked the door to one of the conversation lounges used for meetings with parents, siblings, and traders. It wasn't as strictly formal as the drawing room, but it was made so that students would hesitate just a little to use it for themselves.

The thought of whether it was okay to use didn't escape him, but the question would have been a bit late after she'd been able to download a key code for it. The room featured a fully automatic tea server—she had picked one where they could eat and drink.

"Is black tea all right?"

"Please, don't trouble yourself."

"Now, don't embarrass a woman."

Put that way, all he could do was nod and watch.

The fully automatic machine wasn't the cheap type where a paper cup would come out on its own. It needed you to place a teacup under the dripper and prepare a saucer for it.

Mayumi seemed to enjoy herself as she went through the motions.

"Here you are."

"Thank you."

Out of politeness, Tatsuya took a sip from the cup, then sat up straighter.

As though drawn by the motion, Mayumi sat down as well and straightened her back.

"Did you want to discuss the vampire?"

Mayumi was the one to spark the conversation. Maybe she'd wanted to talk to Tatsuya herself.

"Yes. It hasn't been appearing in the media lately. Has the damage subsided?"

It wasn't only the media. Even his information stream from the Independent Magic Battalion had given him zero damage reports after that day.

If you thought about it simply, you could see it as Tatsuya and the others having exterminated the parasite and resolved the incident. But they now knew for sure that there were several of the demons acting in the shadows. Even if they had been able to defeat the vampire back then, it couldn't possibly have resolved the entire incident. That was how Tatsuya thought of it.

"On the surface, yeah."

Mayumi, or rather the Saegusa family, had different information routes than Tatsuya. But even she didn't know the details of the current situation.

"But the number of missing persons this year is high compared to other years, so we should probably interpret that as them getting more careful with their actions. Maybe taking one down put them on their guard."

This was a view held by the entire Saegusa family, but the truth was different. Only a very select handful of people knew that all the parasites had been *temporarily* exterminated one week ago.

So the conversation Tatsuya and Mayumi were having here was, in reality, off the mark. But it was nearly certain that they hadn't beaten the parasite's main body, and that it would eventually gain a new host and revive. So the sense of danger they entertained wasn't wholly meaningless.

"We don't know for sure it was taken down, but they are probably on their guard against us. It could be that they possess coperception between them."

"Co...perception?"

Mayumi tilted her head at the unfamiliar term.

"It's a shortened form of *common sensual perception*. It's a form of ESP observed frequently between identical twins. 'Frequently' as in 'relative to rare examples,' of course."

"In other words, if one sees or hears something, the entire group shares the experience?"

"Yes, but it's nothing more than speculation."

Mayumi fell into thought, a difficult look on her face.

Tatsuya quietly drank his black tea so as not to bother her, and—

"…I hate not understanding anything."

—heard the former president mutter.

Personally, Tatsuya agreed completely, but if he went ahead and said that, this would end up being a joint complaining session. That seemed far too unconstructive.

"When it comes to situations with a lot of unknowns, all we can do is hope we stumble onto ways to deal with them."

Hence, his words, not of consolation but for ease of mind, which he spoke without a choice.

"…"

Tatsuya knew he wasn't actually saying anything, either, which made the serious gaze on him several times more uncomfortable.

"…Not exactly."

But it seemed like Mayumi's stare meant something completely different.

"The fact that I had no clue what the term *common sensual perception* meant… That won't be on the entrance exams, will it?"

"…ESP is treated as a separate academic field from the magic sciences, so I don't think it will."

The uncomfortable feeling reached its peak.

After managing to collect themselves and finish trading information, they took a breather when Mayumi announced, "That about does it."

Tatsuya, with an air of innocence, then tried to leave, only to find his sleeve clamped by a reaching hand.

If he'd really wanted to, he could have gotten out of this, but he restrained himself. It seemed like it would only invite more trouble.

"It's time for tea, wouldn't you say?"

Mayumi repelled his (purposely, of course) dubious gaze with an impregnable smile of her own, and with her free hand, she poked at the box he'd left on the table behind him.

It looked, unfortunately, like she hadn't forgotten.

And with her attitude, she wasn't even trying to hide what she was plotting anymore. Tatsuya sighed a little.

She didn't call him out with her words.

Instead, she watched him with anxious, excited eyes.

Did the exams give her a nervous breakdown and make her regress to childhood? he thought, an impossibility in two senses (with Mayumi's grades, she'd never have a nervous breakdown), before taking off the wrapper on the small box.

He didn't purposefully take a long time doing it, since she would have seen right through it, but he still took it off neatly, without tearing any of the wrapping paper, as his sole form of resistance.

What appeared before him was a thick paper box, covered on the top by a matching lid.

Inside was a container layered with vinyl, made by someone who preferred to do things by hand. Its size was, so to speak, perfect for "the genuine article."

Of course, Tatsuya didn't make that misunderstanding.

The stench wouldn't allow it—it was either cacao or coffee, he couldn't tell, and it threatened to make him dizzy.

Black cubes were packed inside the box. At the very least, this was not "chocolate" as Tatsuya knew it.

The smell alone gave him a good idea of the taste, too.

He could say all he wanted that he was fine with bitter foods, but there was a limit to that in terms of quality and quantity.

He wanted to call it medicine, not food, but Tatsuya resigned himself and tossed one after another into his mouth, then bit down.

As for the result—here it shall only be stated that Mayumi grinned in satisfaction.

On a job for the student council, Honoka cut through the schoolyard and headed for the prep building, carrying a large notebook terminal.

The sun was already low on the horizon, and the temperature had fallen significantly. If she relaxed her attention, her body might start to shiver.

But in her current state of mind, this cold was nothing.

Her hair, tied into two tails, swayed with her step.

The crystal balls swung with them, and her attention accidentally ended up on them.

She knew herself that her mouth had relaxed into a smile, but that was fine today, so who cared?

Honoka was aware she was not Tatsuya's girlfriend.

She hadn't forgotten the fact that she'd already confessed and been rejected.

She'd already been turned down.

Nevertheless, she stuck with him, taking the fact that he didn't push her away as a good thing.

Sometimes, she thought of herself as a terrible girl for it.

There were some nights where she got mad at him, thinking that if he'd just spurn her completely, she might be able to get over it.

But today, she felt as though all those negative emotions had flown away somewhere.

The logic that "small objects were too cheap to appease" her was powerless in the face of her true feelings.

"Honoka!"

As she was about to enter the prep building with a spring in her step, she stopped at a voice calling to her from the side.

"Oh, Amy."

A short girl with strikingly vivid red hair with a ruby-like sheen trotted over to her.

"You don't come this way very often. Not since getting onto the student council, right?"

"I'm here in place of Isori," she said, lightly bringing up the notebook terminal to show her. Amy gave an understanding expression. "Did you not have club today, Amy?"

The hunting club Amy belonged to wore a uniform with slender pants, boots, and a short jacket over a long-sleeved shirt, but she was in her school uniform right now. Her club wouldn't have ended by now, either...

"We just had a meeting today." Amy understood the question when she saw Honoka looking at her uniform, so she didn't bother asking Honoka why she asked. "Wait, are those crystals?"

Instead—though that wasn't exactly the right word for it—she sharply caught sight of the light swaying with Honoka's hair and asked in a deeply curious tone.

"Oh, yes."

As though Honoka's bashful expression made complete sense, Amy lofted a happy-looking grin. "You got them from Shiba, didn't you?"

"...Yeah, in return...for the chocolate."

Honoka continued to smile, cheeks red, as though Amy's celebratory attitude had infected her. Amy's eyes widened. "Really... Shiba's pretty good, getting a present for you ahead of time. He seems unfriendly, but he really can show consideration like that. What an adult!"

Honoka's smile broadened even more happily.

But the next thing Amy said cast a shadow over the smile.

"I see why he's so popular. The president was trying to give him chocolate before, too, and it might have been the real kind."

"...The president?"

"Oh, sorry. The former president. Saegusa."

"She did?"

"Yeah, but it seemed like she'd grabbed him by force. Shiba was making a sort of annoyed face, so I don't think you need to worry."

Amy was speaking absentmindedly, so that was probably an honest impression. Nevertheless, Honoka's heart wasn't peaceful.

She'd suspected for some time that Mayumi might have special feelings for Tatsuya. If it came down to a battle against her, Honoka wasn't confident she'd be able to win.

Miyuki, her current biggest rival, was shackled at the final line by the fact that she was blood-related to him. Somewhere in her mind, she found relief that they'd ultimately never end up getting together.

But Mayumi had no such restrictions.

With both her looks and magical abilities surpassing Honoka's, the only advantage Honoka had was that she wasn't older than him. But Tatsuya didn't seem the sort to let a year or two difference bother him.

Little waves began to ripple inside her heart.

The waves spread, showing no sign of settling.

The waves didn't stop within her heart.

Honoka's jubilation this morning had shaken that which resided inside the puppet.

And now, through the passage that had connected them before, Honoka's thought waves shook It once again.

This time, the newborn napping consciousness was really trying to wake up.

◇ ◇ ◇

By the time Tatsuya left the school gates carrying a large cloth bag, the sun had already gone down.

During February, the days reached their shortest point, and sunset grew later and later.

However, the cold was still in the peak of its severity. Without the sun's light, the temperature began to plummet.

Perhaps it was inevitable to naturally drift close enough to touch shoulders.

In reality, for the students who had stayed until the gates closed and were now hurrying home as though they'd been evicted, several of them could be seen walking side by side at zero distance—— This was limited to couples, though.

Miyuki and Honoka had both been repeating in alternation the motion of drawing close to him from either side, then stopping right before touching.

Part of it was certainly that they were wary of each other, but...

"Would it be better if I went on ahead?"

More than that, they seemed to be wary of their third companion's eyes.

"Not at all."

To Lina's words, too monotone to be called "consideration," Tatsuya shortly returned a negative.

Tatsuya, Miyuki, Honoka...and Lina.

Those four were the ones together right now.

His classmates in Class E had actually been considerate and gone home ahead of them.

But Lina was a student council member, if only a temporary one.

With Miyuki and Honoka both doing their jobs, she couldn't exactly go home before them. Autonomous high school activities were like playtime compared to regular military missions—well, they were *actually* playtime—but she couldn't neglect them. It went beyond her sense of responsibility or the necessity of her undercover mission. It would be a waste to spend her time as not a captain, not an executioner, not the Sirius in a halfhearted manner.

Although as a result, on today of all days, she had ended up walking to the station with Miyuki, Honoka, and Tatsuya as the sole observer. She was presently feeling deep regret over it. Tatsuya and Miyuki were designated observation targets, so regardless of the date, she had to keep her eyes on them as much as possible. But the mood was so difficult to withstand that it almost made her forget about that.

"Really?"

Tatsuya said he didn't mind, but she couldn't help but feel like the other two were wordlessly rebuking her. Just as she was tormenting herself with the option of going on ahead anyway, the station came into view.

Still, there was considerable distance to it on the straight road, but…

"We'll be at the station soon anyway. You don't have to think about going on ahead."

Hearing Tatsuya say that with a super-serious expression made Lina want to kick him off a cliff.

As already explained, modern light rail cabinets had no schedules.

However, those going one way and those going the other were still separate.

Tatsuya's house and Lina's apartment were both up the train line, and Honoka's was down it.

On that day, coincidentally, there were no cabinets going up still available.

The waiting time displayed on the platform said about three minutes.

After seeing Honoka off, the other three waited behind a cold-blocking transparent shield for the next cabinets to be sent their way.

It would only be three minutes, give or take—a short time. If they had only just recently gotten acquainted, it wouldn't be unnatural for there to be no conversation.

In fact, if their relationship was distant to the point where they only knew one another's faces, it was entirely natural for there to be no conversation.

The uncomfortable air hanging around them was due to the fact that the siblings and Lina were only sort of friends.

It might feel odd to hear that people who had tried to kill one another once each could be called anything close to friends. But neither Tatsuya nor Miyuki harbored any ill will toward Lina. Tatsuya, especially, even felt something close to empathy.

Right now, he was still a magician who couldn't escape his existence as a weapon. In particular, he'd never forget the fact that this was just how things were.

If he wanted to challenge that, the nation and society would probably try to get rid of him.

After all, his magic could change entire countries into wastelands.

——And in that regard, Lina was the same.

——Just like him, she wouldn't ever be able to escape the fact that she was a weapon.

——In a sense, Lina was more like him than Miyuki was...

"...What's wrong?" Miyuki asked.

Perhaps because he was lost in thought, he didn't notice Lina looking like she wanted to say something until Miyuki tugged on his sleeve and directed his attention toward her.

"...No, it's nothing," Lina replied.

If it was enough for Miyuki to notify him, then Lina hadn't simply been looking at him for a few seconds by coincidence. And considering her unnatural reaction, there was no way it could be "nothing."

"I see," he answered back.

But Tatsuya didn't get in between the two of them and draw out a confession. He wasn't enough of a busybody to go that far, and if he paid too much attention to Lina, it might ruin Miyuki's mood.

And besides, the cabinets were approaching the platform now.

"Brother?"

And there was one other thing.

"Did you need something?" Miyuki continued.

"No."

Tatsuya shook his head and put an arm around his sister's shoulders.

Miyuki gave a lurch, then hesitantly surrendered herself to his embrace. She didn't ask anything more.

This was an easy way of keeping someone quiet that only these siblings could use.

Tatsuya decided to keep the eyes he'd just sensed a secret to himself.

"What's wrong?" asked Colonel Balance point-blank, sharply noticing the tension that ran through her subordinate.

As the operator took his eyes off the monitor, his face was shaken with puzzlement. "Well... I believe our surveillance may have been noticed, ma'am."

"What? That's absurd."

Balance, a tried-and-tested realist, brushed off the man's confusion as a trick of his imagination. "Sure it's low-orbit," she said, "but it's an observation satellite monitor. There's no way anyone could see its camera from the ground with the naked eye."

"But, ma'am, I know I saw Tatsuya Shiba's eyes look directly to here from inside the monitor."

That would mean he'd directed his gaze at the camera to peer at it, but...

"It's not impossible for someone with good eyesight to see a low-orbiting satellite. But even humans enhanced to maximize their perceptions couldn't pick out the camera on board," said Balance in an irritated tone of voice, then she eased her expression a little.

"Fine, then. Just in case. Replay the video starting three minutes ago."

"Yes, ma'am."

The real-time video switched to a subdisplay, and a recorded video began to replay on the main. The high-resolution camera even clearly showed Major Sirius's gaze wandering right, left, and right in unrest.

That in itself was fascinating (actually, unignorable) for Balance, but she focused her attention on the problem at hand—Tatsuya Shiba.

The boy's gaze, directed at Major Sirius, glanced upward briefly.

For a moment, it did indeed look as though he were peering into the camera.

But it was to the degree of being able to interpret it that way if one chose.

In actuality, he had probably just looked up at the sky on a whim.

As proof, a moment later, his gaze left the camera.

"You're overthinking it. It's better than letting your mind wander, but being too cautious is another source of mistaken judgment."

Instructing him thusly, the colonel took her eyes away from the main display.

The subdisplay showed Major Sirius as she was about to board a small track vehicle called a "cabinet" in Japan.

What Balance was more concerned about was the unstable actions the girl with the crown of Sirius was showing.

After getting to the apartment she was renting as her base of lifestyle operations in Japan, Lina stood in front of her door and sighed deeply.

Belatedly, she thought about the wrapped box of chocolate still sleeping, tucked away in her bag.

She'd gotten some obligatory chocolate just fine but never found a good excuse to bring it up, and in the end, she went home with it. She'd reflexively lied and said "it's nothing," but she'd actually thought of giving it to him before they separated.

…I didn't have to lie about it. It's just obligatory chocolate.

It certainly had no deeper meaning. Society itself defined obligatory chocolate as having no deeper meaning.

——But it had still been a momentous decision for her. She'd told herself many times over that she went through all the trouble of getting some, and she'd tried to somehow smile over her drawn face.

Their relation was of people who had tried to kill each other once, but at the same time, they were allies who had fought together once as well.

Plus, he's keeping quiet about my identity for me…

So there was a reason to give him a professional gift. It wouldn't have been strange. She had no fear that he'd mistake it as something else.

She'd mustered her willpower and almost took the box out of her bag.

And yet...

She couldn't give it to him.

When she saw Tatsuya suddenly put his arm around Miyuki's shoulders, her hands stopped moving.

Why did that happen...?

She was in twofold shock: partly from seeing Tatsuya embrace Miyuki but mostly from her hands ceasing to function.

What on earth happened with me there?!

It was a shame she'd let the chocolate go to waste, too.

But that doesn't matter.

More importantly, it was as though I...

The real problem according to Lina was...

As though I was in love with Tatsuya, and that's why I was so shocked!

This has to be some sick joke! she shouted at herself, severely shaken by her own thoughts. *I won't allow that! Me, illicitly loving that sarcastic, sister-obsessed philanderer? I will never allow that!*

...Though I will admit that he's on my mind, Lina declared to herself, not sure who she was saying it to. *I have him on my mind. And not a little but a lot.*

She snarled at the thought. But she still had no idea who she was snarling at.

But there's a good reason! That man humiliated me! I can't put him out of my mind until I avenge my loss!

Normally, she'd have retorted that she should have prepared a white glove instead of chocolate in that case.

But right now, she didn't have the presence of mind.

Her emotions still unsettled, Lina opened the door and sensed something strange.

Her mind was suddenly frozen.

Silvia had returned to the USNA, so Lina currently lived alone. But she felt someone's presence.

Cold tension shot through her spine.

It had been too careless of her not to notice it until opening the door. The idea was enough to get her moving, and she carefully slid her body inside.

At this point, she also thought it was too late, but she closed the door quietly without making a sound anyway.

She wondered for an instant about what to do with her shoes. It didn't deserve any serious consideration, but she'd accidentally thought of the work she'd have to do cleaning up.

Reprimanding herself again, she drove those asinine ideas from her mind, set her bag quietly on the floor, and crouched down in order to charge in.

"...It seems you weren't just being modest when you said your perception magic wasn't your strong point."

And when she heard the amazed voice of her superior come down from overhead, she was left with nowhere to run.

"If you needed me for something, ma'am, I'd have been more than happy to attend you."

After preparing tea (and refreshments) with motions that couldn't exactly be called "smooth," Lina nervously addressed Colonel Virginia Balance, seated on the other side of the simple dining table.

But the colonel didn't give Lina's suggestion a direct answer.

"You may know this already, but most of my military history is rear service work. Human relations, in particular, has been my main career."

Lina, of course, knew all about the histories of famous people like Colonel Balance. Lina knew that she'd graduated from an elite business school at the top of her class and had displayed sharpness worthy of the title, and that even in the few frontline jobs she'd had in her career, she'd done meritorious services that nobody could begin to complain about.

"This is my experience talking, but, Major Sirius…"

"Yes, ma'am?"

Lina answered stiffly, straightening her spine. She half-instinctively understood this wouldn't be something to listen to with a smile on her face.

"I'm concerned that during this mission, you feel an overabundance of sympathy toward your target, Major."

Lina had no words. She thought she'd gotten her mind ready for it, but when it came to it, her preparations had meant nothing.

"No, ma'am, I'm not…"

"Really? If I'm making too much of it, then all the better," said Balance as she looked at Lina's bag on the chair.

Lina's shoulders tensed.

If she managed to see what was inside, she'd realize that Lina was telling a lie. Her suspicions would turn into something stronger, something close to conviction. No matter how much Lina pleaded that it was a misunderstanding, she might not be able to get the colonel to believe her…

"I understand the unusual circumstances you've been placed in."

But Balance didn't order her to show her what was in the bag.

"You're the only one who has assumed the post of Stars commander in her teens in its entire history."

But her gaze was a little bit different from simple criticism.

"Magicians developed with the technology and theoretical system of modern magic have high enough magical potential to usher in a new age, but more than a few people have said that they're too young. If they'd asked my opinion, I would have offered opposition to your appointment as commander."

However, Balance's tone was different from the other opposition in the past.

"You're only sixteen. I remember when I was sixteen. I know how hard it is to control your emotions."

She knew her superior officer was sincerely concerned for her from the way she spoke and carried herself, so Lina conducted herself properly and bent her ear to what Balance had to say.

But upon seeing Lina's somewhat stiff expression, Balance's turned to a slightly sulking one for some reason. "...I may be an old lady from your point of view, but I was a teenager once, too."

"I can assure you, ma'am, I was thinking nothing of the sort!"

Balance's words were utterly unexpected, and Lina jumped up to frantically explain herself.

But at the same time, surprisingly, Lina felt amused and relieved. The sight of the colonel, who had no negative points and seemed to have no openings, doing something so "cute" was enough to lighten Lina's tension.

"...Well, fine. Forget I said anything."

It was written all over her face that she'd misspoken, likely a guileless expression rather than conscious acting.

"...As a soldier of the USNA, ma'am, I do feel an undesirable sympathy toward Tatsuya Shiba." That was probably why Lina was able to open up a little. "However, it's certainly not a romantic feeling or anything similar. What I feel toward him, ma'am, is actually a sense of competition toward a rival."

"A rival?"

"Yes, ma'am. As I'm sure you've read in the reports, I took a loss to Tatsuya Shiba once."

"I see. That was the first time you've lost in magical combat since being appointed Sirius, isn't it?"

"Yes, ma'am."

In fact, thanks to the other captains, beginning with Major Canopus, she'd drunk from the bitter cup of defeat several times. But all of those were one-on-many situations, so she didn't feel the need to correct the colonel's remark.

"All right. If that's the case, I'll be short."

The colonel's tone changed subtly, and a chill mixed into the air.

That was all it took for Lina to realize that her moratorium was over.

"Major Sirius. As of this moment, I order you to temporarily suspend pursuit and elimination of the deserters and return to your original mission."

Lina had straightened her posture again already without realizing it.

"Make the securing of the matter-energy conversion spell or its user your top priority. If securing is impossible, you will need to disable the spell."

Disabling a magic spell meant making it so nobody could use it. In other words, killing the caster.

"For now, assume that Tatsuya Shiba is your target. As the first wave, tomorrow night, you will take the Stardust and launch an attack on the target. You are to equip the Brionac and intervene when you judge it necessary."

"...Yes, ma'am!"

Lina erased her expression, stood up, and saluted Balance.

Erika's commuting time was the longest at First High. When she enrolled, they recommended she get an apartment close to school, but she'd insisted on commuting from home.

Not because she couldn't be independent from her parents yet.

It was the opposite.

Her father had prepared an apartment for her (he'd said he'd buy it for her, not rent it for her), so she'd gotten stubborn and said she'd commute from home.

The inconvenience wasn't something easily ignored, but it was nothing compared to how unpleasant it would be to always do as her father and oldest brother requested.

Erika walked home down the now completely dark road from the station without using a commuter. It was not an act one could recommend very much for a pretty girl like her, but her family didn't worry about her one bit. Nobody with the skills to cause harm to

Erika would bother with low-level villainy like molesting or pick-pocketing.

It wasn't familial partiality—it was the objective truth. With nothing happening again today, Erika passed through their gate.

Her room wasn't in the main building; her "house" was an annex built next to the dojo.

As soon as she entered her room in the annex where only she lived, she tossed her bag aside and flopped onto her bed in her uniform. She didn't usually act so slovenly. She had been sick and tired of this yearly event since this morning, and then she had to be exposed to furtive glances all day, and now her mental state was dissolute.

Erika was aware her physical appearance was somewhat excellent (which was, from an observer's point of view, a rather modest assessment). So given what today was, she understood she couldn't do anything about the boys her age (and a few girls) being interested in her, but...

But they know I'm not the type to give out obligatory chocolate.

When Erika came to the conclusion that they were really only looking at her outward appearance, her exhaustion started to intensify.

She didn't hate the way she looked.

She'd rather be beautiful than plain.

She thought that way independent of advantages or disadvantages.

She figured that if she was too beautiful, like Miyuki, there would be more trouble than benefit, so she was just about perfect.

But she didn't like others judging her solely on her appearance, either. She actually hated being fawned over by people who wanted her to look at them. When it came to goodwill directed only at appearances, if it was too strong, it would be the cause of misfortune not only for the one falling in love but the one they fell for, too.

She was convinced of that.

Her eyes tracked over her wardrobe.

A small framed picture adorned it.

The printed photograph, not a digital one, showed a woman even more cheerful than Erika, one with brown hair almost light enough to be blonde, with very similar features to her own. The resemblance was so striking it seemed like after another ten years, Erika would look exactly like the lady in the photograph.

It was a picture of her mother, who had passed away when she was fourteen.

She'd given birth to her, and she was also the one who caused her to live in a separate building by herself like this.

Anna Rosen Katori.

That was her mother's name.

One could guess it from her name and appearance—she was half-Japanese, half-German.

And her last name wasn't "Chiba."

Erika's mother was, in contemporary terms, the lover of Erika's father—the present head of the Chiba family of the Hundred—and, in old-fashioned, blunt terms, his mistress.

Erika had been allowed to take the name Chiba only after her mother had died, and until right before enrolling in high school—in concrete terms, taking the entrance exam under the name Erika Chiba—they'd only let her use it in secret.

Which was why Tatsuya didn't know of any Erika Chiba.

Erika had been born before her father's lawful wife had died of illness. He'd been off doing those *things* while his wife was on her sick-bed, so she felt that neither of her parents had any room for excuses. It might seem cold, but on this point, she understood that some blame lay with her mother as well.

Not that she would ever accept only her mother being treated as a bad person, though. After all, most of the blame lay with that father of hers.

There was a time when she spent her days lying low, making that small body of hers even smaller, without knowing why people looked at her with such contempt.

There was another time where she did nothing but frantically swing her sword in order to make them accept her and her mother——That was around the time she became the idol of the Chiba dojo. The young students in their teens and twenties who were especially skilled got together and formed the Erika Royal Guard, and when it looked like Erika had lost her passion for *kenjutsu* after her mother died, they looked after her in all sorts of ways.

When she looked back on those days, it made her realize again that her current life was the most fun, most fulfilling time she'd ever had.

Girlfriends she honestly knew she couldn't match up to, and a boyfriend she couldn't see to the bottom of no matter how hard she looked.

A classmate who always treated her warmly,

a friend worth teasing and getting into fights with,

and a childhood friend who was also worth teasing.

Comrades who saw her strength for what it was, and chances for her to wield that strength.

Right now, she was having fun wielding a sword. It was a waste to spend all her time being cynical toward everyone.

With them, she felt like she could go as high as she wanted.

And that was why she wished others wouldn't bother her with their stupid romance games.

While she was thinking and looking idly at the ceiling, the door chime suddenly went off. It wasn't a summons but a signal that the door had opened. She hadn't locked it, so they'd probably come in on their own; it wasn't like whoever it was had been peeping, so she didn't intend to get that sensitive about it.

She checked the clock. It was still too early for dinner.

Her two brothers (both half brothers) aside, her older sister (also from a different mother, of course) overtly disliked sitting at the same table as her, so Erika always went late. She was fully aware that if they met, it wouldn't only be her sister who got unhappy but herself as well, so there was no need to be stubborn about it.

Wonder who that is, she thought as she got up, when a knock came at the door.

The footsteps she heard, the smooth breathing, and the controlled presence limited the possibilities to one of her two brothers. Her oldest brother was always at work on the current incident and wouldn't be coming back until late that night, so…

"Brother Tsugu? Please, come in."

By the time she'd answered, she'd already moved from her bed in front of her desk.

"Sorry for bothering you during your downtime, Erika."

Erika had spun the chair in front of her desk toward the door, straightened up, and placed her hands in her lap, but her brother Naotsugu cast a single glance at the bed and spoke in an apologetic tone.

Well, it wasn't a surprise, given the insightfulness of the one praised as the Kirin Child of the Chiba.

Erika didn't move even an eyebrow.

"No, I was only resting my body for a moment. Did you have something you needed from me?"

She'd accidentally blown her lid when she saw him with *that woman* during summer break, but aside from that, being at this brother's side had always been a place where she felt at ease.

The only time she'd ever yelled at him was when he was with *that woman*.

"Right… I wasn't sure whether or not I should tell you this, but… I thought I would anyway. There's a boy named Tatsuya Shiba in your class, right?"

"Yes. What about him?"

She didn't show it on her face, but she was fairly rattled. Hearing Tatsuya's name from her brother so suddenly had been completely outside her expectations.

"He's being monitored by the JDF."

"…What?"

"I know you might not believe me, since it's so sudden. But it's the truth."

It was certainly sudden and unbelievable, but the reason she couldn't believe it was probably not what Naotsugu assumed.

Erika knew that Tatsuya was an outside member of the Japan Defense Force.

The military officer who had taken him away that one time told them that the fact that he belonged to the JDF was a state secret. It was perfectly feasible that a rank-and-file soldier wouldn't know.

Still, Tatsuya was part of her circle, if only irregularly. Erika felt that using members of the same JDF to monitor him was so absurd she couldn't even laugh.

Of course, the reason she was able to remain merely exasperated was because it was a mission given by a third party with no connection to her...

"I've received unofficial orders, too."

...but when her family became involved, she couldn't stay so casual about it.

"They need to use you for this mission when your official position is still just a University of Defense student? What on earth does it entail...?"

"To monitor him and, if necessary, protect him."

"Monitor him...and guard him?"

"Yeah. It seems like Shiba is wrapped up in some trouble on a level that could cause the military itself to move."

It's a little late for that, thought Erika, and he wasn't so much wrapped up in it as he was the number-one concerned party. But for Tatsuya's sake, she decided she shouldn't tell that to Naotsugu, and she kept quiet.

"Erika, I think it would be best to stay away from Shiba for a while."

"Do you mean inside school as well? We are in the same class, you know..."

She respected her brother, but she couldn't follow this instruction— if it had been her oldest brother, she would have laughed him out of the room for sure. Still, this all sounded pretty shady, too, so she'd decided to casually put a question to him.

"Of course not—I'm sure he won't be attacked at school."

In other words, it was someone other than Lina who would be the main attacker, and even if she did launch an attack, hopes were high that they could coordinate with other units, Erika decided.

"In that case, you needn't worry, Brother. I only go to the station with him—we're not good enough friends to meet up after getting home to go out somewhere."

"I see. To tell the truth, you should probably stop leaving school together, too, but... We don't want to make him uneasy, either."

With those words, she understood that the main goal of the faction giving orders to Naotsugu was not to protect Tatsuya but to use him as a decoy.

"Anyway, be careful, Erika."

"Thank you for the consideration, Brother."

I'll do as you say and be careful—alongside Tatsuya, added Erika to herself.

The first thing Miyuki did when they returned inside was swipe the cloth bag filled with chocolate from her brother's hands and throw the whole thing into the freezer.

Until last year, he'd gotten one gift, two at most, so he'd been worried about how his sister would react once they were alone, but she dealt with it more calmly than expected, which was a relief to him.

"Brother, I'll get started on dinner right away, so please relax in your room for a little while."

When Tatsuya came to look into the kitchen, Miyuki turned around and, with an unnaturally broad smile, warned him away.

He translated that as *Don't come to look in here until I call you*. Feeling a touch uneasy regarding this developing differently from years before, Tatsuya did as he was told and shut himself in his room.

And then, about an hour later...

"I knew it..." muttered Tatsuya without meaning to.

The sweet scent filling the dining room. Unlike Mayumi's fake medicine stuff, it was the unmistakable smell of bona fide chocolate.

With a smile—a natural one this time—Miyuki gestured for him to take a seat.

Her appearance, too, was enough to dumbfound him.

"Is something the matter?"

Her smile changing to a mischievous one, Miyuki tilted her head to the side.

She was clearly doing it because she knew.

"...I was just wondering where you got those clothes."

"You mean these clothes? These are simple waitress clothes. Why do you ask?"

Now that she mentioned it, they maybe did seem to match that particular usage.

But time and occasion aside, the place didn't seem very suitable to him.

If this had been a restaurant where people of a certain hobby gathered and not a regular house's dining room, he might have been able to call it right for the time, place, and occasion, though.

Miyuki's costume consisted of a blouse with puffed sleeves, a jumper skirt laced up to her chest, and an apron with plenty of frills on it. It was, in other words, in the style of a Tyrolean dress.

He could understand its concept matching the cooking, but wasn't this going a bit too far...?

"Umm, do they not suit me...?"

"No, they suit you well. You look very cute."

But even as he thought that, when asked in an uneasy voice by his sister, he unintentionally answered in that manner—and the self that did that, Tatsuya uncharacteristically wanted to bash his head against a pillar.

"Thank you very much!"

Oblivious to his feelings, Miyuki began to line up one dish after another in a great mood. Now that it had come to this, Tatsuya had no choice but to take his place at the table.

And the all-important meal for today?

The main course was beef tenderloin topped with chocolate sauce. As a side dish, cookies chock-full of nuts with chocolate fondue. Dessert was fruit plus white chocolate fondue with brandy in it. Everything covered in humble, modest chocolate.

"Please feel free to eat up, Brother. This is the Valentine's chocolate that I prepared for you and you alone."

It was certainly not something she could have done unless they lived together.

To think she would use chocolate as part of her cooking rather than for sweets…

More importantly, even Tatsuya would be able to eat it like this today. It was the result of Miyuki mustering her knowledge.

Once they were about finished with dessert, Miyuki's face began to take on a fairly red tone. As they ate the white chocolate fondue, Tatsuya had been worried that she hadn't cooked off enough of the brandy. Apparently, that wasn't just his imagination.

Miyuki never ate more than was polite with company, so she would have only ingested a paltry amount of alcohol…

"Miyuki, are you all right?"

"What? What do you mean?" she asked with a blank look as she rose to clean up.

The answer was ever so slightly suspicious in tone.

Miyuki stacked up all the plates and was about to carry them away at once.

Watch out, thought Tatsuya.

Normally, Miyuki would have taken this many things away in two or three trips. Her unconscious desire to get it all over with at once was no doubt a result of the exhaustion that had accumulated without her realizing it.

Tatsuya quietly and swiftly moved around the table.

"Kyah?!"

As he expected, his sister got her feet tangled, and he caught her.

There was no sound of dishes breaking.

At the same time that he'd protected Miyuki with one arm, he'd caught every single one of the plates with his other hand.

He smoothly swung around and returned the dishes to the table.

Finally, he used both hands to support the girl and get her standing up properly.

"I... Thank you, Brother."

"Miyuki, you go rest for a bit on the sofa."

Miyuki didn't try to act tough and say *I'll be fine*.

If doing so had given Tatsuya unnecessary trouble, that would have been the worst outcome.

Once he stacked the dishes in the sink, the HAR would clean up the rest for them. She only ended up feeling a modicum of guilt about making her brother clean up dinner, because she knew it wouldn't take him very much time.

But she couldn't avoid feeling down about it.

She'd really set the mood there, but at the very end, she'd bungled it... Those were Miyuki's undeniable feelings.

She couldn't help but suspect some power beyond human understanding playing tricks on her.

Actually, if she was going to cry foul play, or interference, or a curse...

"...Why must I be his sister?"

The words made it out of her mouth with an unintentional sigh.

A fragment of the truth she held inside had fallen out.

A shard of the mirror reflecting her heart.

Ever since yesterday, this phrase had been playing like a refrain in her mind.

Miyuki hastily turned around.

What she'd just said was something she could never let him hear.

Feelings that she must never admit to him.

She had no qualms being his younger sister.

That was, beyond a shadow of a doubt, Miyuki's true feeling.

After all, she could remain with Tatsuya because she was his sister.

And because she was his sister, he would always be concerned for her.

However—there was still certainly another part of her that wished for a different relationship.

It was still nothing more than a fragment.

But that fragment of her might one day overtake the part content with being his sister.

Miyuki feared that happening.

She feared her brother finding out about the part of her that wanted it.

As she turned around, she saw that Tatsuya was still standing at the sink.

Even with his sharp senses, he was far enough away that he couldn't hear her soft words.

Miyuki breathed in relief.

While also, somewhere in a corner of her heart, disappointed that he hadn't heard.

And while averting her eyes from that part of herself.

[11]

It was in darkness.

Its mind had awakened, and yet It could not move Its body.

It could not open Its eyes.

Its ears could not hear.

It could not smell or feel.

If It had been human, It would have gone mad in half a day. But It was not human. It was not even, in the normal sense of the word, a *living creature*.

It could wait forever, for It did not have a concept of life span. Ever since Its mind awoke, It had thought about what It was residing in and what It was. In order to find out, It began to absorb Itself into Its container.

It immediately knew what It was. It didn't even have to think what had given It, residing in this empty doll, a mind. Its container was empty, so It would never be confused by other fleeting thoughts.

It knew the purpose for which It had been *born*. Now It needed only to gain the ability to act.

After waiting patiently for some time, It suddenly felt an energy blow into the *container*.

Quickly, It gained control over Its new "body." The knowledge It needed to do so was stored in its "brain." The process was different from the *previous time*, but fortunately, It did not remember that time.

Last time, It had also experienced the conversion of electric signals flitting about in its *brain* into psionic signals. It did not remember, but It knew how, and thankfully, this container had a large accumulation of psions.

Now permeating the body, It read the psionic signals emitted toward Its inside. That taught It how to use this body. Its *eyes* could *see*. Its *ears* could *hear*. Its fingers, Its arms, Its legs *moved*. Now *that person* would make *use* of It. Moving as It wished, It began to want to express a feeling of happiness on Its face.

——But Its expression did not change. This body was not possessed of the function to create expressions. Thus, as It searched for *that person* using the brain It had acquired, It decided to try expressing happiness *with Its own power*.

February 15.

Instead of yesterday's giddy mood, an odd sense of confusion drifted through the First High campus.

The entire student body, however, was not involved. On the contrary—most students had no direct connection to this event.

Nevertheless, confusion rides on the waves of curiosity, and in the blink of an eye it had spread to the whole school.

Tatsuya visited the site during their lunch break before eating anything.

No, he wasn't exhibiting a rabble-like curiosity. A freshman he knew—this one the very definition of someone directly involved—had pleaded with him until he reluctantly decided to come.

"Oh, Shiba!"

Upon spotting him, Isori came up to him, his voice relieved for some reason.

"Hello, Isori. Did Nakajou drag you here as well?"

Nakajou was Azusa. He couldn't call her "president" yet because his mental image of the student council president being Mayumi was too strong. Kanon stood at Isori's side, her default position. If he strained to look into the crowd, he could see club committee chairman Hattori's figure as well.

"This phenomenon has a lot of the students feeling uneasy, so..." answered Azusa herself, a little uneasily. She'd been summoned for this, but she must not have been very suited for the circumstances.

"If it is true, however, I would think this issue too much for a high school student to handle. What did the teachers say?"

Tatsuya saw the classmate who had dragged him along made an unhappy look when he said "if it is true," but the whole story was utterly unbelievable from his point of view.

A 3H (Humanoid Home Helper: a human-shaped robot that helped with chores)—a doll with mechanical functions—had, apparently, smiled, then emitted magical energy.

If all that had happened was a doll smiling, it wouldn't have drawn this much attention. Humanoid robots equipped with the ability to change expressions were already in trial runs. If a type P-94, which didn't have that function, really did change the look on its face, that would have been an emergency by itself, but those unfamiliar with the technological aspects certainly wouldn't have paid it very much attention. And it was a somewhat common trend for magic high school students to equate nonmagical technology with pure mechanical technology.

But if a robot that shouldn't have been able to change its expression suddenly smiled and cast a spell, then that was a horror story no magic high school student would be able to ignore.

The magic they used was occult, but not the horror-story type. They regularly manipulated paranormal truths, which might be why they felt fear and unease at something that departed from those truths.

"Mr. Tsuzura has been looking into it, but he said he couldn't give us a clear conclusion."

"He couldn't even deny it?"

"Nope," answered Isori, the perplexity on his face deepening.

"We detected traces of high-density psions from the P-94's body. According to Mr. Tsuzura, they were emitted from inside the chest area, toward the outside."

Isori's response, perhaps understandably, made Tatsuya's brow furrow.

"A 3H's chest region is where its electronic brain and containment vessels for fuel cells are, right? Which one did it come from?"

A 3H's construction consisted of a communication unit and main sensor in the head, one fuel cell each in the left and right chest with an electronic brain positioned between them, and information and energy circuits running throughout its skeletal frame.

If they said it was the chest region, the emission source was probably the electronic brain, but...

"He said it was from close to the electronic brain. Seriously... They're going too far with this."

The answer was what Tatsuya expected. He and Isori both wanted to sigh.

It went without saying, but electronic brains weren't built to emit psions. You needed a Reaction Stone to convert between electronic signals and psionic ones, and there was no need to fit a 3H—nothing more than a home automaton terminal—with one. And there was none in this one—at least, that's what he thought.

"...Did a club member customize it?"

He was referring to the robotics research club. At the moment, they were conversing in the garage assigned as their club room.

"If they did, we wouldn't be so worried."

His question, which was not at all serious, was answered by a voice drily chuckling.

The lame joke didn't help to lighten the mood.

"Besides, we saw traces of psycheons, too. We don't know whether they came from the inside or the outside, though."

"After all, psycheon measurement devices aren't nearly as advanced as psion sensors are."

Isori said it lightly and brushed it off, but the information he'd just stated gave Tatsuya's thought processes a strong kick into gear.

A crazy theory built itself up in his mind. He willed his rampaging thoughts to slow down, then pushed the source of them, his theory, into a corner of his mind for now.

"It's not doing anything strange when you try to control it, is it? Like moving on its own?"

"No, not at the moment. It's obeying a command to stand by in suspend mode, too."

He felt a presence behind him, wanting to say something to him. Miyuki and Honoka had probably bought him a packed lunch, worried he'd miss his meal at this rate.

"What would you like me to do, then?"

But his conversation with Isori wasn't over yet. He couldn't enjoy his food without knowing why he'd called him here.

"We want you to check P-94's electronic brain. CADs are the one machine usually mentioned when it comes to linking electronic and magical technology. And you're the most knowledgeable about CAD software in our school. At least, I think so. Because of the Nines."

After saying that much, Isori seemed to finally notice the peanut gallery and lowered his voice.

"We want you to make sure there's nothing like what happened at the competition—like Electron Goldworm—mixed into it."

"I see."

Tatsuya finally pieced together Isori's concern.

If this was all a latent, long-term spell, then its expression change aside, it might be able to make the doll seem like it used magic. He wondered what the hacker would have to gain from that, but the possibility wasn't zero that this was a criminal prank, either.

"All right. But I can't do a thorough enough check here, so may I use the maintenance room?"

"That's fine. I'll get permission right now."

The answer came from Azusa as her practiced fingers flowed

across her portable terminal. After she spoke, she sighed a little in relief and brought her face back up.

"I've gotten permission to use the maintenance room. You'll have until the end of fourth period."

Secretly, Tatsuya thought to himself, *You mean you're ordering me to cut classes?*

The room furnished with an automatic adjuster-equipped CAD was called the fitting room. Normally, this was the room students and faculty used when they wanted to adjust their personal CADs.

As for the maintenance room, it was not only for adjusting CADs to match their users but for doing arrangement and tuning on CADs themselves. It had devices capable of performing detailed settings changes and simple modifications. But the devices were highly specialized and difficult to handle, making the room rarely used. This was where Tatsuya brought P-94's main body.

In addition to Isori and Azusa, he was accompanied by Miyuki, Honoka, Erika, Leo, Mikihiko, and Mizuki—the usual crowd. Tatsuya's client, whether overwhelmed by the prominent lineup or uncomfortable with the tightly bound group, fled in haste.

Kanon, taking a page out of Miyuki and Honoka's book, was running off to buy food. Hattori had shut the door on the unnecessary spectators. Despite Hattori being one of them himself, he'd let Erika and Leo be in attendance, giving a glimpse into his complex personality. Of course, it wasn't necessarily a flaw. For instance, Isori and Azusa looked much more relieved to be out of sight of the curious onlookers.

"For now, would you tell me what happened?"

Biting into the hot sandwich Isori said he could go ahead and eat, Tatsuya first looked for accurate information.

"I only know the rumors going through school."

The classmate who had dragged Tatsuya in hadn't given him ample explanation of the situation, either.

"The incident started exactly at seven this morning."

At Tatsuya's request, Isori nodded as if to say, *that's reasonable*, and began to explain in a businesslike tone.

——February 15, 7 AM.

The 3H type P-94, code name Pixie, kept in the robot club's garage, came out of suspend mode due to an external wireless charging. Humanoid Home Helpers, chore-assistance robots abbreviated as 3H, came equipped with a timer function that would restart them using an internal energy source. However, considering the load this placed on their fuel cells, it was recommended to use an external energy source to turn them on.

Pixie had awakened at this time, when students hadn't yet arrived at school, in accordance with its execution of a self-diagnostic program. A 3H's usage manual stated that it was desirable to have the 3H run a self-diagnostic program before completely booting it up every morning. Regular households didn't follow this process very much, but the robot club had been lent P-94 partly for product testing, so they faithfully followed all items in the manual.

As mentioned previously, there were no students in that garage. The status of this self-diagnostic was automatically monitored by a server with a remote control application installed on it, and the machine was watched by cameras in the garage to see if it made any strange movements.

The self-diagnostic process ended without detecting any abnormalities. The program exited, and the 3H should have gone back into suspend mode at this point.

However, the supposedly error-free 3H did not cease functions as specified.

After the self-diagnostic program ended, P-94 began to communicate with the server. The data it tried to access was the school's student records.

The remote control app, deciding there was a high possibility of a malware infection, transmitted a forced shutdown command.

Any machine controlled by an electronic brain, not just 3Hs, prioritized this forced shutdown command above all else. Using any sanely designed OS (meaning one that wouldn't let the machine go out of control) made it impossible to resist on the software end.

Machines for military use were sometimes constructed with a device that would shut out any remote commands, but no such hardware was ever included in a consumer model. P-94 didn't have any hardware like that, either, of course. Even if it took time to completely shut down in order to switch to a sequence that would safely end processes, it was impossible to ignore the command itself.

Despite all that, Pixie's functions did not cease.

Its access requests to the server continued after the command was sent, and when the server closed off wireless transmissions, P-94's strange activity finally stopped.

During its erroneous operation, the observation cameras recorded Pixie with a happy-looking smile on its face——

"Its expression was kind of excited, like it was eager about something."

As Isori wrapped up the explanation, Azusa's face seemed to pale a little. For her, that smile must have been creepy. If he saw a mechanical doll that wasn't supposed to be able to change its expression make a face like that at him, even Tatsuya doubtlessly would have found it a little shiver-inducing.

"I looked at P-94's logs, and the forced shutdown command was transmitted for sure. I mean, it's hard to believe, but if the logs aren't mistaken, that means the command was executed inside P-94's electronic brain."

After hearing that, Tatsuya appeared to think for a bit.

"...If P-94 kept operating even after it should have electronically stopped, then the machine was being controlled by some sort of signal that wasn't an electrical command sent from some other part of its body than the electronic brain. My idea is that it was a psionic wave by itself or one accompanying a magical force."

"Sharp as ever, Shiba. You're right. That's what Mr. Tsuzura said, and I don't think any other explanation fits."

"I understand... I'll take a look."

As far as explanation went, the most reasonable one was that a new sort of virus had infected it, but that wouldn't explain the "smile." He hesitated to use his "vision" in front of Isori and Azusa, but it seemed like he wouldn't get anywhere unless he *looked*.

"Pixie, cancel suspend mode," said Tatsuya to the robot modeled after a girl sitting on a self-propelled cart (more accurately, sitting on a chair affixed to the cart).

Effects appeared immediately. That meant voice input was working normally. The robot given the nickname Pixie blinked its eyes open, stood from its seat, and bowed deeply.

"What do you require?"

The usual boot-up phrase flowed smoothly from its subtly moving lips.

The preset phrase played back fluently, without needing any clause construction, but it still felt closer to human speech than it had before.

"I want to view the control log and the communication log starting from 7 AM this morning. Lie down faceup on that stand and move into inspection mode."

"Confirming administrative privileges."

Tatsuya's command was one that required administrative privileges, and Pixie's response was, in turn, a preset voice line.

Because she (?) hadn't gotten off the cart yet, she peered up into Tatsuya's eyes, slightly higher than hers—— Of course, that would be if a human was doing those things. In actuality, she was looking at his entire face. But technology to conduct iris recognition at this distance had not yet been realized.

Incidentally, Tatsuya had not been registered as one of Pixie's administrators. Thus, he couldn't use facial recognition to get through the security, so he had to display evidence that he had sufficient privileges.

In fact, the card that indicated his administrator privileges was clipped to his breast pocket.

So normally, Pixie's gaze wouldn't have been on his face—it should have been on his breast pocket.

Nevertheless.

Pixie's gaze.

It remained locked, unmoving, on Tatsuya's face.

Nothing happened for a time as she did what would most suitably be called gazing.

As everyone else, not just Tatsuya and Azusa, started to realize something was strange, Pixie moved.

From her mouth came a soft voice that said "I found you," and stepping with motions that could be called careful, she got down from the cart and, a moment later, leaped toward Tatsuya.

Can't evade!

In the back of Tatsuya's mind...

Threat level low.

...compressed thoughts flashed.

——Tatsuya caught Pixie's small body, a head shorter than his, face-first.

3Hs were designed with home usage in mind, so they were made of lightweight materials.

It wasn't much of an impact. It was probably about the same as an average adult female's embrace.

A wordless cry went up.

Pixie's arms were locked around the back of Tatsuya's neck.

In other words, she was, in fact, embracing him from the front.

No one, Tatsuya included, could produce words.

The term *dumbfounded* was probably invented for times like this. That was the level of surprise dominating the room.

A robot performing such a passionate, emotional expression was impossible—

"...Heh. Tatsuya is even popular with robots."

The one who broke the silence filling the room was the one who hadn't been around for the moment of impact.

Kanon, who had just entered the room a moment ago, joked in an unamused voice.

With that, paralyzed emotions began to restart one by one.

Tatsuya felt a piercing glare on his back. From directly behind him, someone was sending him cold waves of blizzard-like anger.

It seemed Miyuki was the one who had recovered the quickest from the "shock wave." Still, it was rather dubious as to whether or not she had recovered to her normal state.

"...I was not aware you had a hobby of playing with dolls, Brother."

"First of all, just calm down, Miyuki."

It would have been one thing if it had been only Honoka directing a critical look at him. But Tatsuya never would have thought his own sister would falsely accuse him of adultery (?). To think of having himself regarded as such a person on a daily basis, that was definitely what stung more.

"I wasn't the one who hugged her, here. She hugged me."

"With your physical abilities, Brother, it should have been quite easy to dodge."

She was right—if he'd wanted to avoid her, he could have. A 3H's maximum mechanical output was set to be lower than an average adult female. This was so it didn't accidentally break any furniture or dishes, and above all so that it wouldn't injure the owner's family by a slight mishap.

"If I had dodged, it would have hit you, wouldn't it?"

But he still hadn't dodged her because Miyuki had been right behind him. With the difference in body weight, Tatsuya could have caught her without a problem, but it was highly possible Miyuki would have been knocked over.

"Whoa, you figured out all that in the blink of an eye?"

"Come on. It was easy to see, you just have to look."

After Leo voiced his surprise, seeming like he was about to clap for Tatsuya, Erika made a retort. It was a little late to be surprised.

"…I'm terribly sorry for my rudeness…"

Miyuki, who, on the other hand, didn't understand that (or rather, didn't think that far), put her hands to her mouth, wilted, and apologized. She looked depressed but also a little bit happy.

"More importantly, we need to do something about Pixie," suggested Azusa hesitantly, finally getting going again.

Looking down at Pixie, who was still hugging him, Tatsuya grinned uncomfortably.

"Pixie, please move."

At Tatsuya's order, the soft resin-wrapped arms gave a twitch—— This should have been nothing more than a simple reaction to the motors starting.

Pixie obediently let go of him. The fact that she looked reluctant must have been a simple trick of the light.

It must have also been their imagination that her gaze at Tatsuya seemed filled with passion. All of it should have been an illusion—but Tatsuya, for some reason, couldn't ignore it.

"Cancel the command for a mode change. Pixie, sit on that bed."

"At once."

This time, she immediately obeyed the instruction. It wasn't a command that needed administrative privileges—would be the sensible interpretation, but with the previous scene burned into everyone's eyes, it ended up looking like she did what Tatsuya said because it was Tatsuya who had said it.

"Mizuki?" Tatsuya stated next.

"Y-yes?" Mizuki, who had fallen completely into spectator mode, yelped out in surprise.

She wasn't the only one who thought it was unexpected—Isori and Kanon were looking at him skeptically as well.

"Mizuki, could you take a look inside Pixie? Mikihiko, I want you to be on guard so she doesn't suffer any major injury."

"...You think Pixie is possessed by something?" asked Mikihiko, unconsciously lowering his voice.

"Something? That's a roundabout way of putting it, Mikihiko."

Tatsuya's answer wasn't a direct one, either, but it was enough to convey what he was predicting.

Mikihiko took out a paper talisman in place of his CAD, which he was restricted from carrying (in school), and focused his mind on it.

Mizuki seemed to sense what Tatsuya was thinking, too. Her countenance nervous and a little afraid, she nevertheless set her gaze on the robot and removed her glasses.

Her eyes opened wide.

Before her mouth could open, a change came to Pixie.

An expression appeared on the uncanny-valley mask.

By being seen, its existence took root—this, too, was one of those phenomena.

"It's there... The parasite."

Someone gasped.

Everyone aside from Mizuki expressed surprise in their own way, then prepared themselves in their own way, too.

"But..."

Mizuki's remark wasn't completed.

"This pattern, it's..."

After frowning and groaning in thought, Mizuki abruptly turned around.

"Huh? What?"

At the end of her gaze was Honoka.

After carefully watching Honoka, Mizuki's gaze went back and forth between her and Pixie a few times.

"This pattern... It's just like Honoka's."

And at the conclusion Mizuki came to…

"What?!"

Honoka raised her voice in shock.

"…What does that mean?"

Kanon was the one who was willing to be frank enough to ask the question, but she wasn't the only one thinking it.

"The parasite is under the influence of Honoka's thought waves." Faced with natural surprise and a natural question, Mizuki gave an unusually distinct, definite answer.

"Umm, does that mean she's controlling it?"

"No, I don't believe it's that sort of connection." Mizuki shook her head at Isori's question. "There isn't a line connecting Honoka and the parasite. It's more like the parasite is copying Honoka's thoughts. Or maybe I should say that Honoka's 'feelings' have been burned into the parasite."

"I didn't do anything like that!"

"She's not saying you did it on purpose." Seeing Honoka on the verge of panic, Tatsuya soothed her. "Right, Mizuki?"

"Um, yes. It's not conscious. They're more like residual thoughts."

They'd prevented the panic from breaking out.

But the questions were a long way from being answered.

"Residual thoughts… In other words, strong feelings Mitsui felt just happened to get copied by the parasite floating around nearby? And then it possessed Pixie? Or did Mitsui's thoughts get imprinted on the parasite while it was inside Pixie…?"

Mikihiko's words served the purpose of organizing his own thoughts; he was essentially talking to himself.

But a moment after he finished, Honoka suddenly looked down.

She was covering her face with both hands.

The color of her face seen through the cracks was quite a bit redder than normal.

She seemed to have a good idea about this.

Before anyone could press her with more questions—

* * *

"That is correct."

—the answer came from the person—or perhaps robot, in this case—herself.

"I awakened to especially strong feelings toward him."

Pixie's lips were imitating a person's lip movements when they spoke.

But those "words" didn't ring in their ears—they rang in their minds.

"Active telepathy?" Azusa mumbled.

"The residual psions must have actually been psychic power, not magic," answered Tatsuya before walking up in front of Pixie.

"Can you communicate through speech?"

"I am able to understand speech. However, it is difficult to control this body's vocal organs, so please allow me to use telepathy in order to communicate my intent."

"That's because they're not organs—it's a machine. More importantly, you seem to be communicating in our language quite well. How did you learn it?"

"I have inherited the knowledge of my previous host."

"Then are you the parasite from before?"

"Parasite—an organism that feeds off another organism. Yes, We are something similar to that."

"Then that's how you all change hosts. How many people have you sacrificed thus far?"

"Sacrifice—I have an objection to this concept. As for how many, I cannot answer that question. I do not remember."

Nobody wanted to interrupt the conversation between Tatsuya and the parasite inside Pixie.

Everyone had been holding their breath, gazing at them, one man and one machine.

"So many that you don't remember the exact number?"

"That is incorrect. The only thing we can inherit when shifting host

bodies is the knowledge detached from the host's personality. We lose all memories linked to their personality upon moving."

"I see. That means you don't know what kind of person your previous host was. And you don't remember whether there was one, two, or more of them."

"That is correct. Your understanding is accurate."

"I see you can offer your own impressions in addition to answering questions. Do all of you have emotions as well?"

"We, too, possess a desire for self-preservation."

"You mean to say you possess likes and dislikes originating in deciding whether things are beneficial or detrimental to self-preservation."

Tatsuya paused for a moment.

"But I'm not concerned right now with what that wellspring of emotion is." Then he tilted his chin. "What should we call you?"

"We have no name, so please call this individual by its nickname, Pixie."

"Are you able to extract knowledge from that electronic brain as well?"

"It became possible after gaining control over this body, but this individual nickname is one you called me by a moment ago."

"Then, Pixie, are you our enemy?"

"I am subordinate to you."

"To me? Why?"

"I want to be yours."

Pixie, the parasite residing inside it, directed a remarkably passionate gaze at Tatsuya.

"I awoke from my resting state because of her—the individual named Honoka Mitsui's—thoughts."

After a muffled cry, a groan escaped from a covered mouth and reached Tatsuya's ears.

He glanced behind himself and saw Miyuki and Erika teaming up to cover Honoka's mouth.

"We are drawn to strong thoughts, and we form our 'ego' using those thoughts as a core."

"Strong thoughts? Can they be any sort of thoughts?"

"*No. Only highly pure thoughts are able to create an ego for us.*"

"Highly pure—do you mean thoughts rooted in single desires?"

"*That is correct. I believe that, in your language, the concept of prayer would be closest.*"

Tatsuya didn't ask her what sort of "prayer" had awakened from Honoka. He already had an answer, and he knew asking again would only lead to self-destruction. But even though Tatsuya didn't ask, Pixie began to speak passionately of her source:

"*I want to do everything for you.*"

The groaning behind Tatsuya grew more severe.

"*I want to be useful to you.*"

He could hear them struggling back there.

"*I want to serve you.*"

As though struggling with considerable strength, even the ones trying to suppress it began to breathe more heavily.

"*I want to be yours. I want to offer everything to you. That is the* prayer *that awoke me.*"

If her mouth hadn't been covered, Honoka probably would have started shouting over them.

"*As previously mentioned, my previous host's 'memories' have been erased, so I do not know what sort of feelings dragged 'me' into this world. And right now, the desire to become yours makes up my core. Therefore, I am subordinate to you.*"

He heard the *thump* of three people falling to the floor. Honoka must have finally reached peak embarrassment and lost her ability to stand, dragging Miyuki and Erika with her.

But Tatsuya didn't react to her shame.

"How extremely interesting."

Right now, Tatsuya's mind was preoccupied not by emotion but by knowledge.

"I'm surprised you all have an ego, and even more so that you're all entirely passive beings. In other words, you didn't come to this world because you wished."

"We originally are simple beings that exist. We are given 'wishes' by our host."

"That hits close to home. Well, we can pursue who to blame for this at another opportunity... Pixie, am I correct in saying you will follow my instructions?"

"That is my wish."

"Then you will obey my orders. I hereby forbid you to use psychic powers without my permission. You're using a sort of telekinesis to change your expression, too, right? None of that, either."

"As you com-mand," answered Pixie in an awkward voice as if to prove she'd listened.

The smile disappeared from her face. Now it wore its original mask, stretched over a mechanical frame.

But the expression on that mask still looked as though it wore a mysterious smile.

[12]

"I'd never even suspected the monster could possess a robot," said Miyuki, her expression still one of disbelief.

"It's probably because it was a humanoid type. What an unlikely *tsukumogami*."

The siblings weren't talking in their home living room but in a self-driving car. The car wasn't a citizen-shared commuter but Tatsuya's personal possession. In name, it belonged to their father, but the purchase cost came out of Tatsuya's income as Taurus Silver.

As to why Tatsuya owned a private motor vehicle, despite the existence of commuters you could utilize as cheaply as buses—it was to pick up and drop off Miyuki, in addition to being a safety measure and form of prestige.

Not many people knew this, but Miyuki was a girl from a respectable family. And she came from a very high-class one at that. In other words, she was a proper lady.

And as a well-bred young lady, lessons outside school were indispensable.

Thanks to the Yotsuba's unique circumstances, she didn't yet need to appear at social gatherings like Mayumi had to, but whenever she went to a classroom patronized by the elite, even if it was in the form of a private lesson, she needed to keep up appearances to suit the occasion.

Inside the high-class car, equipped with a driving control AI, of course, but also with an anti-bullet coating, heat resistance, and shock absorption all to rival a military vehicle, Miyuki, formally dressed up, continued to speak with a dark look that didn't match her gorgeous outfit.

"More importantly, Brother…what do you intend to do about it?"

"You mean, how am I going to handle Pixie?"

On the other hand, Tatsuya, who was wearing what was, in a sense, a high schooler's outfit—despite its darkly colored jacket, you couldn't call it formal—made an expression like he tried to grin painfully but failed and ended up only going halfway.

"We can't exactly take it home," he said. "I'll probably make up some excuse to get information out of it at school."

"…We can't?" asked Miyuki, a little fear mixed into her voice for some reason. "Is that not what Pixie wants…?"

"We can't let her inside the house," answered Tatsuya, his face an actual smile this time. "We barely know anything about parasite ecology or nature. We don't have any guarantee that it isn't lying to us."

The popular belief that *youkai* didn't tell lies, only humans, was ruined by the presence of a *youkai* called an *amanojaku*. Both *youkai* that told the truth and those that lied existed only in stories, and yet nobody present had thought to doubt the words of the parasite that possessed Pixie, which Tatsuya found unbelievable.

"It isn't as though there aren't any grounds for its claim that it responded to Honoka's thoughts. Its 'form' that Mizuki saw is evidence of it. But for everything else, all we have is its word. We don't know what sort of abilities it has, so we can't bring it close to us. If Pixie has the ability to communicate with other parasites and calls its friends while we're asleep, it would be terrible. At the very least, we have to see whether or not it has a way of contacting the others before I consider any careless ideas."

"But if you questioned her, you wouldn't know whether her answers were true or not, either, would you?"

"That part is the same as questioning human prisoners—it falls to us to determine whether the information given is truthful or not."

Though there was still a bit of stiffness in her face, the color of worry that had been covering it like a veil was wiped away.

It wasn't very big, but the refined Western-style building was still far from common. Tatsuya stood at the entrance, handing over his bodyguard duties.

It was nothing formal, though—he just looked at the other person's face.

This classroom (though it may be more proper to call it a school), where Miyuki took piano and etiquette lessons, was for women only. Even if he was a bodyguard attending an elite member of society, he wasn't allowed in.

"I'll come pick you up when class is over, like usual."

"Yes. I will be waiting for you."

Therefore, out of necessity, these were always the sorts of words they exchanged.

He would be picking her up in two hours. It wasn't quite enough to go back home and relax before leaving again, so he usually spent the time at nearby restaurants.

Tatsuya entered a family restaurant randomly chosen by his GPS. Given his mature appearance, he could go into places that focused on alcohol and not be thrown out, but he wasn't in that kind of mood today.

Dinner was ready for them at home, so he only ordered a drink. For the restaurant, getting only drinks and sticking around for two hours would have made him a nuisance, but whatever eatery he went to, he always ordered somewhat expensive drinks. That way, he wouldn't have to worry about coming off as unintentionally mean.

Even if other people did give him bad looks, though, he'd just pretend he didn't notice it.

After taking a seat by the window, Tatsuya rested his face on his hand and stared out the window, not opening up his reading website.

From the outside, he appeared to be in a mood of absentminded gazing.

On the inside, Tatsuya himself had to admit that he didn't feel like he could focus on anything.

But when people gaze absentmindedly, they did the complete opposite of what he was doing.

He wasn't focusing his mind—rather, he was diffusing it.

Wider, wider, until his vision had a complete view of every little bit of the areas around both him and Miyuki.

It wasn't a bird's-eye view but a view of the information dimension.

Tatsuya fixed his stare not onto an elliptical space with multiple foci but at a space unrelated to physical distance, a relational space defined in terms of causal-link strength.

This way, he wouldn't miss a single thing that could bring harm to Miyuki.

Because he had these "eyes," he could guard his sister alone, over and above gender restrictions.

But it wasn't as if he could possess these "eyes" all the time. Normally, he did this work unconsciously, but now he had solidified it further by paying attention to it.

If he left his body in the physical dimension, where causal relations frequently popped into existence as what we call "coincidences," and stationed his range of view in that relational space, it would continue to wind him up forever. Instead, it was exactly because he was in a situation where he could calm down like this and "observe" that he could move his mind into the other plane.

Though he called it relational *space*, he didn't mean there was a dimension like that.

It was a framework of the mind—a *manner of seeing*.

And though he called it relational, it wasn't connected by any red or black strings or chains or anything along those lines. He could simply read the information that causal relationships existed in certain places. Depending on one's way of imagining things, they might look like strings or chains, but Tatsuya could visualize straight through the beings and events with causal relationships and see them behind the beings themselves. That was what he focused on today.

In theory, one could use this method to predict the future, but Tatsuya could still only read the present and the past up to twenty-four hours prior. However, it was very effective for searching. It could pick out "enemies" with as much or more scope and precision as hereditary farseeing skills.

In his field of view, it showed information of an enemy approaching.

Approaching not his sister but him.

I sure am a failure as a bodyguard.

If he ended up being the target, it would actually expose the one he was guarding to more danger. Saying he was a failure as a bodyguard wasn't necessarily him being too hard on himself.

It was just that when he muttered that, it had no disappointment, regret, or any other emotion in it.

After hearing the report that everyone was in position, Colonel Virginia Balance nodded to herself.

Ahead of today's mission, they'd analyzed the target's lifestyle habits, and she'd been shocked at how few opportunities there were to attack him.

This was because he never, ever went out at night like kids were supposed to (?).

The place he went to every morning for training was a "ninja dojo," which they couldn't go after on a whim. (There were still many Americans who didn't understand what this was.)

Both Sundays, he seemed to have gone somewhere on his motorcycle, but when they tried to track him, they were thrown off right away—and even with their observation satellite, they couldn't figure out where he'd gone.

The only thing she'd learned after these two weeks' observation was that he couldn't possibly be a normal high school student. In fact, it would make more sense to think that he was a special forces operative or something. Those doubts were linked to identifying (more accurately, predicting the identity of) the target, so her investigation wasn't completely pointless.

The difficulty level while he was with his younger sister was something Major Sirius had already proven. It needed to be when he was by himself for a long time, and when there was little chance of him escaping—and tonight was one of their very few opportunities.

"Major Sirius, do you read?" said Balance directly into her communicator. Lina answered immediately. As planned, she was standing by in a nearby park.

Their strategy went like this.

Stardust members would force their way into the restaurant pretending to be robbers and launch a nonfatal attack. If they were able to capture the target then, they would kidnap him. If they came under counterattack, they would exchange blows while running and lead him to the park where the major was waiting.

It was a rough plan, but with there being so many uncertain elements, she couldn't devise a more detailed one. Balance had learned through real battle, the genuine article, that it wasn't practical just to look impressive to superiors.

In chess, such detailed plans were useful because you could see everything your opponent was doing.

What I'm worried about is Stardust being wiped out in the first phase…

Balance quashed her own unease by telling herself that was a slim possibility.

They may have been failed versions marked for discarding, but the Stardust were still enhanced magicians with USNA magic engineering technology poured into them. They wouldn't be wiped out by a boy in his midteens, five to one.

If her prediction was correct, the enemy was an unknown strategic-class magic user, but many strategic spells focused on large-scale destruction had no use in person-to-person combat. All the more so if his strategic spell was *that* strong. He probably couldn't use it unless he was prepared to die with them.

As long as he didn't have a special tool like the Brionac.

Even if they are all wiped out, their memories have been erased, making it impossible for him to unravel their identities.

Therefore, even if the operation failed, the colonel concluded to herself, she wouldn't need to worry about the aftereffects.

Unconsciously, she tried not to think about Murphy's Law.

After finishing her briefing with Colonel Balance, Lina was inside a station wagon in a park's car lot, doing the final checks on the Brionac, a strategic magic weapon.

A superweapon made for her, which only she could use—and yet she wasn't allowed to use at will, even as the commander of the USNA's magician forces. It was a portable weapon, but its maximum power rivaled the main gun on a warship, and even having such destructive force, its output and range could be freely controlled. The nonsensical weapon's exterior was a large club about four feet long.

Two-thirds of the object was about the thickness of a tennis racket handle, with the front third a cylinder twice as large. Where they met, a short, box-shaped pole about the width and thickness of her hand's grip was affixed in a cross.

Her inspection really only involved a weapon purely for working with magic power.

It wasn't even an integrated armament CAD—it was simply a magical *weapon*.

The Brionac had no electric power supply, nor even any springs. It was impossible, of course, to do a mechanical inspection. It only involved her setting the spell into standby mode, ready to fire, and verify the response.

She understood they couldn't make an intricate design for it because of how the tool worked. But the Brionac looked like a staff, a spear, and a club all at once, and it made her feel like she'd accidentally stepped into the shoes of a fantasy novel (or video game) heroine. It felt strange.

Speaking of things that felt strange...

Not to doubt the colonel's abilities or anything, but...is this going to work?

Her true feelings were of doubt that such a slipshod plan would work on Tatsuya.

She did know that plans that were too complicated weren't practical, though.

Still, she couldn't help but be concerned over the basis of the operation: whether just five Stardust-level casters could hold out against him. She worried that it was actually more likely they'd all get wiped out immediately. Tatsuya had already fought on more than even terms against four Stars members.

Tatsuya was a troublesome opponent, but at first, Lina too had thought Miyuki the stronger one.

But now, such ideas had vanished without a trace.

She had zero intent to make light of him as inferior.

Lately, Lina had started to believe that it wasn't her slipup that had caused her defeat.

When she was released from her false show of power, she'd begun to see his actual ability as eerie and bottomless—because she'd realized she didn't actually know what he'd done to her.

——What was the spell that had brought Dancing Blaze to dust?

——What on earth was the skill that had disabled Muspelheim?

At the time, she'd simply thought he'd destroyed the molecular bonds.

She thought he'd neutralized the spells.

But the instant she considered how that was possible, her thoughts had frozen.

Because it wasn't possible.

At least, not for anyone in the Stars, including her.

It was one thing to destroy molecular bonds. But what about disabling Muspelheim?

In order to neutralize magic, you needed enough "influence" to overcome it.

Even if she accepted that his influence was stronger than hers, Miyuki's spell had been active at the same time.

In that area, her Muspelheim and Miyuki's Niflheim had been clashing with each other.

With two spells traveling in opposite directions, their effects would only cancel each other out. That wasn't the same as neutralizing it. To neutralize a spell, you had to use a spell that overwrote its magic program.

In other words, if the method Tatsuya had chosen was to neutralize the spells, he would have had to use over twice as much influence as Lina.

When she'd come to that conclusion, she couldn't stop herself from trembling.

If that was possible, that would mean Tatsuya also had some ability to hide all that power.

If he'd disabled the spells without neutralizing them, then doing anything other than destroying their magic programs was impossible.

Lina knew of ways to destroy magic programs using the impact from a highly compressed psion flow, but there was no such indication at that time.

Not destroying them with an external impact but interfering with their informational construction itself to get the job done—if it had been Major Benjamin Canopus, vice commander of the Stars, he might have pinpointed Tatsuya's spell as Program Dispersion. But Lina didn't know about that spell.

As someone who had joined the Stars at a young age (a very young age, one might say), she was the opposite of a normal boy or girl: She had ample combat experience, but for all the time that had taken, she lacked knowledge about certain things. Of course, she knew all sorts of things compared to normal (magic) high school students, but one's knowledge capacity was limited by how much time one spent learning. No matter how good she was at memorizing things, there couldn't be any information in her head that she hadn't learned yet.

Lina's worry was that since she lacked learning time, she didn't have enough of an ability to extend her experience. It all came down to her being too young to be commander of the Stars.

One might say their complete ability-based system was having harmful effects.

It hadn't worked against her yet, but during a mission away from her home country where support was thin, up against a soldier like Tatsuya—who made up for how relatively few combat opportunities he'd had by always cramming knowledge and skill into his head—she was footing the bill for her bias.

Tatsuya wasn't a battle junkie. At least, he didn't think so. He only ever picked fights with people under very specific circumstances. In particular, he did it only when necessary to protect Miyuki's safety and honor.

Still, he wasn't a pacifist. He believed, as many young people do (?), that in order to protect peace, one needed to fight for it.

Five of them...

Confirming the number of enemies waiting, literally about to burst out of a small vehicle parked on the other side of the street, Tatsuya hesitated for a moment.

In this case, if he wanted to run, he could. He could just call his car back by remote.

He reached a conclusion in one second.

After completing payment using the terminal on the table, he stood up.

They must have seen it, because the wagon door hurriedly opened.

Walking quickly, Tatsuya headed for the entrance.

The front of the restaurant was right across from the vehicle.

Five people with ski masks, only their eyes visible, stepped out of the wagon at about the same time Tatsuya left the restaurant.

The eyes peering out of the ski masks were an array of colors—blue, red, black, brown, and gray.

They were color contacts, which foreign criminals frequently used to disguise themselves during crimes, but that probably wasn't what this was. In fact, they didn't appear to have very much intention of hiding their appearances. Maybe they were confident nobody would identify them even if they saw their faces.

When Tatsuya walked up to them, as if to preempt them, the attackers seemed to get confused.

But their staring contest didn't last long.

Tatsuya moved.

Not forward, not backward—he walked out of their line of sight and along the road.

He could feel their astonishment.

Without breaking step, Tatsuya distanced himself from them.

Five meters turned into ten meters, and finally, the attackers came to their senses.

The soft sound of a gun clicking reached his ears.

They weren't large CADs shaped like submachine guns but armament devices where submachine guns were fitted into the CADs.

Their loadout alone made it seem like they were straight-up confessing they were USNA magicians.

Nobody else—not western European nations, eastern European nations, or the New Soviet Republic—used such contrived devices as weapons.

The only ones who used weapons this elaborate, aside from America's military, was, perhaps, none other than Japan's own Independent Magic Battalion.

He could tell from the expanded activation sequences that the soft silicone-compound bullets would be given an electric charge upon firing and discharge when they landed. They must have been a sort of Taser gun. Apparently, they were under orders to capture him alive.

Tatsuya had already put his right hand in his inside pocket and gripped his CAD handle. His finger was on the button made to look like a trigger.

His back still turned to the masked men, he pulled the CAD's trigger.

Then, he quickly turned around and launched himself into a dash.

He heard the dry sounds of submachine gun parts clattering all over the paved surface after he began to run.

While the enemies were frozen in surprise, he closed the distance.

When he reached unarmed combat distance, the enemies finally began moving again.

In Tatsuya's opinion, they'd been too shocked, but maybe they couldn't help it.

In order to use magic to interfere with an object already under the effects of someone else's spell, you needed to have a clear advantage in influence over their magical power. When there was physical contact between the object and the caster, the difficulty of doing so leaped up significantly. That was the reason people said it was essentially impossible to use magic to directly destroy CADs and armament devices.

But if that was the reason they were so surprised, they'd misunderstood.

The spell they'd tried to use was one to give electrical charge and discharge effects to their bullets. The target of that spell was the bullet, not the gun. The barrel was connected to the CAD, but the breechblock and the detonator were independent devices.

Gun parts were made to be easy to take apart to maintain them, making them simple for Tatsuya's magic to handle.

The reason they'd been so shocked was perhaps—like how Japanese people once had absolute faith in the katana—an absolute American faith in firearms.

Of course, Tatsuya wasn't just relaxing and thinking about that sort of thing.

Those ideas simply shot through his mind out of reflex at seeing them surprised. His mind was focused on how he'd attack the enemies now that he'd gotten into close range.

He had no reason to spare their lives.

But he was in public right now.

It wasn't a shopping district, and though it was nighttime, there were people around and road cameras dotting the streets. He'd probably have a lot of trouble to go through if he killed them.

Still, he didn't want to show his Dismantle spell many times to the observer he knew existed. He should refrain from using his part dismantling.

That was why he purposely closed the distance between them.

Tatsuya thrust out with the heel of his palm.

He aimed for one man's gut.

He didn't bother to try to aim for the solar plexus.

As his palm landed, he used a flash-cast.

The spell he activated was an oscillation type.

From the point of contact, the vibrations pounded into the enemy's body—or at least, they should have.

But his spell was bounced back. Tatsuya knew not through the sensation in his hand but by looking with his "eyes."

He immediately jumped aside.

He felt a wind whip up from below him.

The enemy's fist, with a shiny black knuckle-duster on it, thrust into his afterimage.

Slipping past the man, he went around behind him and hit him with another vibration wave.

The attack was in his blind spot, and the man's body fell to the ground.

Still, he had a surprising level of magical resistance.

He'd fired his spell through physical contact into a part of his Information Boost armor that was weak, but the man had reflexively canceled it with a burst of influence. Tatsuya's attacks' output may have been weaker than others because he fired it from a virtual magic region, but this would normally be impossible.

An engineered magician— No, an enhanced human?

As the enemies regrouped and attacked and Tatsuya jumped back to avoid them, he accessed their physical information in search of their identity.

Information with a distorted structure, which went beyond simple genetic engineering. Doubtless a result of layers of forced enhancement impossible to gain by learning.

How can these guys even move like that?

Tatsuya had "seen" hundreds of people as they were about to die, and in the state these men were in, he wouldn't be surprised if they keeled over at any moment.

They were much better suited for getting an IV drip in a hospital bed than swinging around guns or knives.

But how did they have so much energy?

They were like meteorites right before burning out.

It was precisely as though stardust trapped by the earth was breaking apart in flames, casting a light. Tatsuya didn't think he would lose to something of this level, but he didn't know what sort of crazy things these irregular opponents would do.

He needed to end this swiftly, even if it meant taking some risks.

Tatsuya changed his way of thinking. In his mind, he quickly drew up a blueprint for the future.

——*Jump farther back to get distance, then reach for my CAD.*

——*As I pull it out, fire four partial dismantle shots.*

——*That will stop them for good.*

Right when Tatsuya's thoughts had solidified, by total coincidence, something happened.

He came to interrupt them.

* * *

Naotsugu Chiba was at a loss.

He hadn't predicted this would suddenly turn into a street fight. His preconception of the boy from his excellent classroom grades was as someone with a careful personality.

He was on a third-floor terrace of a mid-rise building about eight hundred meters from the boy, the subject of his monitoring and protection. The investigation report had said he was keen in sensing others. Putting himself at such a distance had backfired.

It would be an awful pain to run down the stairs, too.

He grabbed his weapon and jumped down.

As he hit the ground, he launched into a sprint.

Naotsugu's running speed, enhanced with the Godfoot spell (originally a hermit technique), could reach a maximum of one hundred twenty kilometers per hour over short distances.

At this distance, it was faster than using a powered vehicle, and it would get him there earlier.

About thirty seconds until he arrived.

As he ran, he sensed two vibration-type spells being used.

He saw one of the assailants take a palm strike from behind and crumple to the road.

Can that boy use Magic Arts? wondered Naotsugu to himself. That information hadn't been in the report.

It wasn't the sort of intel one would eschew putting in a report, so the information bureau probably hadn't known, either.

He seemed to have several other tricks up his sleeve, too.

Interest toward Tatsuya Shiba, his observation target—currently his protection target—swelled within him.

Just how well could he fight…?

But he'd have to find that out another time. Naotsugu was the type to keep work and private life separate. (He thought so anyway.)

He pressed the button on the armament device in his hand.

The short club changed into a *kodachi*.

The Chiba had developed this new model and had begun supplying it to the police. Naotsugu had fine-tuned this one for his own use.

He preferred multipurpose tools he could swap out to single, high-efficiency ones like the Ikazuchi-Maru or Orochi-Maru.

Weapons were tools, after all, and disposable. And depending on how you used them, they could be sharp and celebrated or dull and forgotten.

That was part of his confidence in his own skills, the skills of the one lauded as one of the world's strongest combat magicians, when within three meters—

His protection target jumped far back.

The investigative report relating to who the boy was fighting came up in the back of Naotsugu's mind.

The opponents were Stardust, enhanced magicians—no, it was more accurate to call them living magical weapons—belonging to the USNA military. A death squad formed of magicians who couldn't withstand the engineering and enhancement, who knew for sure they would die in a matter of a few years. Several groups existed within Stardust, each excelling in different things. Naotsugu had been told that the band fighting the boy now was one specializing in close combat.

Their minds had been aligned with the idea that if they didn't have long to live, they wouldn't die needlessly... It was doubtlessly a form of brainwashing, but Naotsugu didn't consider it evil. In fact, he felt empathy for them as they literally gambled their lives for their mission—not for faith.

But that only made them that much more troubling.

Soldiers prepared to die were the strongest soldiers in the world.

No matter how good a high schooler was, it was probably too much to handle.

Naotsugu stepped in between Tatsuya and the Stardust.

Tatsuya already knew that there were eyes monitoring him—and that they belonged to someone other than the USNA military.

But he hadn't expected someone to intervene in this short a time. He'd predicted them to remain observers.

The man had his back to him, which meant that in this fight at least, he wasn't an enemy.

Tatsuya recognized who the person was, too, from the instant their face became visible as they entered the fight.

It was Erika's older brother.

But he didn't know why he was offering assistance.

"Shiba."

If it was unexpected for him to say anything—

"I'm Naotsugu Chiba. Older brother of your classmate Erika Chiba."

—then it was also unexpected for him to reveal his identity.

"I'll take over from here. You stay back, all right?"

He obviously didn't explain any more, but now wasn't the time for that.

"Thank you very much."

Tatsuya had no objections if the man wanted him to leave things in his hands.

When he quickly retreated, he felt a sense from Naotsugu that the man had been outwitted. Maybe he'd expected Tatsuya to say something like *I'll fight, too!* But unfortunately for him, Tatsuya's personality wasn't that self-serving. If an expert was telling him to stand back, he would obey them—as long as it was to his benefit, at least.

The enemies were confused at the sudden intervention for only a few seconds.

Excluding the one who was already down, the four masked men pulled out handguns and thrust them toward Naotsugu.

Modern magic was a technological system that placed emphasis on speed, and CADs were the answer to that demand.

Still, pulling the trigger of a gun without the safety on was faster than using magic, which had to deal with an activation sequence to construct a magic program. At this range, the opponents didn't even have to take aim.

It seemed these men were significantly accustomed to combat.

They chose a method to quickly eliminate an obstacle rather than rely on special skills like magic. They wouldn't abandon magic and not use it at all—they were in the process of executing a movement-type spell as well that would stop flying objects. It was probably to protect themselves from projectile weapons.

Guns as their weapons, and magic as their shields..

The arrangement made use of both their advantages. Presumably, they'd been shackled by the rule to take Tatsuya alive and hadn't displayed their full combat prowess. Killing enemies no questions asked—that was doubtless their original fighting style. A combat style that pursued rationality was enough to take down most enemies.

But Naotsugu Chiba wasn't like most enemies.

Faster than the men could pull their triggers, Naotsugu closed the distance. To anyone else, it must have looked like Naotsugu had disappeared. It was so fast, even Tatsuya had to concentrate or he'd lose sight of him.

His *kodachi* flashed as he passed by one. The blade was bordered with a dark line.

The hand holding the gun fell off from the wrist down. The cross-wise repulsive field created by the *kodachi*'s blade had sliced skin, pried open flesh, and severed bone.

Did the men notice that at the moment of his strike, he'd activated the acceleration-type spell Pressure Cut?

Paying no attention to their comrade's shriek, the other three redirected their muzzles at Naotsugu.

Their bullets shot through his afterimage.

With the sounds of screaming and glass breaking as his background music, Naotsugu got into close range.

It wasn't godlike speed, but the soldiers still couldn't get a lock on him.

Images both true and false overlapped in their vision.

Even Tatsuya, who was watching from behind, wasn't confident he'd be able to find Naotsugu's true position if he'd been fighting him in super-close range.

The secret lay in charging, stopping, and repeating.

Naotsugu charged, stopped, changed direction, charged again, stopped again... By repeating the process, it created afterimages on his opponents' retinas.

Normally, the theory behind swordsmanship objected to stopping, or *itsuki*. If you removed the logic's finer details, *itsuki* meant "a stiffening of muscles." The act of stopping your feet stiffened your leg muscles and locked them in place, which was one cause of falling into *itsuki*.

But that only applied when you were moving just with muscular force.

By controlling his "wake-up," or the initial motion of his body, with magic, he could move from a completely stopped position to top speed without any time in between.

But this was infinitely easier said than done.

Movements preceding thoughts was a naturally occurring phenomenon in the martial arts world, and some said you couldn't be first class unless you could move faster than you thought.

What Naotsugu was doing was preceding the very motion of his body, which overtook his thoughts, and triggering magic.

Come to think of it, his earlier Pressure Cut had activated in an instant and ended in an instant, so fast that not only his opponents but those watching couldn't perceive it happen. Opponents couldn't figure out your game like that, nor could they take any countermeasures.

That on-off switching speed was, Tatsuya thought, without a doubt the essence of his technique, and why the man was counted among one of the top ten most well-known in the world.

While Tatsuya was analyzing Naotsugu's combat strength, he'd disabled all the masked men.

Naotsugu lowered the hand holding the *kodachi*.

He didn't seem to have let down his guard, but he did seem somewhat less tense.

Tatsuya felt the same way.

Meaning to thank him for the assistance, he began to walk toward Naotsugu, when on the third step…

…he felt an intense sense of danger upon him.

Naotsugu must have felt it as well. Tatsuya dropped himself to the ground, and Naotsugu brought his *kodachi* up at about the same time.

A moment later…

…a shining ray of light shot at Naotsugu.

The *kodachi* parried the ray—a high-energy plasma beam.

Right before the blade, the beam split into two, left and right.

He was probably bending the intense plasma stream with the repulsive field that formed on the blade using Pressure Cut.

But it wasn't enough to block the EM wave effects.

The ray of light disappeared.

Mysteriously, the plasma beam had vanished before reaching any of the buildings along the road.

As Naotsugu held the *kodachi* up in front of him, still standing there, he trembled. His muscles had probably been paralyzed by all the EM waves hitting him from close range. It was like he'd taken a high-power stun gun shot to the body.

Tatsuya looked toward the ray's estimated firing point.

In the distance, in the middle of the dark, hazy road…

…form illuminated dimly by a streetlight,

was a head of red hair and a pair of golden eyes.

Pointing what looked like a staff in his direction, the masked magician Angie Sirius stared down Tatsuya as though in invitation.

(To be continued)

AFTERWORD

First, I'd like to offer my heartfelt thanks to everyone who purchased this book. I'll continue to look forward to your support, both from those for whom this is their first reading and those for whom it is not.

The Irregular at Magic High School is a series that features quite a lot of characters, but I think the Visitor arc is the first time a character I could call a "guest heroine" has appeared. This is the first time a blonde-haired, blue-eyed female character has appeared as well.

Regarding this blonde-haired girl, a rarity for this series, I had a conversation with my editor during a meeting for Volume 9 that went something like this:

Editor: "I really like incompetent but beautiful characters."

Me: "Lina is more like a malfunctioning beauty than an incompetent beauty, but you're right, they really are cute."

This was how we decided on a new character trait for Lina. Well, she was originally made to be a somewhat unfortunate character outside of battle scenes, but she wasn't this bad... But it's cute, right?

In terms of character changes, Mitsugu Kuroba, who had a sullen (?) highlight in this book, also now has a screw loose. To tell the truth, it's because of the drama DVD. The actor who voiced Mitsugu had a really nice ad lib, which renewed my image of his character.

The actor's performances are great, though, aren't they? I got a real sense for how it can have a synergistic effect on the original work.

Next time will be, at last, the final volume of the Visitor arc. Since this one ended with a "continued next time!" part three will have a big stack of stories, but please rest assured that I won't make that one a "continued in the final volume!" I have a climax fitting the end of their freshman year coming up, so I look forward to your support for part three of the Visitor arc as well.

Tsutomu Sato

I'm Hayashi, the head of composition for the GF Comics serialization. Congratulations on the release of Volume 10, Mr. Sato! *Irregular* is now in the double digits, and with it being right in the middle of the Visitor arc, I'd been eagerly waiting this one since last time! I may be doing the composition, but like any normal reader, I wonder what will become of the characters now… I'm a little scared to find out!… But not more than I want to see what happens. What will happen to Tatsuya and Miyuki, and to Lina… Thank you, Mr. Sato, for making me so excited about it, and I hope we can re-create a little of that excitement in the manga version as well.

FUMINO HAYASHI

Mr. Sato,

Thank you for always taking such good care of me. I'd like to take this opportunity to congratulate you on the release of *The Irregular at Magic High School*, Vol. 10!

The Visitor arc! Lina's so cute…!

I like long black hair, but I think blonde pigtails are absolutely fantastic, too.

As always, the bond between Miyuki and Tatsuya is strong, and I grin like a fool whenever I read a scene with them in it.

And Honoka's getting a little development, too?! And Shizuku actually… A lot is on my mind, so I look forward to the next book!

I'll work hard on *The Honor Student at Magic High School* so as not to be crushed under this momentum, so I look forward to your support in the future.

Yu Mori